2/2018

and the
PERILOUS PYRO-PAWS

Peter Nelson & Rohitash Rao

Balzer + Bray
An Imprint of HarperCollins*Publishers*

Balzer + Bray is an imprint of HarperCollins Publishers.

Creature Keepers and the Perilous Pyro-Paws
Copyright © 2017 by Peter Nelson and Rohitash Rao
All rights reserved. Printed in the United States of America.
No part of this book may be used or reproduced in any manner
whatsoever without written permission except in the case of brief
quotations embodied in critical articles and reviews. For information address HarperCollins Children's Books, a division of
HarperCollins Publishers, 195 Broadway, New York, NY 10007.
www.harpercollinschildrens.com

Library of Congress Control Number: 2017949411
ISBN 978-0-06-223650-0 (trade bdg.)

Typography by David Curtis
17 18 19 20 21   CG/LSCH   10 9 8 7 6 5 4 3 2 1

First Edition

*To David, a talented actor who played the role of
invisible little brother once upon a time, until I was
lucky enough to discover who he'd always been—a
teacher, inspiration, and great friend.—P. N.*

*To all the budding artists in my family
(you know who you are!). Keep drawing, painting,
and telling stories. Don't give up! I can't wait
to read your books one day.—R. R.*

J ordan Grimsley stared at the dark stone in his hand. The bright, ruby-like gem he'd plucked from the snowy ground at the end of his last adventure had since turned a deep, dull red. Almost black. As if a light inside it had died.

Jordan tossed the stone into his duffel bag alongside a keepsake from another adventure: a hand-whittled wooden slingshot his friend Alistair MacAlister had given him. He looked around his tiny bedroom cluttered with his boxed-up belongings. One box was filled with books from his bookshelf: *The Amazing World of Cryptids, A Guide to Mankind's Most Amazing Mythological Monsters, A Complete History of Amazing*

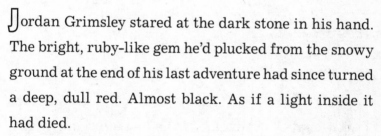

Creatures. Jordan smiled. Nearly every book he owned seemed to feature the word "amazing" in its title. He wondered why he kept them. Given his recent experiences, Jordan could write an amazing book of his own. And the most amazing thing about *his* amazing book was that it would all be true.

He zipped his bag closed. Of course, he could never write his book. What Jordan Grimsley knew had to stay secret, forever. At least that was the plan.

Jordan and his older sister, Abbie, had been given a very important— and very secret—responsibility. They were put in charge of the underground organization their long-lost Grampa Grimsley had created—one that kept the world's undiscovered mythical creatures happy, healthy, and hidden. Jordan and Abbie never got to meet old George Grimsley before he met his fate, but they knew his story. He'd sacrificed everything—his family, his freedom, and eventually his life—to protect and keep the cryptids safely secluded. This responsibility now rested with them—at a time when the Creature

Keepers organization was in very real danger of being exposed to the world.

Jordan slung the bag over his shoulder and glanced around his small bedroom for the last time. He wondered if he would miss living in this city apartment. Then he thought about where he and his family were moving.

"Not a chance," he said to himself.

Jordan's mother and father had been left Grampa Grimsley's old house, located deep in the Okeeyuckachokee Swamp at the southwestern tip of Florida, which they'd renovated into a retirement home. But the retirees who lived there weren't just any old folks. They were the elderly support group who kept the Creature Keepers operation running smoothly, quite unbeknownst to Mr. and Mrs. Grimsley. Jordan's parents would never in a million years suspect this friendly (if slightly odd) group of geezers ran a high-tech mission control center directly beneath their new home. And Jordan shuddered to think what might happen if they ever found out.

It was a strange time for the Creature Keepers. Earlier that summer, they had successfully defeated and captured a horribly dangerous cryptid known only as Chupacabra. This cryptid was like no other Jordan had ever encountered. He was mean, cunning, and dangerous. Chupacabra had hated Jordan's grandfather, and now he hated Jordan—not because he knew they were related but because he thought they were one and the same. He was convinced Jordan's grandfather had secretly de-aged himself using waters from the Fountain of Youth and that Jordan was actually the young George Grimsley.

This terrible creature had succeeded in robbing the three elemental powers from the world's only special cryptids. He'd hijacked the Loch Ness Monster's Hydro-Hide, stolen the Sasquatch's Soil-Soles, and burgled the Yeti's Blizzard-Bristles. The combination of these three gifts would have given Chupacabra the rare and dangerous power known as the Perfect Storm. But the Creature Keepers were able to stop him, capturing Chupacabra alive and imprisoning him in ice.

Before he was defeated, Chupacabra attempted to get good-natured cryptids to follow him by convincing them that they were meant to rise up against their Keepers and join him in destroying the human race and taking over the world. Luckily, none of them did. But a handful found the idea of living openly, freely, and *peacefully* more than a little interesting.

And so, on the very day when Jordan found the glowing red stone lying in the snow, four rogue cryptids respectfully thanked the Creature Keepers for their years of care and protection, then struck out on their own to live as liberated creatures.

Jordan shut the door to his bedroom as he thought about where those rogue cryptids might be. He and Abbie had been checking in regularly with Doris, an old friend of their grandfather's and the head honchess down in Florida. Thankfully, they had yet to resurface, which was quite remarkable. These were not small or subtle creatures. Sandy was a full-grown, brightly glowing Sumatran Golden Liger. Paul, a West African Dingonek, was a dragonlike cryptid with scaly skin and a saber-toothed tiger's head. Not exactly the kind of creature one might trip over if it were lying outside one's door.

Wump. Jordan tripped over Chunk, Abbie's overweight, lazy pet iguana, lying outside his door. Its fat face was munching away inside a half-empty bag of Crazy-Blazin' Jalapeño-Heckfire Nacho Cheezy Puffs.

"There you are!" Abbie burst out of her room with a box of black clothing, which she shoved at Jordan. She gathered Chunk up in her arms and kissed the overweight reptile on its orange-dyed mouth, covering her face with Crazy-Blazin' Jalapeño-Heckfire Nacho Cheezy Puff dust.

Jordan and Abbie's father bellowed from down the hall. "Hello, Doris," Mr. Grimsley shouted into a phone. "Nearly all packed up, yes. We'll all be driving the moving truck down next week. What? I see. . . . Well, how many? Yes, yes, of course! And C. E. Noodlepen approved the funds for the expansion? So long as you're overseeing the construction, Doris. I trust you and no one else, at least until the Grimsley caravan gets down there."

Doris was the only old lady Jordan knew who was tough enough to pull double duty, running both the Eternal Acres retirement home *and* the Creature Keeper central command. She kept both operations running at the same time and one of them a complete secret. She also happened to be one of Jordan's

most favorite people in the whole world.

Mr. Grimsley beamed at Jordan and Abbie. "If you think they'd be helpful to you, I'm sure they'd love to fly down ahead of us. They're right here. Please hold."

Mr. Grimsley shoved the phone into Jordan's hand, then ran off to share the news with Mrs. Grimsley.

"Doris, is everything all right?" Jordan asked.

Abbie put her ear to his and listened in. "Did the rogue cryptids turn up?" she asked.

"No, they didn't," Doris replied to them both. "And no, things are not all right! I had to call on a normal telephone because our entire operation down here is off-line! We had to disconnect everything in the underground command center so we could install a new entrance to fit that Chupacabra-filled glacier in here! You couldn't have just locked him in a small cage?"

"Doris, what's the emergency?" Jordan asked.
"Is Chupacabra secure?"

"Yes, yes. Of course he is! But I could use you both down here. I told your father I needed you to help me make more room for some new elderly retirees."

"Ugh," Abbie said.

"More old people."

"They're Keepers! *Active Creature Keepers*, from all over the world, forced into sudden retirement and turning up on our doorstep!"

"But you said *elderly* retirees," Jordan asserted. "Creature Keepers are kids."

"Not anymore, dearies," Doris said. "The last of their Fountain of Youth elixir finally worked its way out of their systems. Their bodies are catching up to their years, as mine did for me. They were bound to turn old. I just didn't expect them to turn up here!"

Jordan felt an unpleasant wave in the pit of his stomach. Each Creature Keeper lived alone with his or her cryptid, and while they looked like kids, they were much older. Jordan's grandfather had discovered a way to derive an elixir from the magical waters of the Fountain of Youth and used it to keep the Keepers young, so they in turn could keep their assigned creatures happy, healthy, and hidden. A powerful substance, it had an especially drastic effect the one time it was given to a cryptid. But the supply and source of the elixir had been destroyed by Chupacabra. Worse, it had been largely Jordan's fault. Which he still felt pretty horrible about.

"Doris," Abbie said, "if these Keepers are showing up at Eternal Acres, where are their creatures?"

"Best if I explain when you get here," she said.

"We'll catch a flight down as soon as we can," Jordan said.

"Thank you. Oh, and one more thing. In that journal of your grandfather's—is there any mention about . . . *Face Chompers*?"

Jordan and Abbie exchanged a look. "No," Jordan said. "What is that?"

"Like I said, best if I explain when you get here."

2

The Leisureville, Florida, municipal airport had no restaurants, donut stands, or gift shops. It didn't even have an automatic carousel in the baggage claim area. There was just a big hole in a wall through which a man outside on the single landing strip tossed your bags. Jordan and Abbie found their backpacks in the pile on the floor and made their way outside.

"Who's picking us up?" Abbie asked as they stepped outside onto the curb. "Please don't say Bernard. I didn't say good-bye to Chunk if this turns out to be my last day on earth."

Bernard was a Skunk Ape—a Floridian Skunk Ape, to be specific—who was fascinated with human behavior and enjoyed attempting it, often poorly and

sometimes quite recklessly, whenever he got the chance. He was very well-mannered, and not just for a cryptid. In fact, Jordan preferred his company to most humans he knew. And while many of the more humanlike skills Bernard had picked up were very helpful (he was a surprisingly skilled pilot, for example), riding in a car with Bernard behind the wheel was not something Jordan or Abbie was looking to experience again anytime soon.

"Doris said Bernard has been busy flying all over the world," Jordan said. "Answering distress calls from Keepers. He's the one who's been bringing them in."

Abbie scanned the near-empty parking lot. The

only option she could see was the Leisureville Local Line, a public transportation fleet consisting of exactly one shabby-looking bus parked at the curb directly in front of them. It suddenly let out a loud *HISSSSS*, then slowly pulled away from the curb. Parked on the other side was a disheveled old van with a large foot bolted to the roof. Leaning against it was an equally disheveled old man in a T-shirt, cutoff shorts, sandals, and a headband holding back his long scraggly hair. Jordan and Abbie recognized both the van and the man.

"Hap!" Jordan said. "You made it!"

"Of course I did! When you told me what you needed and why, I drove for three days without stopping, man!"

"Wait." Abbie looked concerned. "You haven't slept for three days?"

"I said I drove without stopping." Hap chuckled. "I didn't say I was awake the whole time. Pile in, you guys. *Roadtrip!*"

Hap Cooperdock was a free spirit. For years he dutifully served as the Keeper of none other than the Sasquatch, commonly known as Bigfoot but who preferred the name Syd. During all those years, Hap never drank the doses of Fountain of Youth elixir that were delivered to him by the Creature Keeper central command. So unlike all the other Keepers, Hap had aged normally. When he got to a ripe old age, he decided it was time for him to quit creature keeping and hit the road. Jordan and Abbie had helped him out by Squatch-sitting until they found a very unlikely replacement.

"How's Buck Wilde doing?" Abbie asked as they barreled along the Ingraham Highway, deeper into the swamp. "He'd better be taking good care of Syd."

"You know those two dudes," Hap said. "Buck loved searchin' for Syd on his TV show, and Syd loved watching Buck on TV. So the two of them just wake up every day, point at each other, and can't believe their luck. They're like two peas in a pod."

"How about you, Hap?" Jordan asked. "You still like being on your own?"

"I gotta admit, the open road gets a little lonely. I pop up to Canada to check in on those two from time to time, but it's not my home anymore. To be honest, I've been thinking about settling down somewhere."

"Hopefully those rogue cryptids will start to feel that way, too," Jordan said. "And come home to their Keepers before anyone sees them."

"That reminds me." Hap nodded toward the rear. "I brought the stuff you asked for."

Jordan leaned over the seat and pulled back a muddy tarp. A dusty old wooden box lay beneath it, filled with dozens of tiny glass bottles.

"What is that?" Abbie said.

"Concentrated elixir made from the Fountain of Youth," Jordan said.

"Never touched the stuff myself," Hap said. "Stashed 'em away for years. 'Fraid that's all I could salvage. A bunch were smashed; some were leaking. A few had a snot-green color to 'em. Figured they might've spoiled."

"Fountain of Youth juice has an expiration date?" Abbie said. "That's ironic."

* * *

Hap's Bigfoot van turned off the Ingraham Highway and stopped short. A traffic jam clogged the entrance to the Eternal Acres retirement community, with construction delivery trucks lined bumper to bumper along the dead end road leading to the cul-de-sac where Grampa Grimsley's old house stood.

Hap pulled up on the sidewalk and drove along the edges of the retirees' perfectly manicured lawns, getting as close as he could to the great house at the end of the street. When he couldn't go any farther, Jordan and Abbie hopped out, eager to see what was going on.

"You two go check in with Doris," Hap said. "I'll find you."

Jordan and Abbie jogged to the black iron entrance gate to Eternal Acres. Unlike the little houses that lined the road leading up to it, their grandfather's old house stood three stories tall, with beautiful alcoves, balconies, and windows. It was hard to recall how creepy it was when they first saw it. And now it seemed to be undergoing another facelift.

"There you are!" A plump little old lady in a yellow hard hat worked her way past three delivery men who were loading lumber into the front yard. "Come in! Come in! What in the devil took you so long? It's about time you got here!"

Jordan couldn't help but grin when he saw her. "Hiya, Doris."

"I know, I know, this place is upside down. And it isn't just the remodel, believe me." The front foyer looked like a hardware store clearance sale. Elderly retirees bustled about carrying lumber, paint, pipes, furniture, ladders, doors, tools, toilets, brackets, hinges, windows, light fixtures, and curtain rods. As busy as the old folks were, they all took a second to wave, nod, salute, or say hello to Abbie and Jordan as they scurried past. Doris led the two of them through the mayhem, pointing out old bedrooms, new bedrooms, and expanded bedrooms as they made their way down the long hallway toward the back of the house.

Jordan and Abbie stopped her as they reached the door to the back patio. "Doris," Abbie said. "Where are the new guests? The Keepers—can we see them?"

"Right! Yes, yes, of course. They're out here. After you." She opened the kitchen door. The great brick wall that separated the thick Okeeyuckachokee Swamp from the backyard creaked and swayed, then gave way, crashing toward them, into the yard. Standing on the other side was Peggy, a twenty-foot-tall Texas Jacka-lope. A group of older folks tossed carrots to her and petted her while more loaded up the broken stones and wheelbarrowed them toward the swamp.

Peggy's long whiskers twitched beneath her nose as she sniffed the air. After spotting Jordan and Abbie, she hopped up into the patio yard in one giant bound, then began lick-ing their faces like an excited golden retriever.

"All right, all

right," Doris said. "That's enough, you oversentimental furball." She pointed past the crumbled wall into the thick of the swamp. "In the boathouse. Eldon's keeping an eye on them, and keeping watch."

"For what?" Abbie said. "For *Face Chompers*?"

"Doris, what are these Face Chompers?" Jordan asked.

"Eldon will explain. Now, you'd better hurry along. He's anxious to see you. Just don't bring up the rogue four. He's still a little miffed about those cryptids who went off on their own."

Jordan and Abbie trudged deep into the dense swamplands until they reached the edge of Ponce de Leon Bay. Hidden along the shoreline, beneath the tangled cypress tree branches and coastal swamp grass, the Creature Keepers' boathouse and dock served as a garage and launching point for various odd modes of transportation. In Jordan's short time with the operation, he'd ridden—and even piloted—a seaplane, hot air balloon, submarine, swamp boat, and a rocket thruster–powered military-grade aircraft called a Heli-Jet.

None of these crafts seemed to be there. The boathouse and dock looked empty and abandoned except for a sad, drab-looking little canvas pup tent set up by a tree. Abbie and Jordan knew whose tent that was, but in case they had any doubts, the Badger Ranger flag waving atop it was a dead giveaway.

"Camp Dorkface," Abbie said under her breath.

Aside from being a dorkface in Abbie's eyes, Eldon Pecone was also the former leader of the Creature Keepers and a First-Class Badger Ranger, not necessarily in that order. He was very much a fan of rules, loyalty, rules, discipline, rules, and a few more rules. Despite this, and much to Jordan's surprise, he was also Jordan's best friend. Eldon had introduced Jordan to his grandfather's secret world, and in a way, it was Eldon's world, too. Jordan would never forget the look on Eldon's face when the four rogue cryptids quit the Creature Keepers and made their way into the world. Jordan was surprised Eldon didn't insist they stay, or attempt to go after them. Like the stone in Jordan's bag, Eldon's light began to fade after that day. Soon after, he passed along the leadership of the Creature Keepers to Jordan and Abbie—as well as a special ring that had belonged to their grandfather. Jordan still didn't feel like either was quite the right fit.

He crouched down at the entrance to the tent. "Eldon? Are you in there?"

"*Shh!*" A sound from above came from a lanky boy in a Badger Ranger uniform clinging to the trunk of a tree, staring through a pair of binoculars.

Abbie hollered up at him. "Yo, dorkface! What are you doing?"

YO, DORKFACE!

Eldon slid down the tree. He was clean-cut, from his short cropped hair down to his spit-shined boots. His Badger Ranger uniform was complete with an official sash cluttered with Badger Badges.

"*Shh!*" Eldon repeated. He suddenly jerked his head as if he heard something in the nearby clump of bushes. He whipped out his binoculars and peered upward, slowly scanning the treetops. "Okay. All clear. For now, at least."

Eldon snapped to attention, standing straight and tall before the two of them, and offered a stiff, Badger Ranger Badger claw salute. "Eldon Pecone, First-Class Master Ranger, clan seventy-four, at your service and reporting for duty. In your absence, I thought it would be prudent for me stay on top of the current situation and to keep a vigilant eye for the newest enemy in our midst."

"What the heck are you talking about?" Jordan asked.

"Permission to speak freely."

"Denied," Abbie said.

"Eldon!" Jordan snapped at his friend. "Please just tell us what's going on!"

Eldon relaxed his stiff stance but kept a worried look on his face. "I'm afraid what we're looking at here is an organized, wide-scale abduction of cryptids."

"By who?" Abbie said.

"Not who, *what*."

"These Face Chewers?" Jordan asked.

"The Face *Chompers*," Eldon said somberly. "A mysterious and powerful force with the ability to locate our cryptids anywhere in the world and snatch them from the care of our very best Creature Keepers."

"I don't believe it," Abbie said. "How could anyone— or anything—do that?"

"Eldon, how do you know all of this?" Jordan said. "How can you be sure?"

Eldon stepped to the doorway of the boathouse and reached for the handle. "Their Keepers are on the other side of this door. They all tell the same chilling story. Whatever these Face Chompers are, we've never dealt with anything like this before."

"Open the door," Jordan said. "We need to talk to them."

"All right. But I feel I must warn you. What you're about to see . . . isn't pretty."

He swung open the door. Inside, about a half dozen elderly people looked up. Some rested on cots; others stood chatting. But each and every single one of them, old men and old ladies alike, wore the exact same thing: a bright pink woman's nightie.

"It's kind of pretty," Abbie said. "And I usually *hate* pink."

4

Jordan, Abbie, and Eldon sat with the oddly dressed Keepers, listening as they introduced themselves, then recalled fondly the creature they'd lost.

"Justine," said an old woman with beautiful Asian features. "I keep—er, *kept*, I guess—Clarissa, the Christmas Island Colossus Crab." She bowed her head and sobbed quietly.

An elderly dark-skinned man put his arm around the woman. "I'm Thomas," he said softly. "I was responsible for Gilligan, the Feejee Mermonkey."

"Alice," another woman said in an Australian accent. "The Tasmanian Globster wasn't just my creature. Hogie was my mate."

The next person—a tall, lanky old man—was trying

to hold it together. He kept taking short breaths and holding up a finger, politely and silently requesting a moment. He finally went to speak but shook his head and buried his face in the bulky shoulder of the short, stocky bald man sitting beside him.

"He's Christopher," the puffy, shorter Keeper said in a thick New York accent. "He misses his bird-bro, Gavin, the Cornwall Owl Man."

Jordan looked closer at this last stocky, bald man. Something about him seemed familiar. "What about you?" Jordan said. "Who's your creature?"

The puffy old man's lip trembled. "My creature is— *He's my bestest bro in the whole world!* He burst into tears, then blew his nose loudly on Christopher's pink nightie. Jordan realized who he was.

"Mike! Is that you?"

"You guys gotta find Lou! He's out there some-wheres, and he needs me!"

Mike was the Creature Keeper to Lou, otherwise known as the New Jersey Devil. When Jordan and Abbie had first met the two of them, they came off like tough-talking meatheads. But deep down, they were a pair of big old softies.

"Okay, big fella," Abbie said. "Don't worry. We'll find him." She scanned the sad faces of the rest of the Keepers. "We're gonna find all of them. We promise."

Jordan suddenly understood what Eldon meant when he said this wasn't pretty. "She's right, of course," he said. "And any information you can remember about the nights your cryptids went missing would be extremely helpful."

For the next hour or so, Jordan, Abbie, and Eldon listened to almost the exact same story from each of the distraught Keepers.

"Worst night of my life, you guys," Mike shared. "I woke to a blinding light in the sky. I ran out and felt a hot, swirling wind all around me. I looked up and"—he sniffed loudly—"I saw Lou's little hooves rising away from me. The light cut out, and all went silent. Then this floated down and landed on my head." He stood up and gestured to what he was wearing, turning around slowly. Embroidered across the silk, pink back in neon-blue stitching, it read: *Face Chompers*.

"Lou's tracking collar was cut off, lying on the ground. That's all any of us have left—just their collars, and these lady dresses."

"Actually, I think they're nighties," Abbie said.

"They're *slips*, dearie." Doris stood just inside the boathouse. She lifted her dress to reveal the white, silk material beneath it—along with a little too much of her wrinkly legs. "I wear 'em all the time. See?"

"We all wear them now," the lanky Christopher said in a British accent. He wiped his eyes and stood to join Lou. "In solidarity for our lost creatures. And we will continue to wear them until our cryptids are safely returned to us!"

The others excitedly stood up and joined in a pink-clad, group high five. Almost immediately, they reacted in pain and sat back down.

"What's wrong with them?" Jordan whispered to Eldon.

"They're still aging," Eldon said. "Since the Fountain of Youth elixir has been destroyed, they've been going through uncomfortable regrowing pains."

Jordan felt the guilt flush his face, just like before. It was because of him all the Creature Keepers around the world had been so suddenly cut off from the magical waters that kept them young and vibrant.

"I'm sorry," he said to them. "This is all my fault."

"Yes it is, dearie," Doris said. "But don't kick yourself in the fanny too hard. You also came through with something that will help ease their pain." She turned toward the doorway and hollered. "HAP! GET IN HERE WITH THAT STUFF!"

Hap entered, followed by four new elderly people, all dressed normally. Hap set down the box of tiny bottles. The five of them, plus Doris, opened a few and began administering the bottles of elixir to the elderly Creature Keepers.

"Welcome to old age," Hap said as he served them. "You guys ain't getting any younger—literally. But this'll slow the process a bit and help take the edge off."

"That's right," Doris said. "And you have Jordan to thank for it! Now, just a sip, Keepers! You need to make it last—we don't know how many more of you Bernard will be rescuing. Rest up. Your rooms should be ready in the next couple of days."

The Keepers sipped their elixir. Almost immediately, they

began feeling better, which made Jordan feel better, too.

"Eldon," Abbie said. "Who are those four old fogies helping Doris and Hap? They don't look very happy, either."

"They're not. In some ways, they're more troubled than the other Keepers."

"They're Keepers, too?" Jordan asked.

"Those are the Keepers of Paul, Francine, Donald, and Sandy, the four cryptids who"—Eldon seemed to have trouble with the next part—"*willfully abandoned us.*"

Once again, Jordan felt a guilty flush in his face. This time, however, it was due to a secret he held. Something he'd done willfully, too, and to his best friend. He'd betrayed Eldon.

"They were the first Bernard brought in," Eldon said. "On his way back from dropping Chupacabra at the Yeti's mountain home in the Himalayas. Poor Bernard had to break the news that their creatures no longer needed them. I'm sure they're beginning to come to the same conclusion that the rest of us are—that they've been abducted by the Face Chompers."

"That would explain why the four rogue cryptids haven't shown up anywhere yet, right?" Abbie said. Jordan didn't answer. He was staring at the four Keepers. So she punched him in the arm. "Hey!"

"Excuse me a second," Jordan said. "I need to talk to those Keepers."

The four Keepers were busy tending to the others, fluffing pillows and refilling water glasses. As he approached them, Jordan could tell they were going through regrowing pains, too. But they hadn't taken any of the elixir and hadn't asked for any.

"Here." Jordan pulled out a bottle and handed it to them. "This will help."

The elderly woman glanced at the others, then pushed away his offering. "That's not for us," she said. "It's for them."

A frail-looking old man read the confusion in Jordan's face. "We don't deserve that. Our creatures weren't taken. They left us."

Jordan glanced back at Eldon and Abbie, who were talking with Doris. Then he continued in a lower voice. "I was there when Paul, Donald, Francine, and Sandy left. They didn't mean to hurt you. They just wanted to live free. I saw how hard it was for them to leave."

"That may be," a third Keeper said, "but the fact is, we failed them. We couldn't keep them hidden."

"Or happy," said the fourth, a disheveled old man. "Now we can only hope that wherever they are, they're healthy."

It was clear they hadn't considered Eldon's theory

that the four rogue cryptids had been abducted by the Face Chompers. Maybe they didn't want to. Either way, Jordan had to reveal his secret. At least to them. "Listen to me," he said. "On that day, I did something I shouldn't have done. I disobeyed a direct order and gave Bernard permission to fly off and find your creatures." The four were surprised at this, and Jordan continued. "So I have to ask: when Bernard came to bring you here, did he mention anything to any of you? Was he able to find them?"

"He only told us the terrible news," the frail man said. "That our creatures had chosen to leave us, to live on their own in the world. Then he offered to bring us here, where we could be close by in case there was any news of their whereabouts. He went back out to try to find them, but that's when the distress calls started coming in from all over the world. He's been bringing in these poor Keepers, one at a time, ever since."

"Well, I'm going to make you a promise," Jordan said. "We're going to find your cryptids, and all of theirs. And we're going to bring them back to you safely. You have my word, as the new co-leader of the Creature Keepers." For the first time, a smile crept over their faces. "But in return, I need to ask you all to do something." He held out the bottle of elixir again. "Take care of yourselves. Believe me, it's what Paul, Donald, Francine, and Sandy would want."

The four Keepers smiled a little more. Then they passed the elixir around.

Jordan and Eldon followed Doris and Abbie out of the boathouse and through the swamp, back toward the retirement home. All four of them now kept an eye toward the darkening sky, searching for Face Chompers.

"I can't believe it," Eldon said to Jordan. "But I've gotta hand it to you again."

"Hey, it was nothing," Jordan said. "When Doris mentioned the Keepers were aging, I remembered Hap's stash. You would've done the same thing."

"No. I mean I can't believe it. I have to hand *this* to you, again."

Eldon held out his hand. In his open palm was a sparkling ring. It was thick and crystal clear, filled with a highly concentrated form of the same elixir that was in the tiny bottles, only far more potent.

"My grandfather's ring! Eldon, where did you find it?"

"In Japan." Eldon smiled. "I think someone may have dropped it."

Someone did. Jordan had dropped it into the bowl-shaped head of a Kappa, a cryptid who had turned to stone, then come back to life. "I'm sorry I lost it. But Eldon, I think it may have brought Morris back."

Eldon thought about this. "When your grandfather first gave the ring to me, he told me how the Fountain of Youth elixir flowing inside gave it its power. But he also said its power could be multiplied when given to someone who had made a true sacrifice. I didn't understand what he meant at the time. But I think I'm starting to."

"Morris sacrificed himself for Abbie before I gave him the ring. Maybe that's what saved him."

Eldon smiled and dropped the ring in Jordan's hand. "If that's all true, I can't say I'm unhappy with how things turned out. But this is the third time I've given you this darned thing. Please try to hold on to it."

Jordan slipped the ring on his finger. "I will. Thanks."

"You and Abbie are great leaders, and you're going

to get the Creature Keepers through this crisis. You deserve to wear your grandfather's ring. I just hope if a day comes when you need its full power, you won't have to sacrifice too much."

* * *

The remains of the high brick wall that Peggy the Jackalope had knocked down earlier had been restacked to form a short, rectangular foundation just inside the swamp. The two boys joined Doris and Abbie standing in the center of it, on a smooth, metal floor.

"Well?" Doris said. "Whaddy'all think of my new greenhouse? Now that the foundation and floor are in, all it needs are the glass walls and retractable roof."

"I never knew you had a green thumb," Jordan said.

"With all the construction going on here, no one would mind if I had this built, too. Besides, since Peggy's started living with us full-time, we've been going through a *lot* of carrots."

"Wow," Jordan said. "I nearly forgot the tough road she's had. I mean, she was neglected, then just plain left to die—by her own Keeper."

"*Ex*-Keeper," Eldon said. "Our original traitor. And public enemy number one."

"I'll never forget what that worm did to Morris," Abbie said.

Harvey Quisling was a horrid little old man who had betrayed the Creature Keepers and worked to help Chupacabra. A former Keeper himself, Harvey was guilty of one of the worst sins a Creature Keeper could commit: he'd abandoned his cryptid, Peggy. Harvey had proven himself to be a sneaky, dishonest, dangerous person, but an expert at sewing, knitting, and stitching—skills he oddly managed to use for evil.

"I swear," Abbie continued. "If I ever meet Harvey again, I'm gonna bust him up so badly, the only stitching he'll be doing will be to his own melon-shaped head."

"Stitching . . ." A thought struck Jordan. "What if Harvey Quisling is involved in this somehow? I mean, who else would leave as a calling card those weird, pink pajamas—"

"Nighties," Abbie said.

"Slips," Doris added.

"Whatever! Think about it—Harvey Quisling has stitched furniture out of jackalope fur, tailored a coat out of Nessie's scales, and sewn together a life-sized puppet out of a pillowcase and old clothes! Embroidering 'Face Chompers' on the backs of those dresses—"

"Nighties."

"Slips."

"Whatever! It would be child's play for him. He's gotta be involved. It can't be a coincidence! You watch, any day now, we'll get a crocheted ransom note."

"Jordan, those abducted cryptids were snatched from nearly every corner of the globe," Eldon said. "Quisling barely crawled out of that jungle alive less than a month ago. He could never pull off something like that."

"Not unless he had help again," Jordan said.

"So who's he working for?" Abbie said. "And what are the Face Chompers?"

Doris nodded in the direction of the retirement home. "All I know is his last boss is frozen in a block of ice under that house, locked in a cryogenic cell behind a thick steel door. So it sure as cinnamon sticks ain't Chupacabra."

Abbie thought for a moment. "What about the fourth elemental power?" She turned to Jordan. "You over- heard the two of them planning to find it and steal it, but we caught Chupacabra before they could try. If there's a fourth special power, there's bound to be a fourth special creature who controls it. Could Quisling be working for that creature now?"

"I never did find out which cryptid it was," Jordan said. But it's possible Harvey could have known."

"What if it's a new creature?" Abbie said. "One that's never been discovered?"

"An undiscovered cryptid?" Eldon said. "No way, unless its special power was invisibility. It would have to have somehow kept itself hidden all these years from humans, from Creature Keepers, even from George Grimsley himself!"

"We all know the powers the other three have," Jor- dan said. "Nessie can move oceans with the flick of her tail. Sasquatch can split the earth open with one big foot. The Yeti can cover an entire continent with snow in a single breath. If there is a fourth special creature, who knows what its power could be."

"Whatever it is, it very well could be snatching up

OCEANS

EARTH

WEATHER

4th SPECIAL CREATURE POWER

other cryptids," Eldon said. "And possibly transforming them into something called Face Chompers."

"And Harvey Quisling could be helping it," Jordan added.

"But where in the world is it?" Abbie said. "Did they mention any clues?"

Jordan shook his head. "Harvey may be the only one who knows."

"He and one other," Doris said. "Let's go downstairs and ask him, shall we?"

A loud noise suddenly startled all of them as one end of the metal greenhouse floor began to lower, forming a ramp. They all looked up at Doris standing on a safe edge at the top of the ramp, smiling at them, holding a remote control. "I told you I needed a new entrance to move that frozen Chupacasicle into central command! So I installed a secret back door!"

The floor opened at an extreme angle to a gaping black space below, swallowing them up. Doris slid down behind them, disappearing into the darkness.

Jordan, Abbie, Eldon, and Doris tumbled onto the cool, white, polished floor of the underground Creature Keepers command center, slamming into boxes, chairs, and desks stacked up in the center of the large room.

"Sorry about the clutter," Doris said as Eldon helped her to her feet. "We should start putting this place back together."

"How about you start putting some stairs in that entrance?" Abbie said.

"It's really more for equipment than people," Doris said. "And of course it serves as a nice bunny door when Peggy needs to do her business—"

BOING-BOING-FWOOSH! Before Doris could

finish her sentence, a bus-sized blur of white fluff bounced past them and bounded up the ramp, out into the swamp.

"Boy," Jordan said. "I guess when a giant Texas Jackalope needs to go, she needs to go."

Ed, a bald and bookish old man, stepped out of a side chamber holding an enormous pooper scooper and a large shovel. "You have no idea," he said. "Welcome back."

Eldon stood before a short row of personalized lockers lined against a wall. "Okay, everyone. Safety first." He was wearing goggles and a yellow hard hat and slammed closed the door to a locker marked *Pecone, E.* He opened the one beside it, marked *Grimsley, A.*

Abbie took out her goggles and hard hat. "*Now* you give us these? Where were they when we went down the carrot garden slide of death?"

"Just be sure each of you returns your own equipment to your designated locker before leaving," Eldon said. "This is Creature Keeper property."

Creature Keeper central command was the hub of the entire cryptid protection operation. Thanks in small part to the technological know-how of Jordan and in large part to the small fortune left behind by his grandfather, the secret underground station was crammed full of state-of-the art equipment. Grampa Grimsley had left all of his estate to be managed by a lawyer named C. E. Noodlepen. This mysterious gatekeeper originally notified the Grimsleys they were the legal benefactors of the old house and was also the one from whom Jordan and Abbie's parents could request Grampa Grimlsey's resources as needed for home improvement.

Luckily for Jordan and the Creature Keepers

command center, C. E. Noodlepen was also none other than Eldon Pecone. Even the letters in their names matched up.

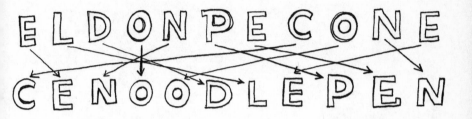

Jordan's grandfather had left Eldon with final authorization on all his savings and estate. Because Eldon was underage, he used the pseudonym to access his accounts by mail, funding what Jordan and Doris needed to bring the CKCC up to modern standards. This included computers, tracking systems, digital display maps, and a really nice coffee maker. It also included the latest addition and Jordan's latest design, which Jordan called "The Cooler." It was a cryonic, vaultlike freezer cell designed to keep its prisoner not only locked up tight but also frozen solid.

Jordan and Abbie were mesmerized as they stepped away from their lockers and approached the looming Cooler on the opposite side of the room. In the center of the door was a thick-glass portal. In the center of the cold, steel cell was a massive block of ice. And in the center of that ice was a familiar silhouette, belonging to the horrible Chupacabra.

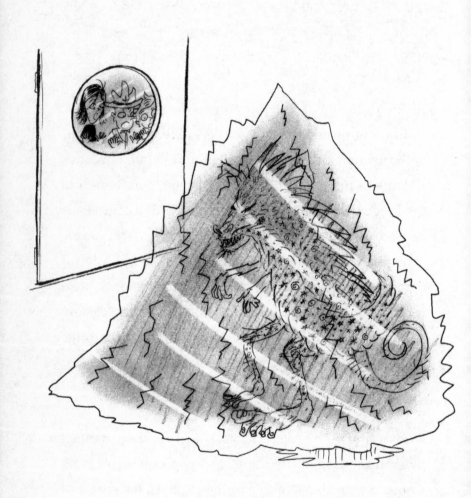

"Wilford had kept him in a perfect frozen state at the top of the Himalayas," Eldon said. "Bernard and Kriss flew all the way back to Mt. Kanchenjunga to pick him up."

Kriss was the West Virginia Mothman, a cryptid who was a little moody and a lot shy. Which may be why Abbie shared a special kinship with him. "The abominable snowman and the introverted mothman," she said. "Sounds like quite a party. Where's Kriss now?"

"He stayed up on the mountain," Doris said. "Bernard said he seemed to take a liking to the solitude."

"That sounds like Kriss, all right," Abbie said.

Doris peeked through the portal, then held up an ice pick. "Well? Let's wake up Sleeping Beauty and ask him about the fourth special cryptid, shall we?"

They all huddled around the portal and stared in at the dark, Chupacabra-shaped blob suspended in the center of the ice. A shiver ran through Jordan, which had nothing to do with the freezer in front of him. "Uh, Ed," he said. "How long to get this place back online?"

"With your help on the computers? Not long at all, I should think."

"Great," Jordan said. "Then I'd like to propose a plan B. Ed and I will get the tracking computer back up and running so we can immediately begin a scan, pinpointing exactly where the Face Chompers struck and see if there's a pattern that might lead us to a location of origin for whatever we're dealing with. Sound good?"

The others looked in at Chupacabra one more time and quickly agreed that Jordan's plan B was much better than defrosting the diabolical cryptid.

Doris tossed her ice pick aside and let out a chuckle. "I knew you'd all chicken out once you saw him again. Ed, if you're going to help Jordan get all this junk up and running, you'll need your rest. Who do we have to take your shift on watch tonight?"

Hap's voice called out from the bottom of the ramp. "Hap Cooperdock reporting for duty!" The shaggy old Keeper approached them. "Need someone to stay up all night gazing at a freezer door? I could do that in my sleep!"

The next few days were busy ones as Jordan and Ed worked to get the mapping and tracking system reinstalled and back online. Abbie helped Doris and Hap put the finishing touches on the new guest rooms, then prepared to move the Keepers from the boathouse into the nicer surroundings of Eternal Acres. Eldon continuously scanned the sky and treetops, watching for any sign of a Face Chomper attack—while also keeping an eager eye out for his creature, Bernard, to return.

The Skunk Ape had been expected earlier, but Doris reassured the others that there was no need for alarm. "His last distress call came in from eastern Europe," she said as she, Jordan, Abbie, and Eldon carried the Keepers' lunch out to the boathouse. "We can't contact him until we get the system online, but he could reach me if there was an emergency. It's also possible he picked up a new distress signal on the Heli-Jet radio and went to rescue another Keeper."

"That's my Bernard," Eldon said, trying to hide the worried tone in his voice. "Always looking to help others."

"I'm sure he'll be here any day now," Abbie said.

"Right," Jordan added. "If there's one thing I learned about that Skunk Ape of yours, he can take care of himself."

Bernard was the first cryptid Jordan had ever met. The two of them had been through a lot together, and Jordan thought of him as sort of a great-uncle—a big hairy, stinky great-uncle. In addition to looking forward to seeing Bernard again, both Jordan and Abbie were eager to find out everything he'd seen and heard while out collecting abandoned Keepers. If there were any sign of Harvey Quisling, or any clues to an undiscovered special cryptid kidnapping other creatures and brainwashing them into becoming Face Chompers, Bernard was just the Skunk Ape to pick up on them and report back.

They all arrived at the boathouse to find Hap staring down at the box of elixir. "Weird," he said. "I could've sworn there were more bottles here." He turned to the elderly Keepers. "Did any of you coots raid my supply? We seem a little short."

"Of course they didn't," Doris said as she set down the basket of food. "The only thing that's short is your memory, Cooperdock. I'm sure you just miscounted how much you brought with you. Now let them eat their lunch. We have some exciting news: you're all moving out of this drafty boathouse today and into your new rooms at Eternal Acres!"

After the celebratory meal, the Keepers gathered up their things and were led out of the boathouse by Abbie and Doris. They were offered fresh pairs of pajamas, but they all refused to change out of their pink *Face Chompers* garments.

"We will continue to wear these in solidarity," Mike said, "until our creatures are safely returned to us."

"Well, at least let us wash them when we get to the house," Abbie said. "They're getting a little ripe."

Jordan and Eldon followed Hap toward the boat-house door. He was carrying the wooden crate of elixir with his head down and lips moving, silently recounting the bottles in the box.

"Hap, look where you're going!" Jordan shouted. Hap looked up just in time to walk into the wall beside the doorway. He fumbled with the box, nearly dumping all the tiny bottles onto the floor.

"Sorry," he said. "That was a close one."

"Give me that," Eldon said, taking the box. "Now that everyone's moved out of here, I'll keep them safe in my tent."

"Your tent?" Jordan said. "Eldon, the Keepers are going to be living in the house now. You don't have to camp out here anymore."

"I prefer it," Eldon said. "Besides, out here I can keep an ear to the ground and my eyes on the skies—for Face Chompers or anything else." Eldon saluted, then disappeared inside his tent.

Jordan and Hap made their way back toward Eternal Acres, and came across Doris's finished greenhouse. Its iron frame had been attached to the stone foundation and held up its glass walls and ceiling.

"This came out really sweet." Hap stepped inside the open door. Bunches of carrots lay on shelves mounted along the walls. Beneath the shelves, long, deep boxes of soil lined the inside perimeter of the little glass house, where new carrot tops sprouted out of the dirt. The center of the floor was empty except for a few crates of even more fresh carrots. Jordan picked one up and took a bite.

"Hey, check this out." Hap reached for one of two buttons mounted on the wall beside the door. "Doris told me the roof opens up!"

CLACK! GRRRR!

"Hap! That's the wrong button!"

The floor beneath them began to lower as before. Jordan leaped to grab the edge of the shelf. Hap was frantically hitting the button, trying to reverse the ramp. It continued to open, sending the crates of carrots tumbling into the darkness below. Hap pulled Jordan up to the secure section of the floor, and they both froze as they heard a stirring sound rise beneath them, followed by an echoing *MUNCH-MUNCH-CRUNCH!* Something down there was chowing carrots.

"*Peggy*," Jordan whispered as the munching sound suddenly stopped. A loud *SNIFF! SNIFF-SNIFF!* echoed up in its place.

"Well, better her than the *other* critter that's down there," Hap said.

"*Shh!*" Jordan glanced at the shelves surrounding them and saw the bunches of carrots. Then he heard a loud *THUMP! THUMP!* It was getting louder. And faster. "Oh, no," he said. "The ceiling! She's gonna crash straight through it! She'll be cut to ribbons! Hap! *Hit the other button!*"

Hap slammed the second button, and a whirring sound began grinding overhead as the glass ceiling began to slowly retract. Beneath them, the *THUMP-THUMP-THUMP*-ing grew closer as Peggy charged up the ramp.

Jordan grabbed a bunch of carrots and flung them into the dark, empty space in the center of the greenhouse. As he did, a large white, fluffy head emerged like a breaching whale swallowing them. Peggy leaped straight up just as the ceiling finished retracting, soaring over their heads and landing outside, a hundred feet from the greenhouse. She sat up and sniffed the air for more to eat. Relieved, Jordan and Hap ran outside and tossed more carrots to Peggy.

A voice shouted out from the house. "Jordan! Are you out here, son?" Jordan froze. It was his father. Mr. and Mrs. Grimsley were just inside the back-porch door.

"Oh, no." Thinking quickly, Jordan shoved the last bunch of carrots in Hap's arms. "My parents! They can't see Peggy! Get her out of here!"

"No problemo!" Hap whistled, then flung the carrots in the air toward the swamp. But Peggy was too

fast and dived at them. The bunch caught on her antlers, dangling just in front of her nose. "Uh-oh," Hap
said. "That's not good."

Peggy burst forward to get the carrots she was dangling in front of herself. Luckily, the direction she was
facing took her away from the house, into the swamp.

"Don't just stand there," Jordan said. "She could run
for days! Go get her!"

Hap tore off after Peggy. Jordan ran toward the house.

Up on the deck, Abbie and Doris spotted Peggy and
quickly stepped in front of Mr. and Mrs. Grimsley. Doris
called to the group of Keepers behind them, and within
seconds, the Grimsleys were surrounded by pink-clad
retirees blocking their view of the cotton-tailed fanny
Hap was chasing through the cypress trees.

8

"Surprise! Are you surprised? We wanted to surprise you!" Mrs. Grimsley loved surprises.

"Super surprised, Mom." Jordan nervously eyed the swamp behind him.

"We met our wonderful new tenants," Mr. Grimsley said, patting Mike on his balding head. "Such nice folks, so happy to have them staying here!"

Mrs. Grimsley leaned in close. "Although their matching pajamas are a little odd," she whispered.

A sudden rustling sound

from the swamp got everyone's attention. The top of a distant cypress tree began to shake and shudder. "Looks like the wind is picking up out here," Doris said quickly. "Storm might be coming. Best to get inside before it rains!"

They all shoved Mr. and Mrs. Grimsley back into the house. Jordan slammed the door and shut the curtain, then peeked out. His stomach dropped.

The giant Jackalope crashed through the trees, hopped over the greenhouse, and landed in the back-yard with a thump. Hanging off her neck, holding on for dear life, Eldon was trying to reach for the carrots still dangling from her antlers. Hap was bear-hugging her fluffy tail, riding it like a rodeo cowboy. Peggy lunged for the carrots, leaping around the side of the house.

Inside, Mrs. Grimsley turned pale. "What was that? The whole house shook!"

"Doris is right," Abbie said. "Thunderstorm coming! Why don't we all go sit in the living room before we get any more, uh, surprises?"

They made their procession down the long hallway, away from the back of the house, past the bedrooms, and toward the great room near the front door.

"The renovations are something," Mr. Grimsley said. "Great work, Doris."

"Thank you," Doris said. "But I couldn't have done

it without the help of Jordan and Abbie." She turned her smile from Mr. and Mrs. Grimsley and shot a secret glare at Jordan. "They really are good at tackling big challenges."

"That's wonderful," Mrs. Grimsley said, smiling proudly at her children. "And it makes our wonderful news for the two of you all the more wonderfuller!"

"Well," Doris said. "Then I'll excuse myself and take our new guests to their bedrooms, and let you have your family time."

The Grimsleys made their way into the great room, leaving Doris and the Keepers. As soon as the coast was clear, Doris and the Keepers ran down the hallway and out into the backyard.

In the great room, Jordan immediately began pulling down the window curtains. As he did, he spotted Peggy running in circles alongside the house, like a giant dog chasing its tail, trying to get at the carrots hanging from her antlers. Eldon hung off the other antler and finally grabbed the carrots. As soon as he did, Peggy stopped short, sending Eldon flying into a nearby hedge.

"Something out there, son?" Mr. Grimsley said as he approached. Jordan took one last look. Eldon tossed the carrots to Hap, who sprinted off toward the swamp like a football player, with Peggy in hot pursuit. Doris and the Keepers came around the corner and had to dive out of the way as Peggy nearly trampled them. Eldon looked up at Jordan. He gave a grin and a thumbs-up, then collapsed into the hedge.

Jordan's father joined him at the window. "What is it?"

Jordan let out a sigh of relief. "Just a pesky badger flopping around in the hedges."

"Well, come sit down," Mrs. Grimsley said. "We've got another surprise!"

"We're going on a vacation!" Mr. Grimsley blurted out, stealing his wife's news. "Just us! Gonna grab some Grimsley Family Fun Time! How great is that?"

Abbie stepped forward. "What? When?"

"Right away!" Mrs. Grimsley said. "Before the two of you start at your new school. "You've worked so hard and done so much for us, and we feel awful that we took away your vacations this past year to work on this old house."

"Uh, that's very nice and all," Jordan said, "but we really don't need a vacation. We're happy to stay here and make sure everything's running smoothly—"

"Ranger Master Bernie said you'd say that!" Mr. Grimsley held up four colorful tickets. "That's why he sent us these!"

"It would be rude not to use them," Mrs. Grimsley said. "He's very nice."

"Ranger Master Bernie?" Jordan said.

Abbie snatched the tickets from her dad and quickly read them. "He's booked the four of us on a cruise across the Gulf of Mexico?"

"Specifically, the Yucatan Peninsula!" Mr. Grimsley said.

Ranger Master Bernie was not an actual Ranger, or a Master, or even a person. He was actually Bernard the Skunk Ape, with his fur shaved off, stuffed into one of Eldon's old Badger Ranger uniforms. Disguised as a Ranger Master, he'd fooled Jordan and Abbie's parents in the past, convincing them to send their children off on secret Creature Keeper missions. It was still slightly amazing to both Jordan and Abbie that their parents fell for it the first time, never mind the two or three times since. But he'd never sent all four of them any-where together.

"Well?" their dad said. "Who's ready for some Grimsley Family Fun Time?"

"Uh, we are," Abbie said. "I guess."

An idea struck Jordan. "But we'd like to bring our friend Eldon along if that's okay." He and Abbie shared a look, and she understood immediately.

"That's your friend you told us so much about," Mrs. Grimsley said. "We'd love to have him join us."

"I don't know," Mr. Grimsley said. "Inviting a non-Grimsley kind of dilutes Grimsley Family Fun Time, don't you think?"

"We're kind of his only friends," Jordan said. "It'd really mean a lot to him to come."

"Please, Roger," Mrs. Grimsley said.

They all looked at Mr. Grimsley, who wasn't thrilled.

"All right," he finally said. "Give him one of our tickets, and I'll order an extra one. I just hope he can muster some of the Grimsley spirit."

"Don't worry, he'll fit right in," Abbie said. "He's a total dorkface."

Jordan and Abbie ran through the swamp toward the boathouse, searching for Eldon. Before they reached his pup tent, they tripped over the exhausted Badger Ranger, who was lying against a tree, sipping from his canteen, drenched in sweat.

"What are you doing down there?" Abbie asked.

"Where's Peggy?" Jordan said.

"She's back down below," Eldon said. "Hap and I were able to wrestle her through the greenhouse entrance."

"You look awful," Abbie said.

"Golly, thanks. Next time I'll let you wrangle a giant Jackalope into submission. I'm getting too old for this stuff." He took another swig from his canteen.

"Eldon, listen to us. Our parents are taking us on a trip. A family vacation. And you have to come with us."

"Family vacation? Me? No, no. I couldn't possibly. I'd be a fifth wheel."

Abbie held up the tickets. "Forget fifth wheels—this might be about the *fourth special*."

"Look at the tickets," Jordan said. "The trip is to the Yucatan Peninsula, just across the Gulf of Mexico. *And Bernard is the one who sent these to our parents.*"

Eldon suddenly looked taken aback. He snatched the tickets and read them.

"Don't you remember?" Abbie said. "Wilford told us how the three special cryptids were born from huge world-changing extinction events that happened over the millennia! The Yeti himself came from a massive ice age. An explosion of new tree and plant life created Syd the Sasquatch from the soil. And it was a shift in the seas that flooded the earth and was responsible for Nessie!"

Eldon looked up at them.

"He also told us about a fourth extinction event," Jordan said. "An asteroid that struck the earth with such impact it left a crater a hundred and ten miles wide."

"And probably wiped out the dinosaurs," Abbie said.

"The Yucatan Peninsula's Chicxulub crater," Eldon said. "But this can't be right. There are no documented cryptids from that area."

"Not *documented*," Abbie said.

"Not yet," Jordan added.

Eldon was catching on. "If this cataclysmic event yielded a fourth special cryptid with a fourth elemental power, how'd it go undetected for millions of years?"

Abbie shrugged. "All I know is every time that Skunk Ape of yours shaves off his fur, squeezes his burly butt into your old Badger Ranger shorts, and tricks our parents into letting us go somewhere, I end up meeting some weird creature."

"It can't be a coincidence," Jordan said. "None of this can."

"You don't think Bernard's in some kind of trouble, do you?" Eldon said.

"I don't think he would've found the time to purchase cruise tickets for the four of us if he were in any kind of danger," Jordan said.

"You're right," Eldon said. "Maybe he found some clue and wanted us to check it out right away!" His smile suddenly turned to a concentrated scowl. "But why invite your parents?"

"Maybe he got another distress call, like Doris said," Abbie suggested.

"I bet he's on his way here with a new Keeper he's rescued, and knew he'd need our folks out of here for a few days," Jordan added. "Pretty smart of him, if you ask me."

Eldon wiped away a tear.

"What's with you?" Abbie said.

"I'm just so proud of that darned Skunk Ape."

"So you'll come with us, then?" Jordan said.

Eldon let out a sniffle, then gave them a Badger Ranger salute. "First-Class Badger Ranger Eldon Pecone reporting for duty."

9

The *Mayan Princess* wasn't exactly a cruise ship—it was more like a giant yacht. It only held a few hundred passengers, but it had many of the same fancy trappings as one of those floating hotel-like ships, including a swimming pool, sauna, multiple decks, and an entire floor of cozy, ocean-view cabins.

Jordan and Abbie made their way onboard and through the various levels, finally exiting onto the top outer deck. A crowd of passengers pushed against the railing, waving good-bye to people on the dock below.

"Where's Eldon?" Abbie asked, pushing through the crowd with her brother.

"He said he had to pack some things, and he'd meet us here on the ship," Jordan said. "But I don't know how we're going to find him with all these people!"

Abbie scanned the sea of tourists. Among the bright blue Bermuda shorts, blindingly orange flowery Hawaiian shirts, and neon-green tank tops, she spotted a drab brown hat floating above the crowd. "I see him," she said.

They found him standing alone near a bathroom door, looking pale and jittery. "Eldon, are you okay?" Jordan said.

Eldon took a sip from his canteen. "I'm just a little seasick."

"We haven't even left the dock yet," Abbie said.

"Our parents are around here some-where," Jordan said. "They're eager to meet you." Jordan looked back at the crowd. "I think I see them." He yelled toward the front of the ship. "Mom! Dad! Over here!"

URP

Eldon suddenly seemed to turn paler. He put his hand over his mouth like he was going to be sick. He rushed into the bathroom, slammed the door, and locked it behind him, just as Mr. and Mrs. Grimsley approached.

"Hey, kids!" Mr. Grimsley said loudly. He was wearing a Hawaiian shirt with a bright goldfish and teal kelp pattern. "Isn't this great?"

"Where's your friend?" Mrs. Grimsley said. "Did Eldon get onboard all right? We're shoving off any minute."

Jordan gestured toward the closed bathroom door. "He's not feeling well."

Eldon's muffled voice came through the door. "It's a pleasure to meet you, Mr. and Mrs. Grimsley. Thank you for including me in your family vacation."

"Oh! Our pleasure!" Mr. Grimsley shouted at the door. "Jordan and Abbie speak very highly of you. Nice to, er, meet you. Sort of." He glanced at Jordan and Abbie, then leaned closer to them. "I thought you said he was a First-Class Badger Ranger," he said in a softer voice.

"He is," Abbie said. "I also told you he was a first-class dorkface."

"Well, he doesn't seem to be cut from the heartiest Badger Ranger material."

"Be nice," Mrs. Grimsley admonished them. "Although I must say, he's not at all like that rugged Master Ranger Bernie, is he?"

"Sorry to interrupt you, Mr. and Mrs. Grimsley," Eldon said through the door. "But you should know that I can hear everything you're saying."

"Well, you just take your time and feel better!" Mr. Grimsley yelled into the door. "And when you're ready, come and join us on the Lido deck by the pool! We'll have plenty of time to talk and get to know one another once we're on the open sea. It's a twelve-hour trip, after all!"

Eldon answered with a horrible retching sound.

Mr. and Mrs. Grimsley made their way off through the crowd. Jordan and Abbie leaned an ear to the door. "Hey, Eldon," Abbie said. "Hang in there, okay?" She was answered with a gagging sound. She shrugged at Jordan and walked to join her parents.

Jordan leaned in next. "Hey, buddy. Listen, before we left the house I told Doris to let us know when Bernard returns to the swamp. She'll have him radio us with whatever info he has on the fourth special creature. Then we can spoor for this mystery cryptid together, just like old times, okay?" What he heard back was more retching. "Don't worry about making it to dinner if you don't feel up to it. You're in cabin B-14, just down the hall from us. If we don't see you tonight, we'll find you in the morning. Rest up and you'll feel good as new for our adventure tomorrow!"

The door unlocked. It opened a bit. Jordan stepped

back as Eldon's hand slowly emerged, with a very tenuous thumbs-up. Jordan slipped the key to Eldon's cabin into his hand, and it disappeared again, the bathroom door locking once more.

That night, after an Eldon-less dinner with his parents and sister, Jordan lay in the bottom bunk of the cabin he was sharing with Abbie. He could hardly sleep. Here they were, on their way to do the one thing Jordan had fantasized about ever since he'd read Grampa Grimsley's journal. He always wondered what it must have been like for his grandfather to go on an expedition and track and discover a never-before-seen cryptid. And this was not any cryptid. What they were looking for was quite possibly the fourth special cryptid, one in possession of the last elemental power. He only wished his grandfather could be with them.

"Hey, Abbie," Jordan whispered to the top bunk. "Do you think when we find the fourth special creature we get to name it? Or do you think it picks its own name?"

"I don't know," her voice came back through the darkness. "Depends on how smart it is, I guess."

"If we do get to name it, is it okay if I pick the name?"

"It depends."

"On what?"

"On whether or not you pick a dumb name."

Jordan thought for a moment. "Well, if it's a girl cryptid, I think I'd like to name her Ellerie Rose. Whaddya think?"

There was a silence. Jordan suddenly hoped his sister had fallen asleep and hadn't heard him. Then suddenly Abbie's voice replied in the darkness.

"Yeah. Ellerie Rose is actually a very cool name."

* * *

The next morning, Jordan opened his eyes to see a horribly familiar face staring at him. He shrieked and tossed Abbie's overweight pet iguana off his chest. Chunk hit the floor like a sack of wet ham. "What is that thing doing here?"

Abbie leaned her head upside down over the edge of the top bunk, still half asleep. She looked at Jordan, then at Chunk, then back at Jordan. "He *was* trying to sleep. We both were. Till you woke us up."

Chunk was safely hidden in Abbie's backpack as the two of them made their way down the hall to cabin B-14. The door was ajar, so they pushed it open and looked inside. There was no sign of Eldon, but his bed had been slept in.

They began searching the ship for him, keeping an eye on the approaching horizon. They came across their parents happily sitting in the breakfast rotunda behind a mountainous stack of all-you-can-eat waffles.

"Pull up a plate!" Mr. Grimsley exclaimed through a mouthful of fried batter, butter, and syrup. "Gotta fill up for Grimsley Family Fun Time!"

"No thanks, Dad," Jordan said. "Have you seen Eldon anywhere?"

Mr. Grimsley shook his head. "We literally have *never* seen him. Wouldn't know him if he served me these waffles!"

"Is he feeling better?" Mrs. Grimsley asked. "I feel so badly for him."

Before they could answer, a voice came over the ship intercom: "*Good morning, passengers. We are now approaching the port city of Progreso, Mexico, and will be docking at el Terminal Remota, the longest pier in the world. Please feel free to disembark and explore this wonderful seaside village on the Yucatan Peninsula. You may contact our lovely and helpful cruise director at the information kiosk for things to do and see on your visit. Buenos dias!"*

"I'm sure Eldon's all right," Jordan said. "But we should probably find him before we reach the port. We'll check in with you guys later."

They didn't want to worry their parents, but as soon as they were out of their sight, Jordan and Abbie ran to the bathroom where Eldon had last been spotted. Finding it empty, they continued searching as the ship docked. He was nowhere to be found. They stood against a railing, scanning the lower decks.

"Hey, you guys! Down here!" Eldon's voice called to them from farther below. Eldon was waving from the pier. He had his backpack on, looking eager to explore. "Let's go!" he yelled up. "That undiscovered creature isn't gonna spoor itself!"

10

El Terminal Remota was indeed the longest pier in the world. Basically a straight, double-laned road that ran five miles out from the coast, it connected the beachy mainland of Progreso, Mexico, to the deep water dock where the yachts and cruise ships came in. At the deep end, a large gathering area served as a parking lot for taxis, buses, and tour guides waiting to shuttle tourists into town as they stepped off their ships. It also served

as a vibrant marketplace and boardwalk, with booths and shops filled with locals selling T-shirts, gifts, and adventurous excursions—from the ancient Mayan pyramid tours in the nearby jungles, to deep sea fishing trips, to cave spelunking, whale watching, and more.

Abbie, Jordan, and Eldon walked past all the touristy wonders, determined to begin an adventure that wasn't likely to be offered by any guide or local vendor.

"I'm glad you're feeling better," Jordan said to Eldon.

Eldon sipped from his canteen. "I just needed to get off that ship. Any news from Doris?"

"I contacted her this morning," Jordan said. "Bernard still hasn't shown up."

"I'm sure he's okay," Abbie said quickly. "I mean, he sent us here, so that probably means he was too busy helping other Keepers or he would have picked us up and brought us here himself."

Eldon nodded. "I know. I just miss him. And I'm worried he took a dangerous risk to discover what he's sent us here to find. What if he got too close to these Face Chompers?"

"Even if he did, we know he's okay," Jordan said. "He wouldn't have booked us on that leisurely cruise if he were in some sort of danger. I bet he's on his way back to Okeeyuckachokee right now with another Keeper he's rescued. When he lands, Doris will tell him we got his secret message, and he'll help us find whatever it is we're supposed to be looking for."

"What are we supposed to be looking for?" Abbie said.

"I don't know," Eldon said, looking past them. "But that might be a good place to start."

A small booth set up along the boardwalk sported a sign that read: *Behold the Chicxulub Crater.* Beneath it an artist's painting depicted an asteroid slamming into the earth, with some very surprised-looking dinosaurs standing around in the foreground.

"That's the extinction event Wilford told us about," Abbie said, stepping toward the booth.

A young girl smiled at them as she offered Abbie a map. "Welcome to Paradiso. Are you interested in learning about the crater?"

"We'd like a guide to take us on a tour," Abbie said. "Is it far from here?"

The girl began to giggle.

"Sorry," Abbie said. "But I wasn't really going for funny."

"You are standing over the crater right now," the girl said. "You are in it." She turned and gestured across the Gulf of Mexico behind her. The others gazed out at the turquoise water. "This area is roughly half the Chicxulub crater," she said. She turned and pointed inland, toward a low mountain ridge curving beyond the sandy beach and green jungle. "The other half is on land, extending along those hills."

"Oh," Jordan said, rather overwhelmed at the size of it. "I see. . . ."

"The best exploring to do is to visit the cenotes that line the ridge."

"Cenotes?" Eldon asked.

"Freshwater swimming pools," she said. "Millions of years ago, the impact of the asteroid resulted in layers of porous limestone. Over time they crumbled and collapsed, forming deep sinkholes that filled with rain-water. They are connected by a series of underwater caves and tunnels. The scuba tours can take you diving if you like. Or you can just do like the local children: jump in and swim."

"Sounds fun," Abbie said.

"And very beautiful. It is said the cenotes are where the ancient Mayans came to communicate with their gods. They were the gateways to a mythical under-world. Now thousands of people swim in the cenotes every year."

Eldon took the map from Abbie and unfolded it. The three of them saw the outline of a great circle laid over a small segment of the Yucatan Peninsula. It was half over the land and half over the water, just as the girl had said. There were photos, as well, of tourists and locals crowding the swimming holes.

"So they're crawling with tourists," Abbie said. "Some secret adventure."

"You're right," Eldon said. "There's no way a cryptid could go unseen all these years in a place as crowded as this."

"Hey, guys?" Jordan called from a few booths down the pier. He was standing in front of a shabby, poorly-nailed-together stand made largely of what looked like found driftwood. They thanked the girl and walked to see what Jordan had found.

Jordan stood beside a thin man in flip-flops, cutoff shorts, and a tank top. His crudely painted sign overhead read: *See—Amazing Creature—El Alebrijes!*

"Guys, meet Sam," Jordan said, grinning. "He has a creature he'd very much like us to see."

"Again, not much of a secret adventure," Abbie said. "This can't be what we're looking for."

Eldon stepped up. "Sam, we're looking for a very unique kind of creature. If what you're offering is a regular old, run-of-the-mill kind of creature, we're not interested." Something stirred in Abbie's backpack. Chunk's scaly face popped out, then sagged drowsily. "See," Eldon said. "We've got the basic creatures covered."

Sam laughed, then patted Chunk, who snapped at his finger. Sam chuckled some more, then pulled a piece of paper out of his pocket. "No," he said, looking around suspiciously. "Not a lizard. I will show you . . . *El Alebrijes!*" His eyes lit up as he described it. "It has a head like your reptile's, but also large feathered wings, a woolly trunk, gold-furred legs, and clawlike feet!"

"Okay," Jordan said. "That does not sound like your run-of-the-mill lizard."

"The Alebrijes is a one of a kind, señor! Trust me, you've never seen anything like this creature in your life! You won't believe your eyes!"

A few moments later, Abbie, Jordan, Eldon, and Chunk were in Sam's clunky old jeep, making their way toward the mainland, away from the *Mayan Princess.* Jordan was watching the stalls rushing past, when something suddenly caught his eye.

"Wait!" he hollered. "Stop the car!"

Sam screeched on the brakes. Jordan stood up in the jeep and looked back.

"What is it?" Abbie said.

"Quisling," Jordan said, scanning the crowd. "I could've sworn I spotted him."

"What? Where?" Eldon stood up beside him. Abbie joined, and the three of them scanned the crowd. Jordan pointed back a ways.

"There. Near those guys."

Sam backed up toward a group of locals who were fishing off the side of the concrete pier. They were crowded near a sign on the railing reading *Prohibido el Paso*—No Trespassing. The sign seemed unnecessary, as the tattered footbridge on the other side was hardly more than rope and cable, its broken and missing planks making it impassable. It ran a hundred feet out over the water and connected to an old wooden structure.

"Are you sure?" Abbie said. "I don't see that little troll anywhere."

"I couldn't have imagined it," Jordan said, looking around. There was no sign of Quisling. His gaze fell upon the structure standing in the middle of the water. It was a dark, rotting, gray platform hosting a cluster of boarded-up, abandoned old buildings with rotted-out scaffolding. Rising from the center was a large wooden tower. "Sam, what is that?"

"The old oil rig. From years ago, when this was the end of the pier."

The three of them looked down. The concrete section of the pier they'd been driving butted up against the older, wood-planked section that ran the rest of the way to the beach.

"When the oil company's expensive drill broke down, they abandoned it."

"It's so ugly," Eldon said. "Why doesn't the government tear it down?"

"It is harmless," Sam said. "Although some think it is cursed. Or haunted."

Jordan stared out at the rig. "Like by ghosts?"

"Not ghosts," Sam said. "By the spirit of the Chicxulub. The name of the crater that lies beneath and spreads all the way to the jungle. It means 'the devil's fleas.'"

"So people believe the devil's fleas are haunting an old oil rig," Abbie said.

"What do you think?" Jordan said to Sam.

Sam smiled. "I think the wooden legs of the old rig attract fish beneath the water. There is very good fishing there."

"Of course," Eldon said. "It likely provides a natural feeding habitat."

"Perhaps, señor." Sam chuckled. "Or maybe the fish like to nibble on the devil's fleas." Sam roared the engine, honked the horn, and pulled out. Abbie and Eldon sat down as Jordan stared back at the haunted oil rig, thinking about Harvey Quisling and wondering how his eyes could play such a strange trick on him.

The jeep rumbled through the beachside tourist town of Progreso, heading straight into the thick jungle that spread out beyond it. Through the trees they saw a clearing in the distance, with incredible Mayan pyramids towering over the canopy. Abbie spotted a sign beside the road that led toward the ruins, which read: *¡Cruce de la Iguana!*

Sam pointed to the ancient construction as they passed but didn't slow down a bit. They barreled past, heading deeper into the jungle. Eventually, they reached another, smaller intersecting road. Sam turned onto the road and entered a small village.

The main road of Flamboyanes was lined with small block houses constructed out of brightly painted slabs of concrete and overgrown with lush, green trees and jungle brush. Something about the way the houses struggled against the bursting jungle reminded Jordan of the way the wall that once stood in his grandfather's backyard seemed to be fighting back the Okeeyucka-chokee Swamp.

They passed open air restaurants and could smell the food being cooked over wood fires. They waved to the people walking along the roads and in the shopping markets. It was a simple, charming little village— certainly not the kind of place one would expect to find a sixty-six-million-or-so-year-old cryptid hiding out.

They jolted to a stop in front of a small warehouse on the edge of town. Children were playing outside, but over their laughter, Jordan could hear voices just inside the sliding metal door and lively music coming from what sounded like a small radio. There were also the sounds of hammering and sawing.

Jordan, Abbie, and Eldon all stared at the door with the exact opposite expression from Sam, who was grinning in anticipation. "You are about to witness something very special and rare!" Sam gripped the handle of the sliding warehouse door. "I sincerely hope you are all prepared!"

"Prepared to be disappointed," Abbie muttered.

Even Eldon agreed. "Uh, sir, what is your refund

policy if we decide at this exact moment that this isn't something we're interested in seeing anymore?"

Sam let out a hearty laugh. "I tell you what, señor," he said. "I do not know what you expect to see behind this door. But I promise you it is beyond your wildest imaginations. In fact, if what I'm about to show you does not make you scream, I will refund your money in full."

"You're on, buddy," Abbie said.

Sam knocked on the door. Immediately, the lively music stopped. So did the voices and the construction sounds. The children excitedly gathered from behind as an odd squeaking grew louder. Something was approaching them. Something large.

Then another knock. This time from the inside. Sam grinned again. "That is the sign. Now . . . feast your eyes on the terrifying . . . *ALEBRIJES*!"

He yanked open the door. Abbie, Jordan, and Eldon screamed at the top of their lungs. Abbie ducked behind Eldon, and Jordan fell backward onto

the ground. Chunk peeked out of Abbie's backpack, hissed, and disappeared inside again.

Looming over them was a terrifying creature standing on its hind legs, fifteen feet tall. It had a green, scaly, dragon head with long, sharp saber-tooth daggers jutting from its horrible mouth. Hanging freakishly above that was a long, white, woolly trunk. Its neck scales ended at its upper chest, which was covered in thick, red fur. Its arms, hands, and fingers were hideous, black, pointy sticks. It also, oddly, had large claws jutting out of its side. Fluttering atop its back were two huge, feathered wings, and its golden legs stood propped on two clawed, golden paws. Finally, a long, white-furred whale-tail rose behind the beast, seemingly prepared to thrash them.

The little children cheered. They jumped over Jordan and scooted between Eldon's legs as they ran toward the creature. They hugged its furry, golden legs and tried to climb on its tail. Inside the warehouse, men and women were laughing and smiling. They dropped their tools and pulled the children back.

"No, *niños!*" An older girl peeled a small boy from the tail. "Alebrijes is not a ride! He is very fragile! You'll break him if you climb on him like that!"

Jordan slowly stood up and gazed upon the creature. Its yellow glass eyes continued to gaze down on him unblinkingly, and its sparkling, glitter-glued teeth flashed menacingly in the sunlight.

"Wait. It's . . . a *float*?" Eldon said.

"It's like giant folk art," Abbie said. "Cool."

"You have to admit," Sam said. "You were scared!"

The girl who'd pulled the little boy off the float stepped forward. "I'm sorry we startled you," she said. "But not really."

"Did you see, Julia?" Sam gleefully said. "They screamed like little *niños*! This year we will win, for sure."

Jordan smiled. "Is that what it's for? Scaring tourists?"

"Not exactly," Julia said. "It is part of a long tradition called *La Noche de los Alebrijes*. It is a grand parade held every fall in Mexico City. Each of the villages far and wide submits a handcrafted creature. The best, most terrible-looking Alebrijes are the ones allowed in the grand parade."

"This is the weekend all the local towns in this area have a mini parade," Sam said. "To show off our submissions. Given your reactions, I am very optimistic."

Eldon picked up his hat and dusted it off. He glared at the others, then stormed back toward the jeep.

"Is your friend all right?" Julia asked.

"I think he was hoping to find an actual creature

hiding in here," Jordan said.

"We all were, I guess," Abbie added. "But I still like this a lot."

"Me too," Jordan said. "Thank you for showing it to us. We should probably be heading back now."

Jordan and Sam turned to leave. Abbie took one last look at the homemade creature before following them out. She noticed the children tugging on Julia's dress, whispering excitedly in Spanish.

A little girl broke free, ran to a nearby drafting table, and pulled a paper off it. She ran outside and brought it to Abbie. It was a children's drawing and appeared to depict the same creature that was looming lifelessly inside the warehouse door.

"That's a very good drawing of the float," Abbie

said. The children shook their heads.

"The children did not draw what we built," Julia said. "We built what they drew." The little girl pointed toward the jungle. The other children joined in. Julia smiled. "You know how children can be. They let their imaginations run wild. They claim they saw this creature and drew its picture. We liked it so much, we decided to use it for our village's Alebrijes." She looked down at the kids. "But it isn't any more real than your imaginations, *niños!*"

The kids all shook their heads and began shouting in Spanish. Jordan couldn't understand what they were saying, but he thought he heard the word "cenotes."

Sam smiled. "They each claim they saw a glimpse of the same creature, down in the swimming holes. One saw a wing; another, a dragonlike head. This one says he saw a tail splashing in the water, and she spotted a furry red behind."

Abbie watched the children pointing excitedly. "How do you know they didn't?"

"For the same reason we do!" Eldon's voice boomed. Everyone fell silent. "There's no new cryptid here. A creature like that couldn't go unseen for a day, never mind a millennium—especially in a touristy location like those swimming holes. And even if it could, I doubt it would let itself be seen by a bunch of little kids!" He glanced at the disappointed faces of the children. They couldn't understand him, but they could tell he didn't believe them, either. "I'm sorry, but this entire trip has been a fool's errand. I'm not feeling well, and I'd like to go back. Right now, please."

Jordan and Abbie said good-bye to Julia and the workers, then got back into Sam's jeep. Eldon sat staring straight ahead. Pulling away from the warehouse, Jordan watched the crew return to the Alebrijes, gluing colorful feathers to its wings. The children placed their drawing back on the drafting table and stood there, sadly staring at it.

The trip back to el Terminal Remota was a silent one. Sam dropped Abbie, Jordan, and Eldon near the cruise ship as the midday sun hung high in the air. They thanked their friendly guide and gave him an extra tip for sharing with them such a special local tradition. Eldon didn't speak a word.

"Eldon," Jordan said as Sam sped away. "C'mon. Let's get a lemonade and talk about what to do next. Maybe those kids might have actually seen something."

"Something fifteen feet tall with a dragon's head, fat red belly, huge colorful wings, and a long furry whale tail? Even if there were such a cryptid, your grandfather would've discovered it. The CKCC would have monitored it. Something like that does not stay hidden on its own without the help of the Creature Keepers!"

"What if it could?" Abbie said.

"This was a waste of time," Eldon said. "I shouldn't have come."

Jordan stared at his friend. "If there's nothing here, why would Bernard have sent us?"

"He didn't send *us*," Eldon snapped back. "He sent *you*! Maybe just to be with your family!" He looked at them both. "I don't belong here with you Grimsleys. My family was the Creature Keepers. But that seems to be falling apart and abandoning me. Maybe I'm just meant to be on my own."

He turned and walked off toward the ship.

12

Eldon had told Jordan his story during their first adventure together. Jordan knew his friend was an orphan, but he never thought of Eldon as sad or alone in

the world. Eldon had the Creature Keepers as his family and Bernard as his best friend. Jordan had always assumed those were enough.

Jordan couldn't help but wonder if Eldon regretted handing the responsibility of the Creature Keepers to him and his sister. Jordan was already worried his grandfather's legacy might be falling apart on his watch. Seeing Eldon so broken up made Jordan more concerned than ever. He couldn't let that happen.

"He's probably right, you know," Abbie said as the two of them walked through the ship looking for their parents. "There's no way a creature that large, that colorful, and that *weird looking* could stay hidden in such a populated place."

"I know," Jordan said. "But I can't shake this strange feeling something weird is going on."

"I mean, look at Syd. You've got a Sasquatch living in total seclusion at the top of a mountain deep in the Canadian wilderness, and that dude has reality shows about him."

"I said *I know*," Jordan shot back.

"Something weird *is* going on," Abbie said. "Everybody's cranky, and I'm suddenly the happy little ray of sunshine."

"There you are!" Mr. and Mrs. Grimsley called out

to them from beside the pool. "We were just about to order lunch."

"Where's Eggbert?" Mr. Grimsley said.

"Eldon," Jordan corrected his father. "He's not here. He's a little out of sorts."

"I'm sorry to hear that," Mrs. Grimsley said. "Well, I hope he's feeling better soon. There's a fun parade on the pier tonight, something called the Ally Beerhays!"

"Alebrijes," Abbie said. "It's a local celebration."

"Betsy, look at our daughter." Her dad beamed. "Enjoying her Grimsley Family Fun Time *and* learning about other cultures!"

Abbie rolled her eyes as she plucked a strawberry from her father's tropical juice smoothie. She tossed it over her shoulder. Chunk's head popped out and swallowed it. Her parents didn't notice as they were flagging the waiter down.

As they ate, Mr. Grimsley said, "So, this Odin—"

"Eldon," Jordan said.

"Eldon. How well do you really know him?"

"He's become a very close friend," Jordan said. "To both of us."

"Your father is just trying to say that even though we haven't met him, he strikes us as a little . . . *different*," Mrs. Grimsley said.

"You have no idea," Abbie said. Jordan shot her a

look. "But in a good way. He's just a dorkface, that's all. And he's going through a thing right now."

"He doesn't have a family," Jordan said.

"Oh," Mrs. Grimsley said. "You didn't tell us that."

"Well, he kind of does," Jordan said. "But it's not a particularly *usual* type of family."

"No family is perfect," Mr. Grimsley said. "Even ours. Although we're close. We're very, very close."

"Again," Abbie said. "You have no idea."

Jordan continued. "The thing is, I think he feels like his family might be slipping away. He was hoping to come here to find a long-lost member of that family. I think maybe he was hoping that might help him feel like his family was still growing and maybe he could keep it together. But it turned out to be a dead end."

Mr. Grimsley set down his fork. "Listen to me. He should never give up on family. No one should. Never, ever. Believe me. I know what I'm talking about."

He looked down at his plate but didn't take a bite. Mrs. Grimsley placed her hand on her husband's. "Tell them, Roger," she said gently.

"Tell us what?" Abbie said.

Mrs. Grimsley looked at her husband, who was still looking down. She turned to Jordan and Abbie. "The truth," she said. "Your father didn't decide to move us all to Florida just to help Doris with the home. That was part of it, of course, but—"

"The truth is I realized there's something special about that old place," Mr. Grimsley said. "It didn't hit me until we got back to the city, but there's a feeling of being connected. To Grampa Grimsley. To what he made. I know it's silly, but it's all I have."

"Wow, Dad," Abbie said. "That's . . . kind of cool.

"The thing about it is, everyone thought my father was crazy, including me," he continued. "And maybe he was. But I'd give anything, including being called crazy right along with him, if only I could be by his side, just for one day."

They sat there in silence for a moment. Mrs. Grimsley spoke up. "So we decided to do something crazy ourselves: quit our jobs and run a retirement home in the middle of a swamp!"

They both chuckled, then clunked their fruity coconut drinks together. Jordan and Abbie smiled at this.

Finally, Jordan cleared his throat. "Dad, there's something you should know. Grampa Grimsley wasn't crazy."

Abbie glared at her brother. Then she kicked him under the table.

"I know," Mr. Grimsley said. "Crazy is an ableist term. Let's just say he was . . . *eccentric*. My point is, you tell that friend of yours not to give up on the people he loves. Because someday they'll be gone. You've gotta enjoy your time together, while you can. That's what Grimsley Family Fun Time is all about."

Mrs. Grimsley raised her coconut again. "To Grimsley Family Fun Time!" Jordan and Abbie raised their glasses, too, and the four Grimsleys toasted.

"And to Edweirdo," Mr. Grimsley said.

"Eldon," Jordan corrected him.

* * *

THUD THUD THUD! Someone pounded on the door marked B-14 as the sun began to sink into the Gulf of Mexico.

THUD THUD THUD! A fist slammed the cabin door again. This time, Eldon opened the door and fell backward in horror, tripping over his packed backpack and falling on his rear end.

Abbie stood in his doorway in full scuba gear: fins, mask, tank, mouthpiece.

"What in blazes are you doing?" Eldon said, pulling himself to his feet. "You nearly scared me more than that fake, homemade dragon critter!"

"Wflbm tkrflu skrbling!" Abbie said.

"Sorry. What?"

Abbie pulled her mask off and spit out her mouth-piece. "We're taking you scuba diving." She tossed a pair of flippers at him. "Now suit up and meet us on the pier, Creature Keeper Pecone! That's a direct order!"

Abbie, Jordan, and Eldon bounced around inside a rickety old taxi cab as it rumbled through the dark-ening jungle. It made Jordan miss Sam's open-air jeep.

"Don't think I don't know what this is about," Eldon said. "You know as well as I do that there's nothing to be found out here. You two feel bad for me so you're just trying to be good friends."

"So not true." Abbie smiled at him coyly. "I would never be a good friend."

Jordan unfolded the map they'd purchased earlier that day. "Look, we know it's a long shot. But we started thinking about what the girl who sold us this map had said. These cenotes aren't just swimming holes. They're all interconnected by a maze of underwater tunnels and caves along the rim of that crater. Who knows how deep or how far they go?"

"And that crater was caused by an asteroid that slammed into the earth and wiped out all the dino-saurs, like, a *bajillion* years ago," Abbie said.

"An extinction event," Jordan added.

"We knew all this when we rode through the jungle

to discover an oversized piñata," Eldon said. "It doesn't explain how a real cryptid could ever live in such a touristy place for a *bajillion* years without being spotted once. Impossible!"

Jordan folded the map. "Maybe you're right. But *impossible* is exactly what I would have said a year ago if you'd told me there was a big black, furry creature— who you could smell a mile away, by the way—living in a swamp behind a retirement community in Florida."

Eldon thought about this. "I must say, it is strange of Bernard to send you on a family vacation for no reason." He shook his head. "But no—how could he even know about something like this?"

"He couldn't," Jordan said. "Unless another creature he'd been visiting told him. A creature who knew the location of every single cryptid on earth and years ago shared that sacred information with our grandfather so he could protect them."

Eldon looked up at them both. "Wilford."

"We've hung out with that old Yeti," Abbie said. "Trust me, he isn't *that* wise and all-knowing. You can't tell me it's impossible he overlooked one lousy cryptid."

Eldon was starting to come around. "A cryptid whose special gift might just be staying hidden, maybe even deep beneath the very crater that created him."

"Or her," Abbie said.

"Of course, you couldn't really blame Wilford for the oversight," Jordan said. "I mean, Wilford may have the power to blow his reflective crystals anywhere on the planet so he can see everywhere and everything at anytime. But he doesn't have what we have." Jordan smiled at his friend. "A First-Class Spoorer."

Night had not yet fallen when the taxi dropped Abbie, Jordan, and Eldon off at the entrance to Cenote Park. But deep in the jungle it was getting dark, even if the sky above the treetops was still lit up orange by the fading sunset.

A large sign that read *Cerrado* told them the park was closed. They flipped and flopped right past it in their scuba gear, along the path toward the edge of the first cenote.

The sinkhole looked like it had been cut clean out of the rocky surface by a giant paper hole puncher. Covered in overhanging green jungle plants, its edges dropped off and straight down, disappearing into blackness.

The three of them switched on powerful waterproof head lamps and looked down. The basin lay hundreds of feet below them and spread much wider than the hole they were peering into. Vines hung down from the edges, and there was a carved-out stone stairway and path circling the pool below.

The water itself had appeared black at first, but when they shined their lights in the same spot, they could see it was deep and very clear. They could almost make out the sandy bottom of the beautiful, natural swimming pool.

"Golly," Eldon said. "I can see why so many people come to swim here."

"And this is just one of hundreds that line the edge of the Chicxulub crater," Jordan said. "If they're all connected, there's bound to be some hiding spot big enough for a cryptid to live in."

"Okay," Abbie said. "Are we gonna blab, or are we gonna do this?" She leaped, flippers first, off the edge of the cenote, plunging into the crystal-clear water.

Eldon and Jordan glanced at each other. Then they smiled. Then they jumped.

The water was chilly but not terribly cold. Looking up at the circle of stars through the opening to the cenote overhead, Jordan could see the size of the pool was at least two or three times the size of the hole at the surface, extending deep below the ground.

This swimming hole was clearly no secret. There were stone steps with a rope-fenced path that ran around the edge of the water, with signs and instructions, rules and restrictions for people who came to swim. One of the signs leaped out at Jordan immediately: *Peligro: Submarinismo Estrictamente Prohibido.*

Jordan couldn't translate exactly, but the picture below of a skeleton in a scuba mask made it pretty clear—for whatever reason, this was not a place to be scuba diving.

"Hm," Eldon said, tightening his mask while looking at the sign. "I don't think your grandfather would have minded breaking a few rules searching for a never-before-seen cryptid, do you?"

Jordan smiled. The two of them put their regulators in their mouths and dived, following Abbie's trail of bubbles.

Swimming below them, Abbie looked like she was floating in midair—until she exhaled. A beautiful burst of silvery-white bubbles engulfed Jordan's head, racing toward the surface. Then all went still again, returning the sensation of gliding nearly weightless through a cool, crystal-clear ether.

The experience of flying deep beneath the jungle floor was surreal, but Jordan had to focus on what they were looking for. He spotted Eldon inspecting a nearby wall that curved upward toward the surface while Abbie was making her way deeper. Jordan flicked his feet and darted toward a small crevice in the wall just beneath Eldon.

He shined his head lamp inside the crack and noticed a familiar glimmering. Abbie and Eldon swam to him as he reached his hand in to snatch it. It was smoother than the surrounding rock and felt to be about the size of a golf ball. It was also stuck. Jordan shook his head to the others, and Eldon took a knife from his fanny pack and handed it to him. Jordan worked the blade into the crevice. With some prying, he dislodged it, and pulled it out of the crevice.

Twinkling there in his hand was the same type of ruby-red gem as the one that he'd found in the snow and had since faded in his bedroom. He looked up at Abbie and Eldon. Their eyes were wide behind their masks. Abbie pointed beneath them. Embedded in the wall farther down were a few more red stones.

Jordan worked to dislodge those gems as well and pocketed the knife as he handed the collection to Eldon. As Eldon slipped the stones into his fanny pack, one fell through his fingers. They watched as it sank slowly through the crystal-clear water toward the floor. But rather than coming to rest on the dusty bottom, the red stone disappeared, passing right through it. The three divers glanced at one another, then swam down to inspect.

The floor seemed to be more of a murky river upon closer inspection, like a layer of foggy particles floating at the bottom of the cenote. Eldon reached out and pushed his hand through. His wrist, then elbow, then upper arm, disappeared just as the stone had. Jordan tried it next. The first thing he noticed was how the water beneath the strange, smoky layer was ice cold, much chillier than the water around and above them. Abbie pushed the others aside. Just as she'd leaped from the surface into the pool, she lunged, disappearing through the misty floor. And just like before, Jordan and Eldon followed.

The frigid water immediately sent a chill through Jordan's body. He had to squint through his mask to find Abbie—the water beneath the strange haze was much murkier. He and Eldon swam in the direction of Abbie's head lamp. Floating debris swirled around them, revealing small currents, which grew stronger the deeper they went. The rocks, too, were rougher and craggier, jutting out in all directions, forming caves and crevices everywhere, more like the bottom of the ocean than the tranquil pool above.

Jordan pulled his regulator out of his mouth and peeked the tip of his tongue out. They were no longer in fresh water. This was a salty, subterranean sea.

Jordan spotted the stone. It lay on an algae-slimed rock below him. He swam to it and picked it up, proudly showing the others before stuffing it into his pocket. Even through their masks, Abbie and Eldon seemed unimpressed. They pointed at something behind him. A large natural entrance to a tunnel or cave glistened with dozens of red crystals embedded in its walls. It looked like a giant gaping mouth speckled with tiny ruby teeth.

As they swam closer to the dark, gem-spotted cave, a

cold current from inside gently pushed them back, like an invisible hand warning them to stay away. Abbie, Jordan, and Eldon pumped their fins just to stay in the same spot until the gentle force subsided.

Without warning, the current violently reversed. The force that had pushed them away from the entrance suddenly sucked them in like a riptide. Bubbles exploded from all three of their regulators as they panicked, swimming and pumping their fins, scrambling to grab hold of the slick rocks around them. Eldon reached out for one but was too late—in a split second, he disappeared into the dark chasm. Jordan couldn't believe his eyes. He looked over to his struggling sister. He grabbed her hand, but his grip on an algae-covered rock was weak and slipping. He held on as tightly as he could, but the stronger his clutch, the faster it slid off the rock. In an instant, he and Abbie were sucked into cold, terrifying blackness.

Jordan tucked his knees to his chest in a cannonball position and held onto his mask and regulator for dear life. It was pitch-black as he careened through the deep, watery tunnel, the current flushing him faster and faster. He struggled to stay in the center to avoid bouncing off the rock wall, terrified but thankful for the widening passageway.

He couldn't see Abbie or Eldon. All he could do was
shut his eyes tightly and hope as hard as he could that
they would all survive the frightening ride.

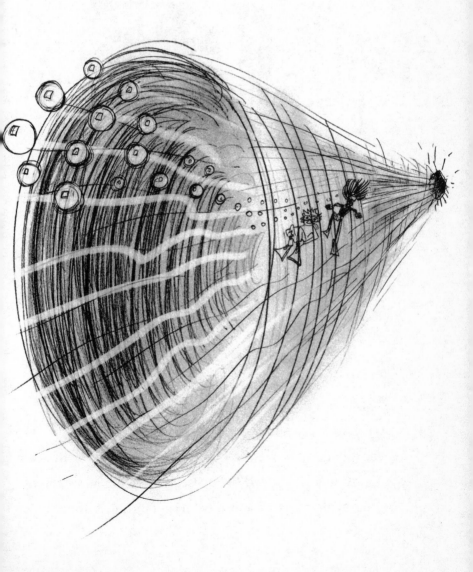

14

WHOOSH!

Just as quickly as the cold
water had snatched him, Jordan felt a sudden
warm gush surround his body. He slowed down to a
gentle glide and opened his eyes. At the bottom of the
sea floor was the crevice he'd been shot out of. Although

slightly dizzy, Jordan got his bearings and righted himself, pumping his fins as hard as he could away from the current pushing out of that crevice, afraid that it might change its mind and suck him back in again.

Eldon and Abbie looked just as disoriented but thankfully in one piece and seemingly okay. They were in open water now, with little or no danger in sight. The surface was only a hundred feet above them. They'd been flushed back out into the gulf. And they were lucky to be alive.

A hand grabbed Jordan, shaking him from his thoughts. Abbie was staring into his mask, checking to see if he was all right. He gave her a thumbs-up, and she responded with the same.

They met up with Eldon near what looked like a small forest of massive, branchless tree trunks sprouting up from the gulf floor, breaking the surface of the water above. Beneath it, on the sea floor, was a thick metal drill, bent and twisted, sticking out of a dug-out hole at the center of the strange, sparse, underwater forest.

Seeing the damaged drill bit, Jordan suddenly realized that the trees surrounding it were not trees at all. They were pier legs, holding up a structure above the surface. Eldon and Abbie were already pulling themselves up along one of the legs. Jordan turned on his head lamp and flashed it at the drill bit. It was bent inside the hole, the sides of which were sparkling red in the shining light. Feeling no desire to enter another tight spot, Jordan quickly swam to catch up with Eldon and his sister.

The three of them burst through the surface into the cool night air and looked around. They could see el Terminal Remota pier in the distance. Looking up, they realized they were beneath the old offshore wooden oil platform standing on its chunky wooden legs.

"Over here!" Abbie was trying to reach the lowest

rung of a rickety ladder nailed to one of the legs. Jordan and Eldon swam to her and helped push her up. Once she grabbed the high bottom rung, they all worked together to climb out of the water, scaling toward the underbelly of the old rig.

Abbie pulled herself through the cutout at the top and helped the two boys through. The three of them collapsed there for a moment, flopping on the wood planks and gasping for breath like fish hauled onto a boat.

"I'll be a monkey's uncle." Eldon was the first to stand and look around. They were standing on the old oil rig Sam had told them about. El Terminal Remota pier could be seen across the water, connecting where the *Mayan Princess* was docked all the way to the beach town of Progreso. And beyond that, in the distance, was the jungle—where their crazy ride had begun.

"Amazing," Jordan said. "The current flushed us all the way back from the cenotes."

"And nearly drowned us," Jordan added.

"At least it saved us cab fare," Abbie said.

The three of them glanced at one another, then burst into laughter, happy to be alive and on a dry dock—even an old, spooky, haunted-looking dry dock. They removed their scuba gear as a cheerful noise caught their attention. Across the water on el Terminal

Remota, tourists and locals were dancing and singing in the distance, slowly parading up the pier from the mainland.

"It's the Alebrijes party," Jordan said.

"I think I see our mysterious creature." Abbie pointed. In the dimming light, a dragon head bobbed among the crowd. "Wait." Six or seven different different Alebrijes were being carried along the pier, surrounded by revelers. "Maybe it's that one."

"Let's figure out how we get off this creepy thing," Jordan said. "Preferably without getting back in that water."

They located the broken old footbridge that at one time ran across to the main pier. The ropes were tattered and frayed, and of the few planks that were left, some dangled high above the dark water.

"Nope," Abbie said. "No way." She walked off, along the inside of the fence.

"Where are you going?" Jordan said.

"To see if there's another way off this thing," Abbie said. "One that doesn't get us wet, never mind drowned. I'll holler if I find anything."

She turned the corner, leaving Jordan and Eldon staring up at the eerie collection of ramshackle buildings that populated the center of the old platform. Overhead loomed the drill tower that housed the machine that at one time lowered the abandoned drill bit to the sea floor.

"I don't care what Sam says," Jordan said. "This place *looks* haunted as heck."

"But it isn't," Eldon reassured him. "If anything, it's just cursed, remember?"

"Right. By the devil's fleas."

A sudden creaking from behind made the two boys spin around. Something caught Jordan's eye—something pink. He looked down just in time to catch a shadowy figure. It slid along a rope and disappeared beneath the platform. A chill shot through Jordan's bones. He looked at Eldon. This time he was sure.

"Quisling," he said. "Don't think I'm crazy, but I just saw him again."

"I don't think you're crazy. I think I saw him, too! What do we do?"

"Find a way to get down there so we can follow him," Jordan whispered. "I'll go and get Abbie!"

Eldon ran off between two of the old nearby shacks. Jordan followed the fence line in the direction Abbie had gone. He turned the corner and made his way through the cluster of old wooden buildings. It was like a tiny town. In the center, connected to the drill housing, was a cottage-sized shack. There were sheets covering the windows, but a light within flickered against the fabric. He found the door opened a crack. He slowly pushed it and entered the little house.

His eyes adjusted to what little light there was, but it was his ears that immediately trained on what was going on inside. Odd grunts and growls, low but steady, came from nearby. He walked through the next door and saw Abbie sneaking toward a wide entryway into the central room, where a large pink swath of material hung like a curtain separating them. Jordan noticed letters stitched across it like a banner:

ꟻACECHOMPERꙄ

The growling got louder as Jordan approached Abbie. He reached out and quietly tapped her on the shoulder. She spun around, terrified.

"Aaah!"

Abbie locked eyes with Jordan and immediately clasped her hand over her mouth. It was too late. The beastly sound coming from the other side of the curtain fell terrifyingly silent. A scuffling and scraping against the grainy wooden floor approached the other side of the pink tapestry. Jordan and Abbie, wide-eyed, slowly backed away, readying for their escape. The light in the second room backlit the creature, casting its shadow against the tarp. Its silhouetted outline resembled the children's drawing and the parade float they'd seen in the warehouse—from its dragonlike head to its great wings that spread as it approached. *It's the Alebrijes!* thought Jordan. Before they could turn to run, a pair of menacing crablike claws raised and snapped violently. Thick, black, spindly tree arms drew back—and sliced the tarp in half, revealing the creature.

Jordan and Abbie fell backward onto the floor. They grabbed each other, shut their eyes, and screamed.

After a second or two of realizing they weren't being mauled, clawed, crushed, maimed, or eaten, Jordan and Abbie peeked out.

The group of cryptids huddling together looked just as confused and frightened as Abbie and Jordan did. They also looked, clustered as they were, capable of casting a silhouette of one very big, very menacing Alebrijes when properly backlit.

But these were not one great creature. They were cryptids of varying colors, coats, shapes, and sizes.

"Way to go, Francine," a guttural voice called out from behind their feet, flippers, claws, and hooves. "You just had to go and destroy our banner!"

Abbie and Jordan looked down.

A Day-Glo yellow glob of goo came sliding to the front of the group. Its dozen or so purple eyes scanned the sliced pink material on the ground. "That was our official flag, with our cool name on it and everything! You're such an oaf!"

"Oh, shut up, Hogie, you puddle of snot," the moss-covered, stick-armed creature said, reaching down and gathering the sliced tarp. This creature Jordan had seen before. She was known as an Australian Bunyip and could have easily been mistaken for an old Okeeyuckachokee Swamp tree come to life. Jordan had last seen her when she and three others handed their collars to Eldon and declared themselves free from the Creature Keepers.

"I don't believe it," Jordan said. "It's . . . you guys."

The other three rogue cryptids were there, too, standing right in the front of the bunch. Paul the Dingonek resembled a sort of jungle walrus, with large tusks and the head of a dragon. Donald was the red-mohawked, orangutanlike Ban Manush of Bangladesh. And leading the pack was Sandy, the stoic Sumatran Golden Liger, still the most stunning and magnificent creature Abbie and Jordan had ever seen.

Jordan stood up. "Sandy? What are you doing here? And why are the kidnapped cryptids here with you?"

"They have not been kidnapped," Sandy said calmly.

"They have been freed. And they have joined us by their own free will."

The others all nodded in unison.

"Joined you in what?" Abbie's fear and confusion had given way to anger. She stepped up to Sandy. "They disappeared without any warning! We've been worried sick about them, and so have their Keepers!" Some of the cryptids looked down at the floor. "Do you guys even know what's going on out there? There's a new evil force, possibly a fourth special creature, and it's got everybody freaking out!"

Jordan spotted something and tried to subtly interrupt her. "Uh, Abbie . . ."

She ignored him. "You all could be in danger! It's something worse than Chupacabra! We think it may have created a horrible army—"

"They're Face Chompers," Jordan whispered.

"That's right!" she continued. "Did you hear him? They call themselves the—"

Jordan tugged her sleeve. She stopped. Francine the Bunyip was holding the pink flag she'd shredded with her sharp, pointy-stick hands. The letters now faced Abbie and Jordan, spelling out clearly the name of their group: *F A C E C H O M P E R S*.

"Oh," Abbie said.

Sandy furrowed her great, golden brow and stepped

closer to them. "You shouldn't have come here."

A large feathered cryptid stepped behind the great cat. He had an owl-like head and huge talons for hands. His wings were massive, even when tucked behind his back. "She's quite right," he said in a British accent. "You'll spoil our plans."

As the others began to gather, Jordan and Abbie backed away. Jordan felt around for the doorknob, ready to make a quick escape. "Okay, our mistake," Jordan said. "We'll just see ourselves out, then—"

"Not so fast!" A high-pitched cackling startled them from behind, followed by the slamming of the door. Two flabby old arms grabbed them both. Jordan turned to look but didn't have to. He knew that cackle. So did Abbie. Harvey Quisling had dropped his bundle of pink silk material and had them both in a bear hug. "What should I do with them, Master?"

"Let them go." Yet another new voice called out from behind the cryptids. It was a voice that made Jordan and Abbie freeze. It was a voice they knew better than Harvey's. But it couldn't be.

"Bernard?" Jordan said.

The crowd parted as a black-furred creature with a white stripe running down his large forehead stepped forward. The Florida Skunk Ape smiled.

"Jordan. Abbie. I knew I could count on you to find us." He looked at Quisling. "Let them go, Harvey. They're not trespassing. They're our guests. I invited them."

Quisling released them. "Yes, Master." He took the torn banner from Francine, joined the others, and began to repair it with his sewing kit.

"And Harvey," Bernard added. "I've asked you to please not call me that."

"Sorry, Master," Harvey said, working his needle and thread. "Old habit."

Abbie looked from Quisling to Bernard. "'Master'? Is he serious?"

Jordan stepped forward. "Bernard, what is all this? What's going on? Please tell us you're here to rescue these poor creatures."

"In a way, Jordan, that's exactly what I'm doing. I'm rescuing all of them.

LET THEM GO.

From the invisible shackles of the Creature Keepers."

Jordan and Abbie were aghast. This couldn't be happening. Jordan struggled to understand. He felt like he was in a nightmare. "But aren't you afraid? You all could be in danger from the—the *Face Chompers*. . . ."

Bernard gently took the half-sewn flag from Harvey. He held it up so Jordan and Abbie could see the words F A C E C H O M P E R S again. He smiled at them both. "Why would we fear ourselves?"

Jordan could feel his heart pounding. "You're the Face Chompers?"

"It's okay, I know this is a shock," Bernard said, moving closer. "But I summoned you both here secretly because I need your help."

"With what?" Abbie said.

"Not what—*whom*," Bernard said. "With Eldon. He made you leaders of the Creature Keepers. He trusts you. And now I need you to *take care of him for me*. . . ."

Jordan and Abbie shared a confused and terrified glance. Bernard and the rest of the Face Chompers were beginning to gather closer to them. Behind his back, Jordan felt around for the doorknob again. This time he found it, and gripped it tightly.

"Sure, Bernard," Jordan said nervously. "We'll take care of Eldon for you, no problem. You won't have to worry about him ever again. Just leave it to us, okay?"

Jordan flung open the door. He and Abbie spun around to run for it but had to stop short. Standing there in the doorway, blocking their escape, was Eldon Pecone.

The expression on Eldon's face was a horrible mixture of anger, confusion, and heartache. Tears streamed down his face as he looked into Jordan's eyes. He looked to Abbie, too. Then he looked past them both, at Bernard.

The Skunk Ape was wide-eyed, shocked to see his Keeper standing there.

"Eldon," Bernard sputtered. "What are you doing here?"

Eldon held back his tears the best he could. "Making the greatest discovery of my lifetime—the awful truth." He glanced back at Jordan and Abbie. "About all of you."

Eldon bolted off, into the night.

Without hesitating or thinking twice, Jordan ran after his friend.

16

The moon sat low in the sky, leaving the old, rickety platform a dark maze of run-down structures. The creaking, distant sound of footsteps was all Jordan had to find his way to Eldon. Through the shadows, he spotted his friend ducking into a narrow alleyway between two supply sheds. Jordan raced after him.

He came out of the shadows and stopped short at the only source of light besides the moon: the main pier, just across the water. Streetlights lit up the festive scene that had now made it nearly all the way to the docked cruise ships. The crowd of people and constructed Alebrijes paraded past. And standing atop an old crate at the edge of the platform, staring across at civilization, was Eldon Pecone.

"Eldon," Jordan said. "Listen to me! I'm just as freaked out as you are, about all of this! You have to believe me!"

Eldon turned and looked at Jordan. "No I don't," he said. "I don't have to believe in anyone anymore." He pulled off his Badger Ranger bolo tie. "Or any*thing.*"

"*Eldon!*"

Jordan ran to the edge as Eldon leaped. He saw his friend sliding away, using his bolo to zip-line across the water on one of the footbridge cables. Jordan watched helplessly as Eldon bumped clumsily into the side of the pier, scrambled onto it, and finally slipped into the crowd.

Jordan looked down. A frayed, weather-beaten rope ran a few feet below the cable Eldon had used, running parallel to it across the span of darkness. Jordan took a deep breath and lunged, baby-stepping tightrope-style across the lower line, half pulling himself along with the upper one.

He was nearly across when—*snap!*—the rope beneath his feet fell away. Jordan dangled from the upper cable for a terrifying moment, then shimmied hand over hand until he reached the pier.

The crowd was happy and noisy, bouncing and laughing, dancing conga lines and swirling about. Jordan made his way through the smiling faces, every so often bumping into a large papier-mâché Alebrijes dancing among them. He had no idea where Eldon was. All he could do was frantically search the crowd of revelers.

"Jordan!" His mother's voice cut through all the shouting and singing. "Over here!" She grinned as she clung to Mr. Grimsley's arm. Jordan noticed his dad had a strange expression on his face, like he was trying to remember something.

"Can't talk, you guys," Jordan said. "I'm looking for someone!"

"Well, if it's that strange Eldon boy, we just saw him," she said.

"You did?"

"Yeah, we . . ." Mr. Grimsley said strangely, trailing off. "We did."

"Eldon bumped into us and introduced himself rather awkwardly," Mrs. Grimsley said. "Funny, we had no idea who he was, but Eldon recognized us."

"He looked so familiar, though," Mr. Grimsley said, staring off. "I just can't place the face."

"Quick, you guys. Which way did he go?"

Mr. Grimsley pointed across the pier, still looking puzzled as Jordan ran off.

He pushed his way through the crowd and came out on the opposite side of el Terminal Remota pier. He looked down the long dock toward the twinkling lights of Progreso. Then he looked in the other direction, toward the nearby *Mayan Princess*. Eldon was nowhere to be seen.

Something caught Jordan's eye. Eldon's Badger Ranger Badger Badge sash was lying on the edge of the dock. He picked it up and peered out over the dark water below. Suddenly, a deep, loud revving sounded somewhere beneath him. There was a speedboat pulling away from a lower mooring. Standing all alone at its controls was Eldon.

Jordan frantically looked for a way to climb down and get to his friend. Before he could do anything, the engine revved even louder, and the powerboat lurched

away from the pier. Eldon disappeared into the dark-ness, the sound of the powerboat's engines fading into the night air.

Jordan stood there staring at the water for a moment. As helpless as he felt, he was pretty sure Eldon Pecone had never taken anything that didn't belong to him ever in his life. And he'd just witnessed his rule-following friend steal a boat. Jordan looked down at the sash in his hands. He felt a presence directly behind him. A large presence. He turned.

"Ahh!"

He nearly fell backward into the water. Towering directly over him was the handmade Alebrijes. Its glass-yellow dragon eyes stared down at him, and its feet, arms, and tail were being carried along by the builders they'd met. Sam and Julia stood beside the homemade creature, chuckling.

"It worked again!" Sam said.

"You looked like you could use a laugh," Julia added.

"Yeah," Jordan said. "That was hilarious, thanks."

"What's wrong?" Sam asked. "You look like you've seen a real monster!"

A horrible thought suddenly struck Jordan. He'd left Abbie alone with Quisling—*and the Face Chompers*!

He bolted past Sam, Julia, and the colorful Alebrijes, back through the parading crowd, toward the other side of the pier.

The tail end of the parade had made its way past the old wooden oil rig, and the party had gathered at the end of the pier beneath the *Mayan Princess*. Jordan leaped off the edge of the pier, grabbing another rope. It snapped as he clutched it, and he swung across the expanse, arcing lower than the platform. He had no choice but to let go or else risk slamming into the wooden scaffolding beneath the old structure.

Rather than plunging into the cold water below, Jordan found himself suddenly bouncing in some sort of strange webbing. A hammock of sorts had been knit together out of a clear silk material, like a spider's web. Looking back toward the pier, he saw a barely visible, thin footbridge knit from the same sturdy, see-through material running across the water, connecting the underbelly of the platform to the underbelly of el Terminal Remota. "Quisling," Jordan muttered. He climbed out of the net and pulled himself through a trap door, then bolted for the cluster of houses in the center of the old wooden rig.

As he approached the old cabin, Jordan heard mumblings and then strange and sinister laughter. He thought he heard Abbie's voice but wasn't sure. Fearing the worst, he burst inside and ran into the central, lantern-lit room.

The rogue cryptids were gathered around in a tight circle, with their backs to Jordan. Harvey Quisling's voice cackled from the center. "Now, my dear, if you don't want to be stabbed, you'd better hold perfectly still!"

"Get away from my sister!" Jordan lunged, grabbing the first cryptid he could—a monkeylike creature with long, tangled hair and the lower body and tail of a mermaid. He shoved the beast aside, wading deeper into the circle. "Hold on, Abbie, I'm coming! I won't let them chomp your face!"

"Ew. What a disgusting thing to say." The Owl Man didn't put up a fight, instead politely stepping out of the way. Jordan found that many of the other creatures did the same. Sandy the Golden Liger growled a bit as Jordan stepped on her huge golden paw, but within a few moments, the entire group parted without much fuss. Jordan stopped short at what he saw.

Abbie stood before Harvey Quisling. The little man was holding a pincushion and had placed pins in an oversized pink silk nightie Abbie seemed to be modeling. It was pulled over her black shirt, and Jordan could clearly read its stitched letters: *FACECHOMPERS*.

Abbie chuckled. "Relax, Jordan. These Face Chompers are cool."

Jordan's eyes went wide. "Oh, no. Snap out of it, Abbie! Don't you see, they've brainwashed you!" He spun around to face the creatures all standing in stunned silence. "That's it, isn't it? The fourth special cryptid's power! Hypnotizing its victims to make them think it's *cool* for all of you to chomp her face!"

"Will you please stop saying that?" The Owl Man looked at the others. "Why does he keep saying that?"

" Jordan, listen to me. These creatures, they were never kidnapped. And they're certainly not Face Chompers."

Abbie glanced down at the blazing-blue embroidery spelling out the words "Face Chompers" across her chest. "Okay. They do call themselves that. But there's actually a pretty funny story behind it."

"Don't you see what they've done to you?" Jordan said. "You're brainwashed! They've made you into one of them! You're even letting Quisling sew you one of their uniforms! Quisling! You said you wanted to bust his melon-shaped head open!"

Harvey looked up from his work. "Is this true?"

"I'm still quite angry with you," she said. "I'm trying to take the high road."

"The high road?" Jordan was near shrieking now. "See? Brainwashed!"

Donald, the large red Ban Manush, puffed out his chest. "If there's a brain that could use a good washing, it might be yours, little man."

Sandy the Golden Liger stepped up. "We are not enemies, Jordan. In fact, we owe you a debt of gratitude. That day we four left the Creature Keepers, it was you who gave Bernard permission to come and check on us against Eldon's wishes."

Gavin the Cornwall Owl Man stepped forward. "You allowed Bernard to come find us, and Bernard helped all of us find one another."

Jordan scanned the room. The other cryptids nodded and smiled, including one he recognized hiding in the back of the group.

"Lou," Jordan said. "What's going on here?"

The New Jersey Devil was short and stocky and had a habit of trying to act tougher than he was. But he couldn't hide his emotions now. "Jordan, you know how much I love Mikey. He wasn't just my Keeper; he's my bestest bro in the whole world. But I got tired of being kept. I never could've told him that, and I never would have left him, if not for Bernard's help and the promise he made me."

"What's that?" Jordan said.

"The same promise he's made to all of us." A clacking near Jordan's feet accompanied the lispy voice. "That our Keepers would be taken care of." Clarissa, a Colossus Crab, continued. "And taken somewhere safe. And he kept his word."

"They only want to live free, out in the open," Abbie said. "When the four rogue cryptids went off on their own, I wasn't sure it was right. But I've listened to their stories. All these creatures stayed loyal to their Keepers only because they couldn't bear hurting them. And that's not really right, either."

Jordan scanned the very different faces staring back at him. The only face that was missing was Bernard's. "I understand you all want to be free. But Abbie and I were given the responsibility of keeping you protected. It was the life's work of our Grampa Grimsley. We can't let his work die."

"We know this isn't easy for you to accept," Sandy said. "But it isn't your choice. It's ours."

Abbie stood up and straightened her pink nightie. "And mine," she said. "And I believe that if Grampa Grimsley were here, it'd be his choice, too."

"Trust me, no it wouldn't." Bernard stepped into the room from outside. "George Grimsley would not have understood this, and he definitely wouldn't have approved. He was my first Keeper, y'know. He was also the most stubborn human I'd ever come across—that is, until I met my second Keeper, Eldon Pecone."

"Did you find Eldon?" Francine the Bog Bunyip interrupted. "Where is he?"

Bernard shook his head. "I looked everywhere. He's not on the platform."

"I saw him," Jordan said. "He's gonna be okay. He just needs time to himself. I know that because—well, he sped off in a stolen speedboat. All by himself."

The creatures gasped.

"First-Class By-the-Book Badger Boy Eldon *swiped*

a boat?" Gilligan said. "Ooh, he's gonna lose a badge for that!"

Jordan held up Eldon's sash. "I don't think he's too concerned about badges right now." Another collective gasp came from the Face Chompers.

Bernard took the sash and stared at it. "I never meant for him to find out this way," he said. "That's why I specifically sent for you two. I needed you to see what we were doing here so you might help me make him understand."

"I'm still not sure I even understand," Jordan said.

Bernard looked at him. "The main thing I need you to know is I didn't do this to destroy the Creature Keepers. None of us did. As stubborn as your grandfather was, I loved him. And I loved what he created. Without the Creature Keepers, not one cryptid in this room would have had the courage even to consider making the choice to be free. And that includes me."

There was something new in the faces staring back at Jordan. It was pride.

"The Creature Keepers don't have to die," Bernard continued. "There will be many who choose to stay with their Keepers. But for those of us who have chosen to leave, all we can do is hope someday our Keepers will understand."

Bernard reached up and draped Eldon's sash over

the Face Chompers banner. They all gazed at the pink flag adorned with Eldon's Badger Badge sash.

A silent, solemn moment passed. And Jordan started to understand. Sort of.

"Um, sorry. But I gotta ask—what's the deal with that *name*? And what's with leaving all your Keepers those pink pajamas—or nighties or whatever they are?"

"Slips," Abbie said. "Doris was right. They're slips."

"Pink slips," Bernard said, somewhat sheepishly. "I thought that was a human thing—when someone gets let go or fired, they get a pink slip. I looked it up."

"He meant to give them *pink slips*," Abbie said, smiling. "But he got confused. He gave them pink *slips*. Get it?"

"You're kidding."

Bernard shrugged. "It seemed like a nice, friendly touch. I sure didn't mean to cause all this confusion."

"Forget confusion," Jordan said. "How about raw terror? I mean, why would you stitch the words 'Face Chompers' on there?"

"That's the name of our group." Bernard scratched his head. "It does sound a bit menacing when you read it a certain way. I see that now."

"A certain way? How else would anyone read it?"

Abbie was grinning now. "That part's kind of a funny story." She gestured to an old chalkboard against the wall. The words "Face Chompers" were written vertically down the side of the board. There was more writing, but it was obscured by the dragonlike Dingonek standing in front of it.

"'Scuse us, Paul," Bernard said. "Could you scooch a bit?"

"Oh, sure. Sorry." The Dingonek politely stepped aside, revealing the rest of the blackboard.

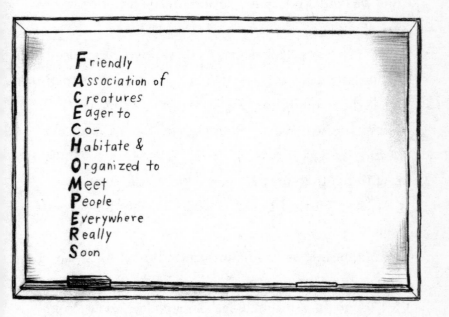

Friendly
Association of
Creatures
Eager to
Co-
Habitate &
Organized to
Meet
People
Everywhere
Really
Soon

Jordan's mouth fell open. He closed his eyes and covered his face with his hands. Abbie began to chuckle. Bernard smiled a little. "I gotta say, I'm a bit surprised I didn't read it that way. I'm usually such a stickler with details."

A giggle sounded out from behind Jordan's hands. He looked up at Bernard and he broke out laughing. Then he stepped up and gave his furry friend a big hug.

"I'm sorry, Bernard. I shouldn't have doubted you. Or your great big, stinky heart."

Bernard squeezed him back. Despite the Skunk Ape's pungent odor, Jordan found Bernard's hugs to be among his favorite things in the whole world. But this one was quickly spoiled as Jordan felt a flabby, wrinkly arm join in.

"Mm . . . yes. This is nice," Harvey Quisling said.

Jordan pulled away. "Hold on. You forgot to explain what you're doing hanging out with this *slimeball*!"

"Whoa, hey." The complaint came from a large blob oozing its way across the floor. "There are some who might find that term offensive. Words can hurt, guys."

"Sorry, Hogie," Bernard said. "Jordan didn't mean you."

"He meant me," Quisling said. "And I must say, I don't appreciate it, either."

"Tough toenails, dirtbag," Abbie said. "You've kinda earned it."

"Harvey had a change of heart," Bernard explained. "And we Face Chompers know the courage that can take."

The Face Chompers nodded in agreement. Harvey smiled at them appreciatively. "True, true," the bald old man said. "After I messed things up in China, I was sure Chupacabra would find me and put an end to my life, once and for all. So I fled, and kept running, quite unaware that you'd captured him."

"He didn't get far," Bernard said. "I picked him up on my way to transporting the frozen Chupacabra up to the Himalayas. I figured we might want to keep his sidekick captive up there, as well."

"When I saw my old master under ice like that, a burden was lifted from me. I explained this to Bernard and begged him for a second chance. He could've turned me in to the Creature Keepers. I know I deserved it. After all, I must admit I had been behaving like a bit of a—"

"Slimeball," Abbie said.

"C'mon!" Hogie the Tasmanian Globster chimed in again. "We just talked about this."

C'MON... WE JUST TALKED ABOUT THIS.

"I decided to give Harvey his second chance," Bernard said. "I suppose I recognized someone who was looking for a fresh start, just like me."

"And us," Sandy said. She, Paul, Donald, and Francine stood close together. "We suspected there were others. Bernard helped us reach out to them. And when they were ready, he helped pick them up and bring them here."

"Why here?" Abbie asked.

"I suggested this place," Quisling said. "My old master sent me here many times, so I knew it would be a safe place for my new friends to gather."

Jordan's eyes lit up. "What did Chupacabra send you here for?"

The old man grinned. "The crater that was forged in this place millions of years ago holds a very valuable secret."

"The fourth special cryptid," Abbie said.

"Or perhaps its elemental power," Harvey said. "I don't really know—you all stopped my master from getting his claws on it. Whatever it is, it's something he wanted more than anything in the world. It was my hope that by giving this secret to my new friends, they would see that they could truly trust me."

"And now we're giving the same secret to you two," Sandy said. "In hopes that you will see we have no desire for power or weapons. We just want to live in peace, on our own."

"The world just might need the Creature Keepers now more than ever," Bernard said. "In ways your grandfather could never have imagined."

Abbie and Jordan sat at the edge of the oil rig platform, putting on their scuba gear, trying not to think
about the dark water below.

"Holy abalone! Can you two get a move-on, please?
I have barnacles growing on my butt that move faster
than you two!" Gilligan the Feejee Mermonkey struck
Jordan and Abbie as a bit of a rude and unserious
cryptid—certainly not the type of creature they felt
comfortable following back down into the depths of
the gulf.

Jordan ignored him and gathered up Eldon's scuba
gear. He walked over to the far corner of the platform,
where Bernard stood staring off at the horizon.

"Don't worry," Jordan said. "Eldon knows you better

than anyone. By the time he reaches the Okeeyuck-achokee Swamp, he'll have come to his senses." He handed the gear to the Skunk Ape. "And if you think we're going down there alone with that salty sea-chimp, you're nuts."

"I'm not very fond of water," Bernard said.

"Neither am I. That's why we're doing this together." Jordan smiled at his friend, then turned and walked back toward Abbie and Gilligan.

Francine and Gavin had joined them on the platform. "Kinda rots you two had such a bad tumble through those sea tunnels," Francine said. "A few of us got a bit banged up going through there ourselves."

"You guys went into the cenotes?" Jordan said.

"Part of our 'training,'" Gilligan said, lowering his voice as he glanced off at Bernard. "He insists we need to work on our 'people skills.' You believe that? Fat load of walrus droppings, if you ask me."

"Yeah," Abbie said. "I see your manners are above reproach."

Gavin the Owl Man chuckled at this. "We'd swim through the tunnels in small teams to spy on the locals at their watering holes," he said. "Taking every pre-caution to remain completely unseen, of course."

"Yeah, well, you may have been spotted once or twice," Jordan said.

"A bunch of local kids caught separate glimpses of you guys," Abbie added. "Thought you were one big monster mash-up. Clashing styles. Not a good look."

Gilligan gestured behind them. "Speaking of which . . ."

Bernard came flopping up, his black-furred feet stuffed in Eldon's flippers, the mask and tank crammed onto his face and back. "Where's Moe?" he said.

Gilligan gestured toward the dark water below. "That overgrown chew toy's down there somewhere, waiting for us."

"Moe?" Abbie said.

"South African Trunko," Gavin said. "Sweet fellow. Keeps to himself."

"Yeah, but not amphibious like me," Gilligan was quick to add. "And not nearly as handsome. Wrap a

hippo in a white shag rug and toss it in a salty bath for a few millennia and boom—you've got Moe."

"Ugh. Shut up already, you soggy ape." Francine

kicked her trunklike leg and shoved Gilligan. The Mermonkey bounced once in the clear webbing just below the platform, then stuck his tongue out as he double-backflipped, diving perfectly into the water.

"I guess we should get down there, too," Abbie said.

"Yeah," Jordan said. "Let's see what you guys found."

They lowered themselves to the hammocklike netting, climbed to the edge, and dropped into the water. When they resurfaced, there was no sign of Bernard. They switched on their head lamps and shined them upward. He was dangling from the net.

"C'mon, stinky!" Gilligan said, floating on his back nearby. "I know bathing isn't your thing, but get in here!"

"Hey, ease off." Jordan knew why his friend wasn't a fan of water, and it had little to do with hygiene. "He just needs a little coaxing, that's all."

"So let's coax him. Keep your eardrums above water unless you want 'em blown out." Gilligan ducked his head beneath the surface. A muffled, piercing screech echoed. Jordan and Abbie could feel the vibrations rippling around them.

Gilligan popped his head back up. "Get ready, kids. It's Moe time."

A surge of water churned beneath the netting,

followed by a large white, furry creature. Moe the South African Trunko was aptly named. About the size of a baby elephant, he had a fat, whalelike body, and protruding from his flat head was a long, white trunk. The appendage, like the rest of him, was covered in shaggy white fur. Below the surface, his tail flared out like that of a lobster. He thrust it back and forth, steadily raising his body upward, stretching his trunk toward Bernard.

Bernard smiled as he clung to the webbing. "Hello,

Moe. How's the water?"

Moe let out a little honk from his trunk, then wrapped it gently around Bernard. He slowed his treading tail, steadily lowering the Skunk Ape before carefully releasing him into the gulf.

Bernard smiled. "Thanks for the hand," he said. "Or rather, the nose."

Moe honked again, then dived along with Gilligan. The other three secured their masks, checked their air tanks and regulators, then followed them all the way to the bottom of the gulf floor, where the drill bit was twisted at the entrance to the large hole it had begun digging long ago.

Gilligan pointed into the dark chasm and gave a webbed thumbs-up. Abbie, Jordan, and Bernard returned the gesture. Trunko swam in circles, staying on watch just above the gulf floor. Gilligan led the others down the abandoned well hole.

The water immediately felt warmer. All along the rock wall, the sparkly red stones glistened like rubies. Jordan pried one loose with Eldon's knife. He pocketed it, then swam down to join Abbie, Bernard, and Gilligan at the bottom of the hole.

At the very center of the shallow hole was a smooth, black surface. Abbie touched it but immediately withdrew her hand. Jordan read her expression and did the same. The strange object was hot—not enough to burn but enough that Jordan couldn't hold his hand against it for more than a few seconds.

Jordan scraped the smooth black surface with his knife. The blade left no mark. He placed the tip against it and picked up a nearby rock, slamming it down on the butt of the knife. The blade splintered,

breaking against the strange stone.

They looked to Bernard and Gilligan for any answers. The Mermonkey shrugged. Bernard pointed to his wrist, then pointed toward the surface.

19

Jordan and Abbie stripped off their scuba gear, stepped inside the little cottage, and came across the weirdest-looking tea party they'd ever seen.

Harvey Quisling, Donald, Lou, and Hogie sat in a circle. Each followed the old man's lead, picking up a small cup and lifting it to their mouths. Hogie went last, and as he tried to

take a careful
little sip, his
cup stuck to
his gooey lip,
sank into his
gelatinous
face, and

slid down the inside of his neck.

"Sorry 'bout that," the Tasmanian Globster said. "I ingest things through osmosis. I'll work on it."

"Please do," Quisling said. "That'll never do in the human world. It's disgusting."

As Bernard entered, Jordan and Abbie broke up the party, taking Quisling aside. "What is that thing down there?" Jordan asked. "Why is it hot?"

"I was hoping the descendants of the great George Grimsley might be able to tell me," Quisling said. "I always assumed it has something to do with the fourth special, but my ex-master never fully explained it to me."

"It's located at the dead center of the crater," Abbie said. "Ground zero of the impact. Could be a remnant of the asteroid Wilford talked about."

"Asteroids and meteorites don't stay hot," Jordan said. "Especially underwater. For millions of years. There has to be some energy source inside it."

"Or something alive," Abbie said.

"So not an asteroid, more of an egg?" Quisling asked.

"Or both," Jordan said.

"An eggsteroid," Bernard said.

"Asteroid, eggsteroid, whatever it is, it's the key to Chupacabra's entire plan to take over the world," Quisling said. "That much I know for certain."

"He had the Hydro-Hide," Abbie said to Quisling. "Why didn't Chupacabra just swim down and take it? Why'd he keep you around? And don't say it was your charming personality. Or your needlework."

Harvey took a deep breath. "It was *precisely* because he wanted what was down there that he kept me around. He couldn't go near it. The effect of the blaststones was too much for him."

"You mean this?" Jordan pulled from his pocket the red stone he'd pried out of the rock. "I found one just like it in the snow the day we captured Chupacabra."

"Yes," Harvey said. "To us they're worthless. Some form of quartz. But to my former master, they were a temporary source of power. And so for me, an opportunity to be useful—and survive." Harvey looked at Abbie. "Even before he stole the Hydro-Hide, Chupacabra attempted to swim down to that asteroid egg. As he did, the blaststones were drawn to him. He said it felt like he was burning from within. Each time he tried, it was too painful, and he'd have to turn back. But he discovered he could withstand holding one or two blaststones, and they provided him with temporary powers. At least until they faded, like used-up batteries. And when that happened, my former master needed his batteries replaced. He entrusted me to dive down and retrieve more for him. I traded those blaststones for my life."

"What kind of powers did the stones give him?" Jordan asked.

"Oh, nothing like the powers he stole from the three special cryptids. But he found he could harness the heat they created in his body and channel it outward."

"To do what?" Bernard asked.

"Maybe to turn the Yeti's crystal map trail into toxic sludge," Jordan said.

"Or melt that tower of ice from within," Abbie added. "Capturing Morris and me."

"Oh, he could do much more than that," Harvey said. "With a fresh blaststone, Chupacabra could step into a fire, soaking up the power of the flame and use it to thrust himself through the sky. He called it fireflying. My idea, that name."

"You must be so proud," Abbie sneered.

"That's right," Jordan said. "I remember Izzy and I saw him firefly—straight up into the sky, and right out of the Amazon jungle."

"Using powers derived from the blaststones I provided him, he was able to steal the elemental gifts from Nessie, the Sasquatch, and the Yeti."

"Again," Abbie said. "Proud of yourself?"

"No." Harvey looked down. "You will never know how sorry I am."

"But it sounds like stealing their powers was just part of a bigger plan," Bernard said. "To get the egg-steroid."

"Or what's inside it," Abbie added.

Harvey nodded. "That's exactly why he needed those three elemental gifts—to get to the fourth. Combining the Hydro-Hide, Soil-Soles, and Blizzard-Bristles, he would somehow access the asteroid egg, crack it open, and take whatever power it holds."

"Well, he can't get to it now," Bernard said. "Because his butt is frozen solid back at the CKCC."

"Right!" Harvey exclaimed. "And you now have the location and know the secret of the final elemental power, all thanks to me, your old pal Harvey Quisling! Case closed, hooray for the Creature Keepers!"

YOU'RE WELCOME!

"Not quite," Jordan said. "If there's an unhatched cryptid down there, it's up to us to get it out, and see that it's kept safe. Especially if it has a power that could fall into the wrong hands."

"But—the only way is to combine the three other powers," Quisling said. "And the only creature with the three powers is—" He began sweating and trembling. "Surely you wouldn't—*release Chupacabra?*"

Abbie smiled at Jordan. "I dunno," she said. "I bet he'd be happy to see you, Harvey. We could throw a little reunion party."

The old man's eyes grew wide. He looked at Jordan pleadingly. "Y-you can't! Please! *You mustn't!*"

"Calm down, Harvey." Jordan seemed lost in thought. "She's messing with you."

"Consider it payback," Abbie said. "For what you did to my friend Morris."

"Chupacabra isn't the only one with those powers," Jordan said.

"Nessie, Syd, and Wilford," Abbie said. "Working together, they could do it."

"But how would you get those three together?" Bernard said. "They're in different parts of the world."

Abbie smiled coyly. "If only we knew an ace pilot with a supersonic Heli-Jet."

Bernard smiled back. "I'd be honored. But not before I find Eldon and try to explain everything. I never should have kept the truth from him. He may never speak to me again. But I have to try."

" Bernard!"

Jordan called out as loud as he dared. He'd been trying to keep up with the excited Skunk Ape as Bernard
ducked between the dilapidated shacks and storage
sheds on the platform, disappearing into the shadows.

Across the water, the late-night revelers at the Alebrijes parade were singing and laughing at the end of el
Terminal Remota pier. They were far enough away, but
Jordan knew one stiff breeze carrying his voice across
might alert them to the strange squatters hiding out
just a hundred feet away.

He came to the edge of the platform and looked
down. He spotted Bernard bouncing across the webbing that connected the platform to the pier. The Skunk

Ape disappeared beneath el Terminal Remota. "What is that maniac doing?" Jordan said to himself.

A moment later, a sudden, whipping breeze blasted Jordan from behind. He spun around. Hovering silently just off the deep end of the platform was the Heli-Jet. And sitting in the cockpit was Bernard. Jordan realized Bernard had stashed the state-of-the-art hybrid flying machine in such an obvious place, no one would think to look there—beneath the long pier crowded with humans.

Jordan laughed as he ran toward the Heli-Jet and leaped on board. He shot his hairy pilot an impressed glance. "Not bad, Bernard," he said. "Not bad at all!"

The Heli-Jet had two amazing features: a stealth rotor system that worked like a helicopter but was almost completely silent and two massive rocket thrusters that weren't silent at all but could jettison the craft at incredible speeds.

Bernard kept the copter in stealth mode, flying it low and farther out over the water until they were a safe distance from the pier and the cruise ship. "Ready?" he said. Jordan nodded. "Hit it, copilot."

Jordan slammed the big red button marked *Boost Thrusters*. The engines roared. Jordan sank back deep into his seat as the Heli-Jet's rocket engines blasted them across the Gulf of Mexico, toward the Okeeyuck-achokee Swamp.

Francine stood before a small gathering of Face Chompers listening intently on the floor of the cabin. She held a notebook in her twiggy hands. The title on the cover was written in scraggly handwriting: *FACECHOMPER Guide to Proper Human Interaction— Property of Bernard.*

"Okay, let's try another one," she said. "This time, Donald, I want you to engage me in a normal human-type conversation."

"Sure thing," the apelike Ban Manush said as he stepped up to Francine.

Francine cleared her mossy throat and read from the journal. "'Say, fellow citizen. Did you catch the popular sporting event that recently occurred?'"

"I have seen it!" Donald blurted out. "I am quite pleased that the team for which I was rooting was victorious!" The rest of them nodded in agreement, lightly applauded, then fell into a sort of depressing silence.

"Okay, that was good, probably," Francine said, flipping through the journal. "I wouldn't really know. Let's try another one."

Abbie sat in the corner trying not to laugh as Francine read from a new page. "Ooh, here's a good one. 'Human Transactions.' For this I'll need an object. Any common object will—*Ow!*" A scuba flipper hit her in the head. Clarissa was grinning ear to ear, snapping her claws, eager to play.

"Sorry," she lisped. "This is so exciting. Use the flipper!"

"Fine." Francine took the flipper and turned to the Tasmanian Globster, who, as usual, was lying in a pile. "Okay, Hogie, you're up. Pretend I'm a human, and I have this flipper. You pass me on the street, and I'll give it to you as a gift. Ready?"

Hogie formed himself into a more vertical blob and grinned. "Wow. Okay."

He took a deep, gurgling breath, gathered himself up a bit more, then pretended to casually ooze past her. "Oh!" He suddenly seemed surprised to see Francine. "Greetings there, human person," the Globster said. "I see you have a flipper as a gift. How wonderful I am for you."

Francine held out the flipper. Hogie's many eyes lit up, and a goopy, armlike protrusion snatched it from her. "Flipper! I find this to be most appreciating, with many more to *you!*" Hogie admired the flipper for a moment, sniffed it, then tossed it in his mouth, swallowing it whole. He belched loudly and smiled up at her. "So pleasantly I have met you. Someday later!" With that, he oozed away from her.

The other cryptids applauded as the Tasmanian Globster attempted some version of a bow. "And *scene*," Francine said. "Not bad. Let's try again. Who's next?"

A roomful of wings, paws, blobs, and claws shot into the air. Abbie was laughing so hard, tears were running down her face.

Bernard stared out the front window as he piloted the Heli-Jet across the Gulf of Mexico. "This is all my fault," he said. "I should've found the courage to tell Eldon on my own. I lied to him, and I deceived you and Abbie. I hate that I was so dishonest, but I didn't know what else to do. When Harvey shared what was at the center of that crater and what Chupacabra had wanted it for, I knew I had to alert the Creature Keepers. But I wasn't ready to tell Eldon about the Face Chompers. Once you and Abbie became leaders of the Creature Keepers, I thought I could trick you two into coming— without Eldon."

"It's okay," Jordan said. "I understand. And so will he. You'll see. Eldon will go right back to being the way he was."

"I'm afraid he and I will never go back to the way we were," Bernard said. "And maybe I deserve that. But I just hope it doesn't mean he's done with the Creature Keepers, too."

Jordan looked straight ahead. He didn't say it, but he hoped the same thing.

The shadow of a land mass in the distance began to grow clearer. As they approached Ponce de Leon Bay, the inlet on the edge of the Okeeyuckachokee Swamp, Jordan and Bernard peered out at the Creature Keepers' dock and boathouse. They both let out a sigh of relief when they spotted the stolen speedboat beached on the shore, as if Eldon drove it right onto the land and abandoned it. Jordan was overcome with happiness, knowing his friend had made it home.

Bernard lowered the Heli-Jet over the dock and set it down near the boathouse. Then the two of them split up. The Skunk Ape headed into the swamp, and Jordan ran toward Eternal Acres. He reached Doris's greenhouse and hit the trap door switch. The floor jerked and began to lower, and Jordan leaped onto his belly, sliding down into the darkness among the loose carrots that had fallen to the floor.

He rolled into the command center and quickly looked around. All seemed normal. He ran to the port window of the Cooler and peered inside. Chupacabra was safe and sound, still frozen in the block of ice.

Hap was sitting in an office chair with his feet up, sound asleep. The elevator door in the corner swooshed open, and Jordan ran toward it, hoping to see Eldon on the other side.

What he saw instead was Doris. She rushed out in her nightgown, her hair in curlers, with a thick, white goo covering her face. She held a large whisk and waved it around like a weapon.

"Jordan!" she cried. "What in blazes are you doing here? I got a breach signal that the greenhouse entryway had opened! Is everything all right?"

"Everything's fine," he said. "Doris, have you heard from Eldon?"

"It's nearly dawn! Why would I have heard from Eldon? He's supposed to be with you!"

Doris looked over at Hap, still snoring away near the Cooler. She rushed to him and swung the whisk, batting his feet off the desk. He stumbled forward, woke with a start, and stared wide-eyed at Doris's face.

"*Aaah!*" he screamed into his walkie-talkie. "Mayday! Mayday! I'm under attack by a hideous lunch lady covered in corn chowder! Get down here, anyone!"

Doris rolled her eyes and pulled out her walkie-talkie. Hap's walkie let out an ear-piercing *squeeee!* Doris screamed into it, "Get your lazy butt up off the floor!"

Hap looked closer at her. "Doris? Oh. Sorry, ma'am." He rose to his feet.

"You slept through an intrusion!" Doris snapped.

"Jordan slid in here, easy as you please! What if it hadn't been Jordan? What if it had been a Face Chomper?"

"Hey, Jordan. Sorry about that."

"It's okay." Jordan turned to Doris. "The Face Chomper threat isn't a threat anymore. We found the missing cryptids. They weren't kidnapped. They joined the Face Chompers."

Doris gasped. "Goodness me, no!"

"Bummer, man," Hap said.

"No, no," Jordan shook his head. "I mean, they *are* the Face Chompers. The Face Chompers are a friendly outreach organization made up of rogue cryptids. They gather, welcome, and train any creature who wants to quit the Creature Keepers to come out of hiding and join the human world. And Bernard—is their leader."

Doris's mouth fell open. A glob of the thick, white moisturizing goo on her face dripped onto the floor. "Are you sure? What about the Creature Keepers?"

"They're not looking to destroy us," Jordan said. "They just—well, they just want to be free of us. They really mean us no harm."

"Then they should really think of another name," Hap said.

Doris glared at Hap. "Let me remind you, Mr. Cooperdock," she snapped authoritatively. "Falling asleep on Cooler watch is *still* grounds for termination,

Face Chompers or not. Assuming we're still an organization in the morning, you'll be lucky to not be free of us yourself. You are dismissed of your duties, for now."

Hap lowered his head and slinked off toward the elevator. Jordan called after him, "Hap, could you please be responsible for gathering all the staff and the Keepers tomorrow morning? House meeting, front hall, nine o'clock."

"Sure thing," Hap said. He glanced shamefully at Doris as he stepped onto the elevator. "G'night, ma'am," he said. Then the doors closed.

"Don't you try to help him," Doris said. "He's still got a lot of shaping up to do to become part of my team. That is, assuming there's still any need for us."

Jordan told Doris about the mysterious eggsteroid that lay at the center of the crater and how they needed to get it to a safer place. She was still in shock about hearing that Bernard of all creatures had decided to abandon them and was particularly saddened to hear how Eldon had found out.

"Go," she said. "You need to find that poor boy. I'll keep watch down here—and gather up all the carrots you spilled all over the floor."

"Sorry about that," Jordan said.

"It's okay. Peggy will be up soon and in need of breakfast, so you did me a favor."

As Jordan ran toward the ramp, he thought of one last request. "Oh, and contact Alistair and get him to bring Nessie in as soon as possible. If we have any chance of cracking that eggsteroid at the bottom of the Chicxulub crater, we're going to need the help of the Loch Ness Monster—and her Hydro-Hide!"

OH... AND CONTACT A LISTAIR!

21

Abbie let out a big long yawn and looked around the small dimly lit Face Chompers hideout. In the corner, Harvey was quietly stitching another pink slip. Unlike Abbie, he seemed perfectly able to ignore what was beginning to strike her as an endless rehearsal for a

RING RING

AAAHHH!

horribly acted and very weird play.

Gavin had taken command of the notebook and held it in his large talons. "Lou, you're up next. Remember, in this practice exercise, Bernard is trying to get us to learn how to interact with humans and their, uh . . ." He peered at Bernard's notes. "'Celery phones.'"

Gavin reached into a cardboard box with the word "props" scribbled on its side. He pulled out a bunch of celery and handed it to Lou. "Okay. From the top."

Lou took a deep breath and carefully held the celery stalk against one of his pointy devil-ears. He glanced nervously at Gavin. The Owl Man was staring back at him intensely. The tension mounted. Gavin suddenly screeched, *"RING-RING!"*

Lou screamed, then threw the celery out the window.

"Hey, not too shabby, Lou," Hogie said. "Lot better than I did." A stalk of celery was sticking out of the side of his gelatinous head.

"Okay, I've seen enough," Abbie said. "Guys, you have to stop this."

"Bernard said we have to practice if we want to meet people," Francine said.

"And do what? Show them you're a bunch of clueless freaks?"

Gavin held up the notebook. "This is Bernard's exercise regimen. And until he gets back, we shall keep working with it to refine our people skills."

"We all love Bernard," Abbie said. "But trust me on this—he's a little fuzzy on his human terminology." She gestured to her silk nightie. "Just look at his attempt at leaving 'pink slips.'" She pulled her smartphone out of her pocket. "Also, this is called a 'cell phone,' not a 'celery phone.'" She turned to Gavin. "May I?"

Gavin handed her Bernard's notebook. She began flipping through it. "Let's see. . . . Okay, wow. See, with candles on your birthday cake? You blow them *out*; you don't blow them *up*." She flipped to another page. "Yeah, and it's a 'soccer' ball, not a 'sock-hair' ball."

Donald quietly reached into the cardboard box of props. He pulled out a nasty, woolly sphere made of his red hair, then tossed it out the window.

"Oh, gross." Abbie stared down in disgust at another page. "This is *so* not what 'sham*poo*' is made from." She tossed the notebook out the window.

"What'd you do that for?" Francine said. "Now we'll never learn how to fit in!"

"You don't have to learn how to fit in, guys," Abbie said. "You need to be yourselves. It doesn't matter if you learn how to bathe a poodle or dance the Macarena or make a banana split—you'll never be human because you're cryptids."

"I dunno," Lou said. "Bernard's pretty into teaching

us all this humany stuff."

"I'm sure he was," Abbie said, "because that's what he's all about. I mean, the dude plays the tuba. He's practically more human than I am! Being humanlike is Bernard's thing. Each one of you guys has to figure out what your thing is. What makes you . . . *you*?"

They all stared blankly at her for a moment. Finally, Hogie raised an armlike protrusion and cleared his throat. "I'm, like, all goopy and stuff, . . ."

"Really?" Francine said. "We hadn't noticed."

I'M, LIKE, ALL GOOPY AND STUFF.

"That's good," Abbie said. "That's the thing that makes Hogie whatever it is that he is. Why act like something else? Especially something *human*. Trust me, I've been around humans my whole life, and they're not so great. Who's next?"

Abbie looked around the room. They didn't seem to be getting it. As she took in how unique each of them was, she thought about a very dear friend. "Listen," she said. "I met this cryptid. He had his own thing that made him different, too. A bowl built into the top of his head. And that bowl had to stay filled with water at all times or he had this annoying habit of turning to stone."

"The Japanese Kappa," Gavin said softly. The others nodded. They all knew about Morris.

"At first we thought it was just a weird thing. Then it was a nuisance. Later, it became a real threat to him and everyone around him. But in the end, it was that trait, that funny little thing, that not only helped us defeat and capture Chupacabra, it saved my life."

Lou stepped forward. "I can bench about three hundred times my own weight. And I can throw stuff around pretty good."

"That's true," Abbie said to the others. "He can. I've seen it."

SNIP! CLICK-CLACK SNAP-SNIP! Abbie and the others looked over to see Clarissa wildly snapping away her claws. *"Hiii-yaaah!"* She reached over and snipped a table leg in two. Harvey's stitchwork slid to the floor. Harvey gathered it up and walked out of the room, grumbling about how no one respected his handiwork.

"It seems that Clarissa has a pair of pretty menacing claws. Good!"

All the other cryptids showed off what made them unique. Francine had strong, branchlike arms with sharp sticks for fingers. "Great for roasting hot dogs," Abbie said. "You'll be a big hit at human barbecues."

Gavin flapped his great wings, creating a windstorm

that whipped around the entire cabin and also slamming his beaked head into the ceiling. "Ow!" he cried.

"Watch it there," Abbie said. "See? You don't know your own strength!"

Suddenly a blinding light filled the room, as if a shooting star had fallen in through the window. They all covered their eyes and turned away until it faded. In the center of the brilliant radiance stood Sandy the Sumatran Golden Liger.

"Very impressive," Abbie said. "But let's keep it on low beams for now, okay?" She looked around the room. "See, you all have things that make you special. People are gonna love you guys. Don't change who you are for anyone, especially anyone *human*." She looked over at Donald, who was sitting on the floor, his legs crossed. He was lifting his foot up to the side of his head. "Wow. Look at Donald, you guys! He's into yoga!" They all applauded.

Donald looked up, turned his head, and pulled his big toe out of his ear. "Sorry, I was just clearing out some wax. What are you guys talking about?"

"Nothing, Donald. Keep digging. We'll find your best quality yet."

Jordan stood at the shoreline of the Okeeyuckachokee Swamp. Both the speedboat and the Heli-Jet were

still parked there, but there was no sign of Bernard. Jordan turned and bolted into the darkness of the thick cypress trees.

He hadn't gone far when he nearly tripped over a pair of boots in the muck. "Badger Ranger regulation, size eight," he said to himself. A few hundred feet ahead he picked up a muddy sock. Deeper into the swamp, the dappled moonlight revealed a few more items of Eldon's. Jordan suddenly knew where he'd find his friend. He broke out running past a Badger Ranger shirt, pair of khaki shorts, and Eldon's belt.

The round wall of tree trunks protecting the Puddle of Ripeness was impenetrable, like a natural turret rising high into the night sky. The air was thick with the musky, woodsy smell from the trees, the perfect disguise for the nasty, gooey, stinky puddle they protected.

Jordan tried to remember where the secret doorway was from the last time he was here. This time was much easier, however—halfway around the circle of trunks, he found the passageway had been left wide open.

Inside, Jordan ran along the circular path that coiled around and around, leading deeper toward the center of the cypress grove. He knew the rare and rancid substance he would find there. The Puddle of Ripeness was a small, bubbling pool of nasty-smelling goo. Jordan had seen with his eyes how powerful an antidote to the Fountain of Youth it was. This time, however, he was more anxious about who he hoped he'd find standing over it: the only two who knew of its existence besides him. Bernard and his Keeper, Eldon Pecone.

He was elated to hear their voices as he made his way around the final circle. But when he heard what they were saying, he stopped before he reached the center, and listened.

"Eldon, please try to understand." Bernard's voice sounded strained and nervous.

"Oh, I understand," Eldon's voice snapped back. "You betrayed me. You, of all cryptids, abandoned me. After everything we've been through together."

"Eldon, it doesn't have to be like this. I just want to be free, without someone keeping me in the shadows. That's what all of us want. But it doesn't mean we can't still be friends. You'll always be my friend."

"You have new friends now, Bernard. You and the other traitors. The Face Chompers. Go be with them. I don't want to see you. Not ever again."

Jordan couldn't believe he was hearing this. As he approached the voices, he nearly slammed into Bernard rushing out along the same path, looking quite upset.

"Oh, Jordan," the Skunk Ape said, more angry than Jordan had ever seen him. "He won't listen to me. He's as stubborn as a squirrel."

"Mule," Jordan said. "I think you mean *stubborn as a mule*." Bernard nodded. "Let me talk to him. I'll bring him around. But while I do, I need to ask you to fly the Heli-Jet to Canada and bring back Syd. Deliver him to your Face Chomper hideout. Do you think you can do that?"

"Sure I can do that," Bernard said. "I'll fly all night if I have to. Then I'll show Eldon that he's wrong about us. That we're not traitors. We just want to live our own lives."

"I know you will," Jordan said. "Just like you showed me."

Bernard gave Jordan a big hug and trudged off. Jordan watched him disappear around the curved path. Then he turned and faced the entrance to the center of the grove, where Eldon would be waiting for him.

22

The clearing in the hub of the cypress cluster was very small, with a mossy patch encircling an even smaller green pool of thick, stinky, bubbling liquid. Sitting there, staring into the Puddle of Ripeness, was

Eldon Pecone. And he was wearing nothing but his boxer shorts.

"Eldon, what are you doing? Where's your Badger Ranger uniform?"

"Don't need it anymore. Don't need anything—or anyone."

"So you're out? Just quitting the Badger Rangers?"

"Badger Rangers, Creature Keepers. I'm out of the whole human race."

"You can't mean that."

"Why not? It's all a lie! There's no honor, no loyalty, not in any of it. Everyone just does as he, she, or it pleases, with no regard for the sacrifices others have made or the years they've given."

"Those cryptids didn't want to hurt you. Especially Bernard. They just want to stop having to hide all the time and to join the real world, that's all."

"They can have at it. And as they check in to the world, I'll be checking out."

"You can't do this, Eldon. Not now. We need you."

Eldon glanced up at Jordan for the first time, then quickly scowled again and pretended that he hadn't.

But Jordan had noticed, and he moved closer. "Listen to me. You were right. There is a fourth special cryptid. I think it's in this weird rock, or egg, at the center of that crater. If it's an unhatched cryptid, it needs the Creature Keepers' help. And if it's a special, its gift may need protecting, too. We have to crack that eggsteroid open, and Abbie and I have a plan. But we're gonna need First-Class Badger Ranger *and* Creature Keeper Eldon Pecone."

"Sorry. They're both gone for good."

Jordan studied Eldon a moment and tried to summon feelings of sympathy. But he could only feel what Bernard had felt—a growing feeling of anger at what a stubborn squirrel Eldon was being.

"Y'know what," Jordan said. "You're right. The Eldon I know isn't here. Certainly not the Creature Keeper I knew. You're not worthy to be a part of what my grandfather started. Not anymore."

Eldon glared back at Jordan. "Oh, you think so, do you?"

"I know so. My grandfather wouldn't sit here feeling sorry for himself. He'd understand that the years of protection he provided those cryptids are what gave them the confidence to be free. If my grandfather were in your shoes, he'd cancel the pity party and help us!"

"First off, I'm not wearing any shoes. And second, your grandfather *isn't* here. I am. It was me who helped build his Creature Keepers into what it is today. Me who kept it running even after he was gone. So don't tell me what your grandfather would do because you never knew him. I knew him! I helped him! So I get to say when the Creature Keepers is dead. *And it's dead!*"

This hit Jordan like a punch in the stomach. Finally, he spoke up. "Well, then no wonder this old thing keeps finding its way back to you." He slipped his grandfather's ring off his finger and stared at the powerful elixir swirling around inside it. "You once told me the Fountain of Youth power streaming through this ring is multiplied by the wearer's sacrifice. But I think it also has a way of finding those who need to sacrifice the most. And I think maybe it's not done with you yet, Eldon."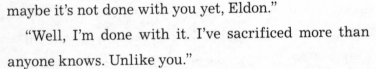

"Well, I'm done with it. I've sacrificed more than anyone knows. Unlike you."

"Maybe. But as of right now, I'm sacrificing the thing that's most important to me. My grandfather's legacy. To prove to you that I don't believe it's dead."

Jordan tossed the ring toward Eldon. It flew through the air but not quite far enough. They both watched it land in the Puddle of Ripeness.

Plop! Grampa Grimsley's ring sank, disappearing into the thick, gooey liquid.

"Nice catch," Jordan said.

"Nice toss," Eldon said.

"Well, you know where it is. If you need it, you can just fish it out."

"Or maybe I'll just let it rot in there while I do the same out here."

"That's your choice, Eldon, but I hope you find that ring one more time and let it help you believe again in what you and my grandfather created. And I hope when you do, you won't have to sacrifice too much."

Jordan swallowed hard. He could feel tears welling up, tears he didn't want Eldon to see. He took a long last look at his friend Eldon Pecone, then turned and walked out.

Jordan wiped his cheek as he ran toward the boathouse. Something crushed beneath his feet. He picked up Eldon's smushed Badger Ranger hat and popped it back into shape. A small wet stain fell onto the brim. Jordan felt his cheek. They were both dry. Another small stain appeared on the brim, then another. Snowflakes were drifting down, gently landing and melting on Eldon's hat.

The small swirling snow squall was concentrated directly over Jordan's head and nowhere else. It trailed upward through the treetops, high above and out of the swamp. It took no time at all for Jordan to recognize this sparkling spectacle as one of many very useful skills belonging to his friend the Yeti. But Jordan wasn't impressed. He threw back his head and hollered at the tiny storm.

"Wilford! Quit spying on me! Come down off your mountaintop and help us!"

The squall swirled around him, retreated above the trees, and disappeared into the warm, starry sky.

Abbie woke with a start and looked around. The sun was up, but the Face Chompers were all snoring after a long night of human *un*training. She smiled at her odd-looking pupils, then suddenly thought of her mother and father.

She rushed back to the *Mayan Princess* and knocked on their cabin door, trying to imagine where she would tell her parents she had been all night or where she'd say Jordan had gone.

Mr. and Mrs. Grimsley were still sleeping, having been up quite late themselves, celebrating the opening night of the Alebrijes weekend festival.

"What are you doing here?" Mrs. Grimsley whispered over Mr. Grimsley's loud snoring, which was almost as loud as Lou's. "Jordan said you'd met some friends and were staying with them."

"What?" Abbie said. "When did he say that?"

"He called early this morning. From Florida. Said he had to see your strange friend Eldon home. He let us know so we wouldn't worry. He said he'd rejoin us before the end of our vacation and to tell you Eldon was back, safe and sound."

"Grimsley Family Fun Time . . ." Mr. Grimsley mumbled in his sleep.

"Good," Abbie said. "And uh, yes, I am staying with friends. I just missed Chunk and thought I'd take him back with me.

"All right, well, why don't you meet us by the pool for lunch and shuffleboard?" her mother said. "And bring your friends. We'd love to meet them!"

Abbie rushed off to her cabin and opened the door to find Chunk right where she'd left him, in his travel crate, snoring almost as loudly as her father. She crouched down, opened the crate, and lifted his plump body. "I'm sorry, Chunkster. I was up all night helping creatures learn how to live free."

She looked down at the small travel crate, then around the dark, cramped cabin. Then she looked into the eyes of her pet iguana.

* * *

It took Jordan a moment to realize where he was when he woke—his Eternal Acres bedroom. Not helping were the retired Keepers, still in their pink Face Chompers nighties, surrounding his bed. Doris stood in the center of them and set down a plate of pancakes.

"Good morning, dearie. I told them that you've found their creatures. They're very anxious to hear how they are but didn't want to wake you."

Mike, the New Jersey Devil's Keeper, stepped forward. "Bro. Give it to me straight. Is Lou okay?"

Jordan sat up. All the former Keepers were longing for news of their cryptids. He knew they deserved answers, but he couldn't help feeling a little irritated. It had been a long night. "Abbie, Eldon, and I found your creatures. And yes, they're perfectly fine."

A collective sigh filled the room. Then the questions came.

"Where are they?"

"Are they being taken care of?"

"Who kidnapped them?"

Jordan suddenly snapped at them. "No one, all right? No one kidnapped them! I'm sorry to tell you this, but they all left on their own."

Confusion erupted from the Keepers.

"Those are what you have on," Jordan continued. "Pink slips. You've all been let go."

"I don't believe it!" Alice shouted out. "Hogie wouldn't leave me!"

"What can we do?" another said. "What *will* we do?"

"You'll all stay here," Doris said. "Everyone is welcome."

Christopher looked angry. "Where's Eldon? This wouldn't have happened under his leadership!"

"I'm afraid Eldon is retired," Jordan said. "Like all of you."

"We didn't retire! We were fired! You said it yourself! These aren't pink slips! They're *pink slips*!" The British-accented Thomas tore his nightie off and stood defiantly in his Union Jack boxer shorts.

"Okay," Jordan said. "I know you're all angry, but the Creature Keepers organization is in good hands. My sister, Abbie, and I are in charge now, and—"

"Crudcakes!" Mike hollered. "We want Eldon! He'll know what to do!"

Jordan was growing more impatient by the second. He hadn't even had his breakfast yet, and he was being yelled at by a room full of angry senior citizens in pink nighties. "Well, y'know what? I would've liked Eldon's help, too! But unfortunately, he's too busy feeling sorry for himself, sitting alone by a puddle in the middle of the swamp, wearing nothing but his underwear!"

The Keepers all fell silent at this. Suddenly, Mike stepped forward and pulled his pink slip off. Beneath it he was wearing tighty-whitey underwear. He dropped his pink slip on Jordan's bed and crossed his arms defiantly. Alice the Australian Keeper did the same. She had frilly bloomers on underneath. They all followed suit until Jordan was lying beneath a pile of pink nighties, surrounded by a group of old people in their underwear.

"This is just great," he said calmly. "Just what I need this morning. Thanks."

"We now stand in our underwear," Mike said. "In solidarity. For Eldon." He raised his fist and walked out. The others did the same, filing out behind him.

"That went well," Doris said, collecting the discarded pink slips before exiting. "Eat your breakfast, now. You seem a little grumpy."

Abbie's taxi reached its final destination, after spending much of the day driving her and Chunk to a number of stops around Progreso and the surrounding area. She'd let the children of Flamboyanes tickle his fat belly, she'd let him float in the cool water of the cenotes and then nap in the warm, Mexican sun. She even bought him a jumbo-size bag of Crazy-Blazin' Jalapeño-Heckfire Nacho Cheezy Puffs and let him have it all to himself.

Finally, she stepped out of the cab and looked down at a sign she'd read before: *¡Cruce de la Iguana!* She carried Chunk up the road toward the looming Mayan pyramids, where other tourists and visitors were wandering around the open field. Everyone's gaze was directed upward at the incredible structures rising toward the late afternoon sky. Only Abbie had her eyes on the ground.

As she approached, a lizard scurried past, disappearing into an overgrown path leading off to the side of the ruins, into the jungle. She set Chunk down on the ground. "C'mon, buddy," she said. "Time for you to make some new friends."

The path led deeper, through a smaller, crumbled monument. She and Chunk followed it down a small ravine, where they abruptly stopped. Twenty or so iguanas were draped over the crumbled, vine-covered blocks of stone. They were mostly sleeping and lounging and paid very little attention to their visitors.

Abbie looked at Chunk, and Chunk glanced up at Abbie. She had tears in her eyes. "Don't look at me like that," she said. "Don't you want to be free? You'll make new friends and be happy here. And who knows, maybe— *Ouch!*" Chunk was suddenly clinging to her leg. She peeled him off and set him down again, taking a step backward. "I'll miss you, too. But this is for the best. I've come to realize that all creatures are meant to be free— *Ow!*"

This time the reptile leaped into her arms. This was the most exertion she'd ever witnessed from him. Chunk stared up at her with his big bulging eyes. She stared back. "Don't you understand? You're not meant to live in a cage, or a city apartment, or even a large retirement home by a swamp. You're meant to be here, in the world, with your own kind." She sniffed back a tear as she set him down on one of the rocks. This time the reptile just stared up at her as she slowly backed away. "Good-bye, my friend. I'll miss you."

She turned and ran out of the jungle before he could latch on to her again—or she changed her mind. She entered the ravine with tears in her eyes, not watching where she was going. She passed through the small ruins, ignoring a small sign: *Prohibido el Paso—NO TRESPASSING!* Abbie stepped on a boarded-up excavation site, and it gave out beneath her.

CRACK! WUMP!

Abbie fell just a few feet through the brittle wood and landed on the cool dirt floor of some sort of antechamber. As Abbie's eyes adjusted, she could make out worn carvings on the walls. There seemed to be a story line told in pictures like ancient cartoon panels. They depicted an asteroid striking the earth, the aftermath of the collision, and the crater. It was difficult to make out the last panel in the dim light, but there was some sort of figure moving away from the crater. The form was small and crawled on four legs. Beneath it were strange Mayan letters:

Abbie took a sheet of paper and a pencil from her bag and did a quick pencil rub of the last panel. She tucked it back into her bag, then climbed out. She glanced back in the direction of Chunk's new home, then quickly made her way back to the main road.

24

Jordan and Doris stood at the end of the boathouse dock, staring out at Ponce de Leon Bay.

"Don't you worry about Eldon," Doris said. "He'll come around."

"You didn't see how angry he was. He may come around, but I don't think he's coming back. It feels like the Creature Keepers is ending, Doris."

"That may be true about Eldon, but let me tell you something I've learned: nothing ever truly ends. Everything just evolves, turning into something else. Look at me. I'm living proof."

Jordan smiled at his friend and thought about all the changes she'd been through, before and since he'd met her. Maybe that's what made her such a no-nonsense person. But for such a tough old cookie, Doris had a sweet and gooey center. Jordan certainly didn't see her going anywhere for a long, long time.

The sound of footsteps on the dock from behind got both their attention. Hap was running toward them. He saluted Jordan, then turned to Doris. "Finished clearing the lunch dishes, ma'am. I'm going to do turndown on all the guest rooms, then start prepping for dinner."

"That would be very helpful, Hap," Doris said. "Thank you so much."

Hap smiled nervously, saluted Jordan again, and scurried back down the dock, running off through the swamp toward the house. Doris smiled at Jordan.

"See? Evolution. He's been demoted to guest services, and now he's working his tail off twice as hard, trying to get back into my good graces."

"Wow. You run a tight ship. Whatever happens, I hope you never retire, Doris."

A burbling in the water just off the end of the dock began to stir. "Speaking of tight ships . . ." Doris checked her pocket watch. "Tsk. Forty-one seconds late."

A periscope broke the surface of the bay, followed by the turretlike "sail" of a submarine, and finally the deck of the craft. The hatch opened with a squeak, and a tubby old man in a kilt clambered out with some trouble. The top of his head was bald, with orange, curly hair above both of his droopy ears. Jordan would have likely thought he'd never met this curious person before if not for the large grin that spread between those ears, which he instantly recognized.

"Mac?" Jordan said. "Alistair MacAlister, is that you?"

"Aye!" The old Scot stepped off the submarine and onto the dock. "In the flesh!" He grabbed his bouncing midsection. "More flesh than last time you saw me!" He gave Jordan a great hug, then pulled away. Jordan couldn't believe his eyes. He was right. The last time he'd seen the Loch Ness Monster's Keeper, Alistair was a boy, just a little older than he.

"That Fountain of Youth elixir took its time working its way through my hearty system," Alistair said. "But once it left, *fwhoosh*! My body caught up to my years faster than a highland mountain hare!"

"Oh, Mac, I'm so sorry," Jordan said.

"Ach! I'm still young at heart! And besides, as old as I got, I'm a spring chicken compared to ol' Haggis-Breath!"

A splash from beside the submarine doused Alistair in water.

"SKRONK!"

The Loch Ness Monster raised her long neck out of the water, snorted proudly, and dived back down, whipping her tail and splashing all three of them this time.

Alistair yelled after her. "Of course, that don't mean she's matured any!"

"I'm glad you and Nessie are here, Mac," Jordan said.

"Came as quick as we could when we got your distress call. We were halfway around the world, cleaning up an oil spill in the Sea of Okhotsk. She's a bit cranky after such a long trip. Could use a wee nap, if you wanna know the truth."

Jordan looked at Doris. The old woman shrugged. "You're the boss."

"There's really not much we can do until the other two specials turn up," Jordan said. "And that egg-steroid we've got to try and crack open has been lying at the bottom of the Gulf of Mexico for about sixty-six million years. Another day or two won't make much difference. Besides, Abbie's in Mexico with the Face Chompers to help keep an eye on things. Let Nessie have a rest, and we'll all embark in the morning."

Nessie snorted her thanks, then shut her eyes and collapsed on the shore.

"Much appreciated," Alistair said. "Say, where's Eldon?"

Jordan and Doris hesitated. "He's locked himself away, feeling sorry for himself," she said. "I was going to try and talk some sense into him. Mac, why don't you come along? He may listen to you."

"Sure, if you think I can help," Alistair said.

"Good luck," Jordan said. "But don't get your hopes up."

"Have you talked with him?" Alistair asked.

"I'm afraid Eldon and I have said all we have to say to each other."

The sun sat low in the Mexican sky as Abbie made her way along el Terminal Remota. She chose to walk much of the way back, to give herself time to reminisce about her last day with Chunk.

Out near the horizon, something caught her eye. It was small but moving very fast across the water and flying very low. As she watched, it dived even lower, dangerously close to the waves. There was only one pilot Abbie knew of who flew like that. When the piloted craft suddenly dived beneath the pier, ducking out of sight from any onlookers, she was convinced. It was Bernard.

She broke into a sprint, heading toward the ramshackle oil platform.

Down in the Creature Keepers Central Command, Jordan peered through the portal window of the Cooler. Chupacabra's silhouette was perfectly preserved within the block of ice. Jordan was about to turn and go when something struck him. He scanned the distance between the Cooler door and its prisoner. A chill ran down his back. *Was the block of ice closer than before?* He roughly calculated the distance at six or eight feet. The ice block looked exactly the same, as did the shadowy figure it entombed. It had to be his imagination, he thought. But then he remembered that's what he told himself after spotting Harvey Quisling.

Jordan turned toward Ed, who was working on the computers. "Ed, have you noticed anything strange in that Cooler?" Jordan said.

"Nope, why?"

Jordan hesitated, then decided not to mention the

idea of Chupacabra sliding closer to the door. He didn't want anyone to think he was crazy. "Nothing. Never mind. Just making sure everything's okay in there, that's all."

The greenhouse entry ramp suddenly hissed as it opened. Doris and Alistair came sliding down, along with bunches of carrots.

"Pretty fancy garage door you got there," Alistair said, chewing on a carrot.

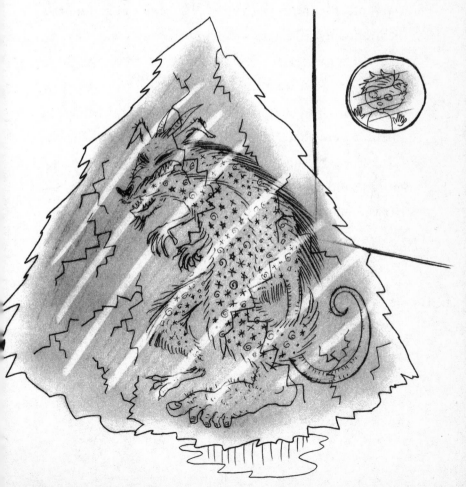

"Any luck with Eldon?" Jordan asked.

"He's got himself sealed up behind those trees," Alistair said. "Stubborn fool's gonna starve himself to death if he doesn't come out."

"I have a plan to take care of exactly that," Doris said, gathering the carrots from the floor. "As well as one to pull him out of his slump. But I'm going to need to recruit some helpers. If you boys will excuse me." She took the elevator up to the main level of the house.

Alistair let out a big yawn. "I suppose I should get a little shut-eye. I'm not the spring chicken I was a month ago. Strange feeling, getting so old so suddenly. But a quick rest and I'll be raring to go."

Jordan gestured toward the elevator. "C'mon upstairs. I'm sure Hap's got a nice, cozy bed set up for you." As Alistair made his way, Jordan glanced one more time through the portal, eyeballing the distance between the door and that ice block.

25

The darkening sky made it relatively easy for Abbie to climb across from the pier to the platform, even as a few vendors and local author-ities were setting up for the next day's final Alebrijes celebration.

The voices coming from inside the central shack were a bit louder than they should've been for a group of cryptids not quite ready to be discov-ered. Abbie entered to find all the Face Chompers she'd been up late helping. They

were excitedly crowding around another cryptid—one whom she knew very well.

"Syd!" She leaped into the Sasquatch's outstretched arms.

"Hey there, kid!" He grinned as he hugged her tightly.

"It's so good to see your big dumb face again," she teased.

"Thanks. I was just telling these dudes how much fun we had when you came and stayed with me up in Canada."

"You mean when we lost your Soil-Soles, destroyed your treehouse, almost got you broadcast on live television, and nearly caused a megathrust earthquake?"

"Good times." Syd plopped himself onto an old couch and put his odd-sized feet up on a table. One was enormous, the other tiny—a sad reminder of how Abbie, Jordan, and the Creature Keepers were able to steal back only one of the Sasquatch's Soil-Soles from Chupacabra.

"Syd, what are you doing here? And how'd you find us?"

"Bernard picked me up! Filled me in on this whole Face-Chompy scene he's started with these guys. Told me how he left things with Eldon, too. Big bummer. But now he's more jazzed than ever to introduce these crazy creatures to the world!"

The Face Chompers reacted to this news enthusiastically, smiling and giggling and high-fiving one another.

"Syd, are you gonna come with us?" Hogie asked. "We'd love to have ya!"

"Aw, thanks, but I'm good. I've had more than my share of human contact over the years. You guys got this."

"I've been working with them," Abbie said. "And they're gonna be—"

"They're gonna be a bigger hit than my 'All-Star Celebrity Squatchin' Special'!" The loud, obnoxious voice exploded like a bomb as Buck Wilde, the onetime-famous host of the popular reality TV show *Buck Wilde: Squatch-Seeker!* suddenly burst in.

He slapped Syd on the back. "Season four finale episode. Highest ratings *ever*!"

He and Syd high-fived as everyone laughed and cheered. Everyone, that is, but Abbie. She'd never been a huge fan of Buck's, especially back when he was hunting Syd. He'd since quit his show and come over to the other side to take care of his former nemesis. Which was nice. But she still thought he was a loudmouthed jerk.

"Hi, Buck," she said flatly.

"Howdy, little lady! Listen, that smelly fella,

Bernard, filled me in on what he and his crazy crew of critters are lookin' to do. And I told 'em I want in. In fact, *I couldn't be more in love with this project!*"

He threw his arm around her and pulled her tighter. "But I also said to him, 'Listen here, Stinky. You're going about it the wrong way, trying to behave like people—'cause you ain't people!'"

This surprised Abbie. "That's right. In fact, that's exactly what I told them—"

"Of course I'm right! You can hand a possum to

a chimpanzee, but you can't ask him to act like a banana!" He pointed to Hogie. "Yo, Squirt! You ever try to peel a possum?"

"Uh," Hogie said.

"Exactly! And that's my point!"

Abbie couldn't believe she and Buck Wilde were on the same page. Kind of.

"So obviously the first thing we're gonna need is a catchy brand name!"

"Sorry," Abbie said. "What?"

Buck stepped into the center of the room. "A brand name! A catchy title! Basic promotional marketing! Trust me, I was on TV! You think *Buck Wilde* is my real name? I made it up! And then my fans ate it up! Human fans! You all need to call yourselves somethin' that'll get their attention! So what's it gonna be? C'mon, start spit-ballin'!"

Donald, taking this literally, hucked a loogie on the floor.

"Okay, that's a start!" Buck said. "Anybody else?"

"Like a name?" Clarissa said.

"Right!"

They all looked at one another, then slowly pointed together at the banner that was back up on the far wall: FACE CHOMPERS. Buck studied it for a moment. He burst into a grin. "Heck yeah! I love it! It's catchy, edgy, and you already got a banner made! Perfect! Now let's get to work!"

Abbie sidled up to Syd as she watched Buck continue his spiel to the other cryptids. "Sheesh," she said to the Sasquatch. "You believe this guy?"

"I know," Syd said. "Isn't he great?"

Jordan was up early the next morning and made his way to the cypress grove fortress that held inside its impenetrable wall of tree trunks the Puddle of Ripeness—and his old friend Eldon.

The retired Keepers were there, too, all in their underwear, still in solidarity with the fellow Keeper on the other side of the trees. They tied bunches of carrots to pink strips of silk, which had been fashioned from slips into small parachutes. Peggy was sitting obediently, kept still by Alistair MacAlister, who was dangling a shiny silver kitchen spoon in front of the hypnotized jackalope's dazed eyes.

Once the retirees bundled together a carrot-filled parachute, they placed it in a slingshot-like harness attached with bungee cords to Peggy's antlers. They pulled back the slingshot and let it go—*boing!*

The care package flew high above the top of the cypress tree walls, then opened up, gently floating down inside the fortress. The old folk broke out into cheers before packing up the next one.

"Great job, you guys," Jordan said. "I'm sure Eldon appreciates it."

Mike sat on the mossy ground with a couple

other Keepers, writing notes, which were then placed into the parachutes. "Hey, Jordan," he said.

"Hey. What are you guys writing?"

"Thank-you cards. To say we really appreciate all Eldon's done for us and our creatures over the years."

"And how we really, really wish he'd come back," Alice said, a bit coldly.

"And how we really, really, *really* prefer him as a leader over you," Thomas said, quite rudely. "No offense."

"No, no," Jordan said sarcastically. "How could that possibly offend me?"

Lou offered a sheet of paper and a pen. "Hey. I'm sure he'd like to hear from you, too. Why don't you jot down a note?"

Jordan smiled sadly. "Thanks, but I'm pretty sure he doesn't want to hear from me." He turned and headed back, scanning the ground as he walked, keeping an eye out for bits of Eldon's uniform. He stopped at the spot where he was sure he'd tripped over Eldon's boots. But they were gone.

Hap came running up to him. "Hey, Jordan! I finished my morning chores for Doris. Need me to do anything?"

"You've been working so hard. Take the rest of the day off."

"No can do, boss," Hap said. "I feel awful about the other night. Totally uncool of me. I gotta get the Creature Keepers to believe in me again."

"Hap, you've been running around the swamp. Have you seen any of Eldon's clothes? They were scattered near here, but I can't find anything now."

Hap smiled proudly and saluted. "Helpful Hap Cooperdock at your service."

"Oh. You have them?"

"I figured when Eldon comes out of his slump, he's gonna want to wear something more than just his underwear. So I washed and pressed his uniform. Shined his boots, too. Then I put everything back in his locker, down in the CKCC." He looked around, then spoke in a lower voice. "I'm not technically authorized to go back down there, but I know how Eldon likes things being returned to their proper places. I thought he'd appreciate it. Y'know, when he returns to his old self again."

Jordan smiled at the scraggly ex-Keeper. "He sure will, Hap. Great job."

Abbie woke with a start. She'd stayed up late telling
Syd of her adventures since they last saw each other:
how she'd befriended Morris the Japanese Kappa and
had even climbed to the top of the Himalayas and met
Wilford, the elusive Yeti. To say nothing of finally
defeating and capturing Chupacabra.

As her eyes adjusted to the morning light, she spotted Syd snoring away. He wore a sleeping mask on his
head and a fluffy bunny slipper on his tiny left foot. His
great right foot stuck out from under a small blanket.

Abbie crept into the main cabin. Clarissa the Christmas Island Colossus Crab was helping Harvey by
holding a roll of pink material in her claws. Gilligan
the Feejee Mermonkey was relaxing in an old washtub

that was filled with seawater and mounted to a pull cart. Gavin the Owl Man of Cornwall was using his long talons to clean and unruffle his feathers. Hogie was gathered in a puddle in the corner, his various eyes staring off in different directions. And Lou the New Jersey Devil was repeatedly lifting Gilligan in his rolling washtub over his head.

"Hey, look who decided to join civilization," Gilligan said.

"Morning," Abbie said. "Where are the others?"

"Out," Gavin said. "That awful Buck Wilde chap got them up early.

"Out? What do you mean, out? Out where?" A panic gripped her. "Please don't tell me—"

"Mr. Wilde said today was 'Brand Launch' day," Clarissa lisped. "So I expect they'll be getting back with some brand-new lunch anytime now. Gosh, I hope it's shish kebabs."

"Not 'lunch,'" Harvey said. "'*Launch.*' As in, launching their brand and introducing themselves to the human race."

"Oh, no." Abbie glanced around the room. "Where's Bernard? Has anyone told him?"

"Told him?" Lou set down the washtub wagon. "He and Buck were working together to convince Francine, Donald, and Sandy to make their big debut! Personally,

I think Bernard was just excited to show off his banner."

Abbie looked up at the wall. The Face Chompers banner was gone. "Oh, this is bad. Why didn't you all go with him?"

Hogie oozed over to her ankles and gazed up at Abbie with his dozen or so glassy eyes. "We wanted to wait for you," he said.

"Yeah. We don't need some grandiose branding campaign," Gavin said. "You taught us in order to get humans to accept us, all we need to do is be ourselves."

She smiled at this and felt less panicked. "Right," Abbie said. "And you're also going to be the ones who don't let that idiot Buck endanger the others. Whaddya say? Who's ready to meet the world?"

A silence fell over the room. Finally, Clarissa spoke up. "Uh, we are?"

"That's right!" Abbie said. *"You are!"*

They let out a loud cheer. Syd appeared in the doorway, yawning. His sleeping mask was crammed up onto his forehead.

"This is it, Syd!" Hogie said. "We're gonna finally meet the humans!"

"Great," Syd said. "Just remember, humans like to take lots of pictures. Might wanna come up with a signature pose." The Sasquatch turned sideways and broke into his classic Bigfoot midstride stance. "This one worked for me, but you can borrow it."

Hogie strained himself, then fell back into a blob. "I'll work on it," he said.

Abbie led Hogie, Lou, Clarissa, and Gavin out of the building. Harvey followed along, pulling Gilligan's washtub wagon. They made their way across the platform to a trap door, where they stopped and peered down through the nearly invisible mesh netting and the water far beneath it.

"Will it hold all of us?" Abbie asked.

Harvey grinned. "High-polymer, stealth-mesh weave," he said. "Some of my best work." The old man jumped through the trap door, followed by Hogie, Lou, Clarissa, and Gavin.

Gilligan lifted himself out of his rolling bathtub and sloshed over to the edge. "Good luck," he said to Abbie.

"Moe and I will keep an eye on your progress from the water. Once we're convinced it isn't a suicide mission, we'll proudly join you."

"Gee, thanks," Abbie said.

The Feejee Mermonkey waved a webbed hand, then leaped into the water.

Abbie, Harvey, and the four remaining cryptids made their way across Harvey's near-invisible, weaved water bridge, which led beneath el Terminal Remota. They could make out the Heli-Jet parked in the shadows beneath the pier as they climbed up and through a hatch that led them directly to the light of day—and the human world.

They all collected themselves at the edge of el Terminal Remota, slightly hidden behind a wall of carnival games, food booths, gift stalls, and small stages that lined the pier. It had grown more crowded, and a river of people passed by. The Face Chompers readied themselves for their big introduction.

"All right, you guys," Abbie said. "Just remember, get out there, be your very best selves, and you'll do just fine. And remember, keep an eye out for Buck Wilde and the others. Okay?"

Hogie, Gavin, and Clarissa traded nervous glances. "Perhaps we're being too hasty," Gavin said. "Maybe we should step back and look at the best possible—*oof!*"

Lou suddenly shoved the Owl Man out toward the pier. "Enough gabbin'! Who's next? *Who? Who?*" He chuckled and glanced at Abbie and Harvey as the others followed Gavin before Lou could push them. "See what I did there, with the 'who, who'? 'Cause he's an owl. Get it?"

"Yes," Harvey said. "We get it. Now it's your turn."

Lou flashed a pointy grin and gave a thumbs-up. "Go big or go home." He confidently stepped out into the sunlight with the others. "Yo, humans!"

Abbie and Harvey stepped out next and stood beside the line of grinning cryptids. Oddly, the parade of people nodded and smiled as they passed, more amused than amazed. It was as if they'd seen a Colossus Crab, Tasmanian Globster, Owl Man, and New Jersey Devil every day.

"I must say," Gavin said. "This is going remarkably well."

Abbie wondered why the crowd was so unfazed until she noticed even wilder and more colorful creatures walking among them. Some were people in Alebrijes costumes; others carried larger, homemade monsters like the one Sam had brought them to see. These four actual cryptids, standing in their midst, fit right in.

"Of course," she said to herself. "They all think you're just part of the celebration."

Hogie heard this and blinked. "I like celebrations."

27

Jordan slid down the hydraulic ramp on his backside and rolled onto the floor of the CKCC. Ed was in the break room getting a cup of coffee, so Jordan walked over to the Cooler and peered into the portal window.

His heart stopped.

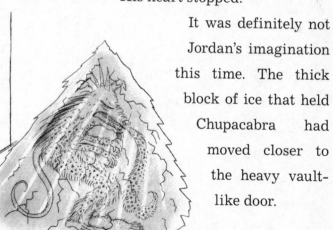

It was definitely not Jordan's imagination this time. The thick block of ice that held Chupacabra had moved closer to the heavy vault-like door.

"Hiya, Jordan. What's up?" It was Ed.

Jordan spun around. "Ed, did anyone open this vault door?"

"No one's been down here but me." He gestured toward the opposite wall with his coffee mug. "Well, me and those annoying gophers back there."

"Gophers?" Jordan said, looking around frantically. "What gophers, Ed?"

"Jeez, calm down, willya?" Ed said. "You can't *see* 'em. But sitting down here all night while those varmints are creaking and thumping inside the walls . . . They'll drive you bonkers!"

"That's a short trip for you, Ed." Alistair chuckled as he and Hap stepped off the elevator.

"Very funny," Ed said. "Don't believe me? Have a listen!" Ed led Alistair and Hap over to the opposite wall lined with the Creature Keeper lockers. Jordan continued to monitor the ice block inside the Cooler.

"Give 'em a minute," Ed said. "You'll hear 'em tunneling around in there." They all put an ear to one of the lockers. *Crreeeaaaak . . .*

"Y'see? I'm not crazy! Danged gophers must be in the walls behind the lockers!"

"Or inside them." Alistair stepped back and read the sign above the locker. "'Pecone, E.'" He ran his hand down the door. *Crreeeaaaak . . .* Alistair pulled his hand away quickly and took another step back. "Uh, Jordan," Alistair said. "You might wanna come here. This door . . . is *warm.*"

Jordan turned.

Crreeeaaaak . . .

"Wasn't warm when I put Eldon's stuff away," Hap said.

"Wait," Jordan said. His mind was reeling. "Eldon's things—you put his fanny pack in there, too?"

"Of course. See?" Hap lifted the latch.

Jordan's eyes went wide. *"Hap! No!"*

BANG! The locker door slammed open. A dark object shot out of it, zooming across the room, straight at Jordan's head. He ducked just in time as the projectile slammed into the metal Cooler door. Jordan stood back up. Eldon's fanny pack was stuck to the metal door like it was filled with high-powered magnets.

Smoke was streaming from its seams, and Alistair yelled to Jordan from across the room. "Jordan, get away from that thing! It looks like it's gonna explode!"

Jordan remembered what was in Eldon's fanny pack. He knew this had the potential to be far more dangerous than a bomb. He leaned in closer to the portal window. Just as he feared, the block of ice was now moving—slowly but steadily across the floor—toward him.

"*The blaststones!*" As Jordan went to grab the fanny pack, it burst into flames, turning to ash. The blaststones inside it, the ones Jordan had given to Eldon, were glowing bright red, and sinking into the thick steel door.

"Get over here!" Jordan shouted to the others. "Quickly! We need to get these stones out of the door and away from him!"

Alistair, Hap, and Ed rushed over to the door. Inside, the ice tomb was just a few feet from them. The Scottish Keeper tried to grab a blaststone. "Oy! They're like hot coals!" The stones continued melting into the steel door. Inside, the ice was beginning to glisten as it slowly melted. Cracks began to spread around Chupacabra's frozen tomb, now just a foot away from the glass.

Hap ran up with a crowbar and tried to pry a stone as it melted deeper into the door. The tip of the tool glowed red hot as it made contact, and the stone disappeared along with the others, burning straight through the door.

"Oh, no," Jordan said. "This can't be happening." Inside the Cooler, the stones burst through the other side of the door and slammed into the ice, sinking quickly. Jordan could only watch as they made their way straight toward the center of the thick tomb, straight for Chupacabra.

"*Go*," Jordan heard himself say.

"Jordan," Hap said. "I'm so sorry. I didn't—"

"GO!" Jordan shouted, startling him. "There's no time to waste!" His mind was racing. "Hap, Ed—the retired Keepers are with Doris, deep in the swamp. Get them back to the house, *NOW!*"

Hap and Ed sprinted up the ramp. Jordan and Alistair pushed desks and heavy equipment against the Cooler door. "Okay, Mac," Jordan said. "Go and get Nessie ready. We may need a quick getaway across the Gulf."

"I'm not leaving you here alone with that monster," Alistair said.

"I can lead him out of here, toward the swamp, away from the house," Jordan said. "What I can't do is fight him off when I get out there. I'm gonna need a getaway cryptid. It's the only way. Now go and get her ready!"

Alistair's voice trembled. "You lead that beast to the boathouse. Haggis-Breath and I will be ready for him." Jordan nodded to Alistair. They both had fear in their eyes. Alistair pulled from his pocket a hand-whittled slingshot.

"Thanks, Mac," Jordan said. "But I'm not sure it'll do us much good this time."

Alistair tucked it back away, then ran up the ramp, into the swamp.

28

Abbie, Harvey, and the four cryptids moved slowly along with the current of swirling tourists, locals, and fake creatures. Many admired the Owl Man's beautiful plumage, and some did a double take at the sight of a giant crab walking alongside a slimy blob.

"I feel so alive!" Clarissa said through her lisp.

"I can't believe I was nervous about this," Gavin said. "Although I confess to feeling a bit offended they're not paying us *more* attention."

"What'd I tell you?" Lou replied as he nodded to a passerby. "Nothin' but a thing."

"This is going great," Hogie said, looking up at Abbie. "Don't you think?"

"These people have no idea you guys are real," Abbie

said. "But yes, that may turn out to be a very great thing." As she and Harvey scanned the crowd for signs of the others, Abbie realized that Buck had picked the biggest cryptids for his brand launch: Bernard, the large, smelly Skunk Ape; Donald, the Bangladesh Ban Manush red ape-man; Francine, the stick-limbed, slimy Bunyip; Paul, the ferocious-looking Dingonek jungle walrus; and of course, Sandy, the giant Golden Liger. The ones Buck would think would get the biggest cheers.

The flow of the crowd moved down el Terminal Remota toward a judging stage stationed near the *Mayan Princess.* The revelers spilled onto the widening area at the end of the pier, forming one of the strangest-looking gatherings Abbie had ever seen. And she'd once been in the middle of a real, live Squatch-fest.

"Abbie!" a voice called out over the heads of the crowd. "Abbie, over here!"

"Oh, great." Abbie's mother and father were waving frantically as they cut through the crowd, moving toward her. Mrs. Grimsley was wearing a gorilla costume with a bright, feathered hat that made it look like she had a toucan sitting on her head. Mr. Grimsley was dressed in a shimmering, scaly mermaid outfit with a fin and tail on the back. For some reason he also had rabbit ears on his head.

"Wow," Abbie said. "You guys look . . . Just, wow."

"Thanks!" Her father eyed the odd-looking crew standing with his daughter. "Are these your friends? Great costumes, gang! Way to get into the Alebrijes spirit!"

"Guys, these are my parents."

Lou grabbed Mr. Grimsley's hand and crunched it. "Nice to meet ya!"

233

"I love your plumage," Mrs. Grimsley said to Gavin.

"Why, thank you," the Owl Man replied awkwardly. "You . . . seem to be an ape."

"Uh, Mom, Dad, these guys aren't exactly from around here."

"Oh," Mr. Grimsley said. "Fellow tourists! Where do you all hail from?"

"We're from all over," Harvey interjected. "And we really should start heading back." He was gesturing to Abbie to look across the edge of the pier at a small makeshift stage with a showy curtain made from the old bunkhouse tarps. Onstage, preparing to address the crowd with a bullhorn, was Buck Wilde.

"Uh, yeah," Abbie said. "We should really go—"

SQUEEEEEEE! A horrible noise emitted from the megaphone in Buck's hand. The entire crowd turned. Buck was grinning ear to ear, overjoyed to have an audience again.

"*¡Hola, amigos!* How y'all doin' today?" Buck began. He was met by murmurs from the crowd. Abbie glanced around. A few people began to recognize "Señor Wilde" from TV. Then a few more. As they did, the crowd grew more excited.

"Say, I don't know if y'all know me, but my name is Buck Wilde, and I used to have a show called *Buck*

Wilde: Squatch-Seeker!"

More people cheered, and a few even hollered Buck's catchphrase: *"GET YER SQUATCH ON!"* The crowd gravitated closer to Buck's sad little stage, pulling Abbie and the others along with them. She felt a knot in her stomach as Buck continued.

"I hung up my Squatch-hunting hat a while back but not my love for crazy creatures! I see a lot of you dressed up like fantastic critters here today! I guess you love 'em, am I right?" More cheering. "Well, that's just super-*bueno*! I've got a real treat for you folks!" He made his way to the side of the stage and took hold of a rope that ran up the side of the curtain.

"Oh, no," Abbie said aloud. "Please, Buck. Not like this. They're not ready!"

"Who?" Lou said. "The creatures or the humans?"

"Both," Abbie said.

Buck continued. "So without any further ado, humans of the planet Earth, get ready, because the Face Chompers are here and they're *ready to meetcha!*"

He yanked the rope. Abbie heard her mother say, "They're ready to 'eat' us?"

The curtain fell away. Gasps erupted from the crowd. Standing there, beneath the large pink Face Chompers sign, were Paul, Donald, Francine, and Bernard. The crowd stood in shocked silence.

"Wait," Abbie said. "Where is Sandy?"

A trap door in the wooden stage suddenly popped open. Sandy the mighty Golden Liger leaped straight up in the air, landing in front of the crowd. She let out a horrible roar, which cued the other cryptids to introduce themselves, as well. Donald the red-mohawked Ban Manush flexed his great muscles. Francine the Bunyip waved her strange stick arms around as she moaned from her swampy mouth. Paul the Dingonek gnashed his long teeth and thrashed his dragonlike head. And Bernard the Skunk Ape stood in the back and waved.

The crowd screamed in panic as they realized these were not costumes. They retreated toward the *Mayan Princess*, to escape the terrifying monsters.

Confused, Buck added to the panic by shouting at everyone through his distorted bullhorn. "Wait! Don't run away! Stand still so the Face Chompers can meet-cha!"

"*Aaah!*" Someone in the crowd screamed as they rushed past Abbie and the others. "*Did you hear that? They're going to eat us!*"

Abbie pulled her parents out of the way of the stampede. Lou stepped in front of Harvey, blocking the old man with his beefy, red body. Gavin scooped Hogie and Clarissa up in his talons, spread his massive wings, and fluttered in the air, hovering just over the crowd. The large godlike bird holding two even weirder-looking creatures in its talons as it hung overhead incited the crowd even further.

"We're surrounded!" someone yelled.

"The Face Chompers are everywhere!" shouted another.

"They're here to *eat us!*" still another said.

Backed up to the very end of el Terminal Remota, some leaped into the warm gulf waters, while most ran for the *Mayan Princess*, plowing up her gangplanks.

"Well, that sure could've gone better," Abbie heard a voice say behind her. She spun around. Buck stood with Bernard, Donald, Paul, Sandy, and Francine.

"Krikey, people sure are jumpy," Hogie said. "They took off faster than a long-finned Tasmanian river eel!"

"Except for those two," Donald pointed his long red-haired arm at a disheveled Roger and Betsy Grimsley. Their costumes were torn, and they stood staring at the strange creatures before them—and one in particular.

"Master Ranger Bernie?" Mrs. Grimsley stammered to the Skunk Ape. "Is—is that you?"

"Uh, yes—and no," Bernard replied.

29

Jordan pushed against the heavy desks and equipment barricading the Cooler door, straining to see what was happening just inside the portal window. Every survival instinct in his body told him to turn and run while he still had the chance. But he thought about his responsibilities as co-leader of the Creature Keepers. He thought about what his grandfather would do. And he stood his ground.

Inside the Cooler, the blaststones had melted through the ice, causing cracks and fractures in the glacial tomb. One thick fracture suddenly splintered so violently that it could be heard through the door.

CRACK!

The sound startled Jordan. He heard bits of ice shrapnel blast the inside of the Cooler door, followed by the sound of something heavy hitting the floor, and finally a horrible scratching sound, like the metal floor was being scraped by a rake—or a set of cold claws. Chupacabra was free of the ice tomb. Jordan shut his eyes and pushed as hard as he could on the barricade, hoping the Cooler door would hold him in.

SMASH! The force hit Jordan along with a freezing cold blast of air, sending him flying backward, along with all the desks and equipment. When everything settled, Jordan gathered the courage to peer out from beneath the pile that had been his barricade.

Chupacabra stood in the smashed-open Cooler doorway, his half Blizzard-Bristle moustache sparkling with ice. The Hydro-Hide he'd hijacked from Nessie was slick and glistening from his melted tomb, and his one stolen Soil-Sole was perched atop what was left of the bent metal door that lay on the floor, complete with a Sasquatch-shaped-footprinted dent in it.

Chupacabra sniffed the air. "Come out, come out,

wherever you are. . . ." Chupacabra sniffed again. "My senses are half frozen, Grimsley, but I know you're nearby. I saw you peering at me in my chilly cell. This is so rude of you. Why don't you just come out and save me the trouble of tearing this room apart?"

Jordan carefully shifted his weight and Chupacabra quickly raised his oversized foot. "Ah-HA! There you are!" Jordan scurried out from under the metal just as, in one Soil-Sole stomp, Chupacabra flattened the desk Jordan had been hiding under.

"Look at you," Chupacabra said. "Like a frightened little cockroach about to be squashed." He stumbled awkwardly on his thawing legs, giving Jordan time to stumble to his feet and run up the greenhouse entry ramp. He clambered up the dark tunnel, the horrible cackling of Chupacabra echoing from behind.

THUMP! THUMP! THUMP! The cryptid was getting strength back in its legs, and Jordan could hear it running up the ramp, gaining speed as he approached. Jordan reached the greenhouse and slammed the retractable-roof button, closing the glass ceiling that had been left open. He rolled under the shelves as Chupacabra came flying up the ramp floor.

SMASH! Chupacabra blasted through the ceiling, raining a shower of glass down all around Jordan, landing outside the greenhouse in a lump. Jordan stayed under the shelf until all the glass had fallen, then he carefully reached up and hit the other button, closing the ramp and sealing off the CKCC—and hopefully the rest of Eternal Acres.

He looked outside and saw where Chupacabra had landed on the mossy ground—but the cryptid was gone. Jordan tore out the greenhouse door, hoping with all his heart that Ed and Hap had gotten Doris and the retired Keepers safely back to the house in time.

He followed drops of blood and bits of broken glass far deeper into the swamp, until the trail of clues abruptly ended.

Jordan looked around, then shouted across the Okeeyuckachokee. "All right, you mangy dog, where did you go? Show yourself!"

"Up here, Georgie boy," Chupacabra's voice came

from a tree, above. He took a deep breath and blasted an icy squall from his Blizzard-Bristles, blowing Jordan to the ground, pinning him flat on his back. Jordan was encased from the neck down in a cocoon of ice.

Chupacabra dropped to the ground and loomed over him. "How do you like it, Georgie? Not very comfortable, is it?"

Something caught Jordan's eye. Two red stones, embedded in each of Chupacabra's claws. He squirmed and wriggled, but it was no use. Jordan was completely trapped. One thought ran through his head: *Eldon, please, where are you?*

"Go ahead," he said. "Kill me. But know that you've been betrayed. The Creature Keepers know your plan, and they're gathering to stop you. Killing me will do nothing because the Creature Keepers is bigger than any one person or any one cryptid. And they won't let you win. As an old friend of mine would say, you can bet your bottom dollar on it."

"I have a much smarter bet," Chupacabra said. "Two things will happen today. One, I will at last control the power of the Perfect Storm, allowing me to begin Operation Pangaea. And two, I will have my revenge on you, George Grimsley, and personally end your life. Both these things will happen. Unfortunately for you, just not in that order."

He raised his claw. "Good-bye, George Grimsl—*ooof!*"

A blur of white fur sent Chupacabra flying as Peggy plowed into him with her great antlers, slamming the nasty cryptid into an old, dead swamp tree. She bowed her head close to Jordan and licked his face. He smiled up at her. "I'm okay, Peggy. Thank you. If you could just let me out of here."

She smashed his icy cocoon, and a smoky smell immediately caught Jordan's attention. He leaped to his feet. An enraged Chupacabra had grabbed a dead tree trunk and pulled himself up. As he did, his blast-stone grip grew hotter against the dry bark. In a fiery blaze, it suddenly ignited.

"Peggy, look out!" Jordan leaped out of the way as Chupacabra swung the blazing tree trunk like a lit torch. Peggy leaped straight into the air, but her fluffy cotton tail caught the flames. She landed and began running in circles. As she did, she began lighting small fires around the swamp. Chupacabra lifted the trunk and prepared to swing at the distracted Peggy again. Before Jordan could shout to warn her, a freezing, snowy blast from above engulfed the giant torch, extinguishing it immediately and knocking Chupacabra backward again.

Fluttering in the sky just above Jordan was Kriss the West Virginia Mothman. And in his arms was Wilford the Yeti of the Himalayas and owner of the other half of the Blizzard-Bristles. He took a deep breath again to blow out Peggy's tail, but a similar wintry blast suddenly struck him, knocking him and Kriss out of the sky.

Chupacabra blew again, but his next cold-shot was met with Wilford firing back. As the two of them blasted each other in an explosion of ice and snow, Kriss and Jordan ran over to Peggy and used some of it to extinguish her tail. There were a few small fires throughout the area, but Peggy was safe.

BOOM!

The ground shook violently as Chupacabra slammed his Soil-Sole on the mossy ground. He'd been pushed backward by Wilford's blasting, and as he stumbled toward the boathouse, Chupacabra decided to put his foot down. The tremor knocked Wilford off his feet, and Chupacabra eyed the water behind him.

"Enough of this!" Chupacabra shrieked in anger. "Why am I wasting my gifts on you fools when I should be using them to take what is rightfully mine!" He took another step toward the water, and his Hydro-Hide scales fluttered. "The next time you see me, it will be too late. You'll be powerless against the Perfect Storm!"

"Stop him!" Jordan cried. "We can't let him get away!"

Peggy and Wilford made a move toward Chupacabra as he dived into the bay. The water immediately rose like a mountain and spit him back onto dry land.

Chupacabra tumbled across the ground, sliding on the snow left over from his battle with Wilford, coming to a stop near a few of the small fires Peggy had set. He shook his head. The water had formed a high, liquid wall at the shoreline, with Nessie balanced atop its crest. Standing on the foot of the dock was Alistair, his hands on his hips. "Over our two old, dead carcasses!" he hollered.

Peggy, Wilford, Kriss, and Jordan slowly closed in on Chupacabra. He crawled backward until he reached a small fire behind him. He let out a horrible laugh.

"I don't know what you're laughing about," Jordan said. "You're surrounded. You're outnumbered. You lost the bet."

"Oh, Georgie boy. Our bet is still on. The only thing that's changed is the order in which I'll carry out the terms. But don't worry. The first thing I'll do when I have the power of the Perfect Storm is terminate you, once and for all. I promise you that."

They all braced for battle as Chupacabra slowly stood up and stepped backward—into the fire. "Killing you is a promise you can bet your bottom dollar I'll keep."

The blaststones in his claws glowed a hotter red, and the flames engulfed his body. *FWOOSH!* Chupacabra suddenly blasted in a streak of fire, shooting up past the tops of the trees, disappearing across the sky.

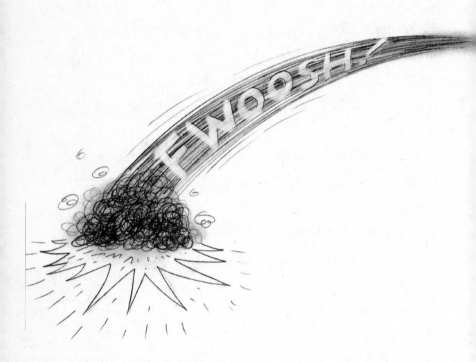

"He's headed for the Yucatan to get that eggsteroid!" Jordan shouted. "We have to warn everyone and get the specials to the bottom of that crater before he does!"

Kriss swooped and grabbed Wilford around the midsection. "We're on our way!" Wilford shouted down to Jordan.

"Us too!" Alistair called out from the water's edge. He was standing in the speedboat, and he tossed a lasso around Nessie's neck. "We'll beat him there, laddie!" he hollered as he tied the other end of the rope to the front of the boat. "We got us a single water horse–power engine!"

Jordan ran to Peggy. "Great work, girl. Put out these fires, then go and keep watch over Doris and the retired creatures. It's all going to be okay." The giant Jackalope gave Jordan a big lick on the face and started hopping on the little fires.

As Jordan ran toward the boat, he glanced to his right, hoping to see Eldon running toward him, ready to join him on what could be their last adventure together. But the deep swamp remained dark, and quiet.

The approaching sirens grew louder as the Mexican authorities rushed to the scene. "Hooray!" Hogie said excitedly. "More celebrations!"

"Not this time," Abbie said. "Pretty sure they're on their way to put an end to this celebration." She could only imagine how many hundreds of calls the local police had received, each one weirder than the last. From aboard the *Mayan Princess*, the frightened people stared down at them from every deck.

"Bernard, get everyone on board. I'll talk to the police." Abbie glanced at her mother and father. "It's okay, guys. You'll understand soon, too, I promise. Just go with Bernard. Everything's gonna be all right."

Mr. and Mrs. Grimsley turned their blank stares to

the Skunk Ape. "Wh—where's your uniform?" Mrs. Grimsley said softly.

"It was just a costume," he said. "Why are you dressed like a gorilla and a pigeon?"

Bernard led them along with Harvey, Buck, and the other cryptids up the gangplank, onto the ship. Within moments, a boatload of shrieks and screams erupted from inside, and the panicked crowd came running off again. Some leaped into the water while most ran down the gangplank toward the police as they came screeching onto the scene.

"Oh brother," Abbie turned to face the authorities. "What a bunch of scaredy-cats."

The police seemed immediately confused and overwhelmed. Abbie wasn't going to have much luck explaining the situation, especially if she had to fight through a throng of hysterical people to get to them. She decided to retreat to her friends and family.

"*¡Detengas! ¡Detengas!*" the officers shouted out as Abbie bolted up the gangplank, onto the *Mayan Princess*.

She ran through the empty ship in search of nine creatures, an old man, a washed-up TV personality, and her mom and dad. She finally located them at the very top Lido deck, standing around an untouched all-you-can-eat buffet.

"That brand release couldn't have gone any better!" Buck was grinning as Sandy, Paul, and Francine loomed around him. They didn't look happy. "Help yourself, fellas," Buck said. "It's all you can eat!"

"You made us look like fools," Sandy snarled.

"Worse than that," Donald added. "You made them afraid of us!"

"Are you guys kidding? You came out with a bang! You can't put a price tag on that kind of publicity! Just look at all the free media down there!"

Among the crowd and the police below, a few news reporters were already setting up, pointing their TV cameras at the ship.

"Great," Abbie said. "Just great."

"Hey, it's what I do," Buck said. "You guys are gonna be on every TV on the planet! And I was afraid I'd lost my touch, sitting around in the woods with ol' Syd. . . ."

Down on the pier, more police had arrived. They were surrounding the ship and keeping the onlookers back. In the distance, more and more people were making their way to see the spectacle. Abbie was lost in thought when a faint voice from behind got her attention.

"Uh, sweetie . . . ?" Abbie's mom looked shell-shocked.

Mr. Grimsley didn't look much better. He spoke in a slightly trembling voice. "Is this all . . . actually happening?"

"Mom, Dad, I'm so sorry!" She rushed to them and hugged them both. "Listen to me. It's all okay. And yes, Dad. It's all very real."

Mr. Grimsley examined the cryptids standing around him. "Then . . . it was all true. My father, his stories, they were real, too. He wasn't crazy."

Gavin stepped forward. "Sir, George Grimsley was a great man. He found me, saved me, and protected me. I owe him everything."

Sandy stepped forward next. "As do I," she said.

Hogie oozed toward them. "Yup. Same here," he said.

They all crowded closer, each paying respects and showing thanks. Abbie's mother smiled. But her father's smile slowly faded.

"Dad," Abbie said. "Are you okay?"

"Forgive me, but this is a lot to take in." Mr.

Grimsley's eyes were full of tears. "To me, my father's life was a mystery. Then it was an embarrassment. Finally, it became a joke. But I see the joke was on me. And the worst of it is, my father died alone, with no one believing in him. Not even his own son."

"Dad," Abbie said. "Jordan and I have learned a lot about Grampa Grimsley. He chose to keep all this a secret. He spent nearly his entire life in the company of creatures. And in the end, that's how he died. Y'know, in the mouth of one."

"She's right, Roger," Mrs. Grimsley said. "There's nothing we could've done. He didn't want anyone to know about all this. Not even his own son."

Mr. Grimsley nodded. "But what . . . is *all this*, exactly?"

"The Creature Keepers," Bernard said proudly. "Sworn to protect all cryptids everywhere and to keep them healthy, happy, and hidden. Mr. Grimsley, I knew your father. We all did. He founded the Creature Keepers. In order to protect us."

Mr. Grimsley turned to his daughter. "You and your brother are part of this?"

"They're not just part of it," Bernard said. "Abbie and Jordan are our leaders."

"Abbie," Mrs. Grimsley said. "Is this true?"

"Jordan and I have been proud to help continue Grampa Grimsley's legacy, and even prouder to help the ones who want to come out of the shadows. And I know that when the people down there understand what's inside the hearts of these Face Chompers, they'll see what Grampa Grimsley saw in them, and the whole world will welcome them."

Mr. Grimsley put his hand on Abbie's shoulder. "Thank you. Your mother and I couldn't be prouder of you."

"Of *all* of you," Mrs. Grimsley said to the cryptids. "But have you considered calling yourselves something other than 'Face Chompers'?"

"*¡ATENCIÓN! ¡ATENCIÓN!*" The booming officer's voice came rising over the railing. Abbie gestured for the creatures to stay back. She, Buck, Harvey, and the Grimsleys walked to the edge and looked down. The crowd and the news crews had been pushed back, and a line of police cars surrounded the ship. The Mexican authorities stood in a line, with one holding up a megaphone.

"Hey!" Buck yelled down. "That's my megaphone! Not cool, amigo!"

"*Okay,* señor*! I'll speak* en ingles*! Send the monsters down with their hands—or paws, or fins, or claws, or whatever—in the air!*"

"You got it!" Buck winked at the others. "Don't worry, I know what I'm doing. This is a classic negotiation technique. You give up something, but you ask for something in return. Observe." He studied the buffet table, then turned back to the railing. "We're sending you down the little squishy guy under one condition: send up more breakfast sausages!"

Abbie pushed Buck away. "You're a moron." Then she hollered down, "Excuse me! I know a lot of you were scared before, but there's nothing to fear. These creatures are peaceful, and they only want to be your friends! If we come down, can you all please be nice and not totally freak out?"

The officer turned to the crowd behind them. They shrugged and nodded. He turned back. *"¡Sí! ¡No problema!"*

"That was easy," Francine said. "Welp, let's head down and meet some folks!"

"Hold up," Abbie said. "Clarissa, Bernard, would you come here, please?" Abbie gestured to Bernard. He understood completely. The Skunk Ape lifted Clarissa over his head, exposing her to the crowd below. She enthusiastically waved a giant claw to them. The crowd burst into a state of sheer panic. They screamed. And cried. A few more leaped into the water.

"This isn't going to work," Harvey said. "What were we thinking?"

"It's true," Sandy said. "Those humans won't accept us. They're too jumpy."

"I'll say," Francine said. "Even George Grimsley's son couldn't stick with us. And he seemed really nice. I liked that bloke."

"What?" Abbie whirled around. She looked over the edge. Her father was marching down the gangplank, straight toward the police and the frenzied crowd.

31

Abbie ran out onto el Terminal Remota to find her father standing on top of one of the Mexican police officers' cars, fiddling with Buck's megaphone.

"Dad, get down from there! What are you doing?"

"What's it look like? I'm trying to turn this durned thing on!"

Buck yelled down from the top deck. "It's the red button, Mr. G!"

"Ah, yes," Abbie's father said. "That makes sense."

The main officer glared up at him. "*¡Señor!* I must ask you to—"

SQUEEEEEEEEEE! The megaphone let out a burst of feedback, unsettling the already unsettled crowd and causing the police to duck and cover their ears.

Mr. Grimsley turned his amplified voice on the crowd. "Listen to me, all you people! Not too long ago, I was just like you—I thought those creatures up there on that ship were monsters—ferocious beasts who wanted to chomp my face and do other bad stuff to me! But my daughter here—" He looked down at Abbie and held out his hand. "Come up here, Abbie; let the people see you. C'mon!"

"This is so embarrassing." Abbie climbed onto the car and stood next to her father. "Okay, I'm here. Now would you please stop—"

SQUEEEEEEEEEE! Mr. Grimsley let out another burst of feedback, cutting her off, seemingly to Abbie, on purpose.

"This is the granddaughter of the late, great George Grimsley, the world's foremost and widely misunderstood cryptozoologist, founder of the Creature Keepers. He was also my dad. But not a very good one. Although I see now that maybe that was a two-way street. Life is funny that way—"

"Get back to the point!" one person in the crowd yelled.

"Yeah, you're really drifting off topic!" hollered another.

"More about the monsters!" a third shouted.

"Dad, stop this," Abbie said. "It's not working.

They'll never understand."

Ignoring her, Mr. Grimsley continued. "My daughter is not crazy! And neither was her grandfather! We all need to believe in them both! If she says these creatures want only to be friends with us, I believe her! Who's with me?"

There were some murmurings in the crowd. The reporters all had their cameras trained on them. People were actually doing something Abbie had spent much of her life making a point of not doing: they were actually listening to her father.

Mr. Grimsley sensed it, too, and kicked it up a notch. "That's right, people! There's nothing to fear! Cryptids aren't evil! They're good!"

"Uh, Dad . . ."

Mr. Grimsley waved her off. He was clearly on a roll. "I can't stress enough how *every single cryptid* has nothing but goodness and joy and love in their heart!"

Abbie interjected again. "Dad, I never said every *single* one. . . ."

He put his arm around and held her closely as he went for the big finish. "In fact, we give you our Grimsley Family word that *no cryptid* would ever do *anything* to harm, endanger, or otherwise destroy any of you, ever!"

Cheers went up from the crowd. Mr. Grimsley was

beaming. Abbie leaned in toward his ear. "Uh, Dad, I probably should've told you—there is this *one* cryptid who's not very nice—"

"There's a what, now, sweetie?"

WHOOSH! A fiery red streak suddenly burst overhead across the clear, blue sky. The crowd's cheers turned to screams of panic again.

"It is the return of the Chicxulub!" someone hollered.

"Run for your lives!" screamed someone else.

The crowd and the police scattered down the pier, away from the incoming comet. Only Abbie and her father stood their ground as the fireball smashed into the docking area of el Terminal Remota with a sharp explosion. The live fireball shed sparks and embers as it bounced down the concrete section of the pier toward the fleeing crowd.

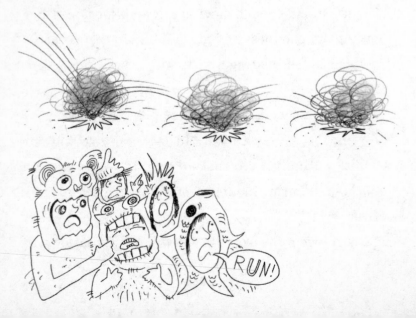

Although helpless to do anything to stop it, Abbie and her father chased after the projectile, hoping it wouldn't engulf the panicked people. The flaming ball slowed to a stop halfway between the *Mayan Princess* and the old wooden platform that served as the Face Chompers' hideout.

When they realized they were no longer being chased by a fireball, the tourists, locals, authorities, and news reporters all stopped running. Some turned back and approached as the flame subsided. The smoke cleared and the ash settled. A figure stood before them. Abbie's eyes grew wide, and she felt her heart sink.

It can't be, she thought.

Chupacabra's Hydro-Hide, single Soil-Sole, and half a Blizzard-Bristle moustache had been untouched by his blazing entrance. He looked down and opened his claws. Two grayish red stones fell onto the pier with a pair of dull thuds. He let out a loud cackle that sent a shiver down Abbie's spine.

Mr. Grimsley leaned in closer to her. "I'm guessing this is the not-so-nice one you were talking about?"

Chupacabra turned toward the broken-down, wooden oil rig platform just off the side of el Terminal Remota. He smiled. "At long last I've returned, armed with the tools I need to take what is rightfully mine!"

The crowd stood in stunned silence, afraid to run,

afraid to scream—until a single voice suddenly cut through the air.

"I told you before, you mangy mutt! There's no way we're letting you get to whatever is lying at the bottom of that crater!"

The crowd parted. Jordan stood near the railing on the opposite side of the pier. A few locals helped Alistair up onto the structure, then the two of them made their way straight for Chupacabra.

One of the locals who'd helped Alistair looked down at the water. "Hey, my boat is back."

Chupacabra laughed as Jordan came to a stop a good distance away from him. "And who would stop me, Grimsley? You? These *humans*?"

Alistair stepped up beside Jordan. "There's someone who would never forgive me if I didn't let her have first shot at you." Alistair put his fingers to his lips and whistled. Nothing happened. He whistled again. "Haggis-Breath!" he shouted back

YEP.

toward the railing. "Ya got kelp in your ears?"

Nessie erupted from the water below, soared over the crowd, and flopped onto the pier with a thud. She reared up her chest and stretched out her long green neck, glaring at Chupacabra. The stunned crowd slowly recognized her and burst into gasps, pointing and calling out her name excitedly.

"The Loch Ness Monster!"

"Ooh! The Loch Ness Monster!" Chupacabra mocked the crowd. "I hope she's not all you've brought to try to stop me, or these people aren't in for much of a show!"

Kriss the Mothman swooped overhead and released his furry, white cargo. The mighty Yeti hit the pier in a perfect superhero-style three-point landing, then slowly stood up beside Nessie.

The crowd fell silent for a moment, then turned their attention back to screaming Nessie's name. *"The*

Loch Ness Monster!" A few in the crowd took selfies.

Wilford scratched his face where half his moustache was missing. "Really? Nothing? Not even for that entrance?" Nessie stopped posing for the crowd and snorted, then the two of them turned to face Chupacabra.

Chupacabra snickered. "Is this all you got? An overgrown guppy and some scraggly mountain hermit?"

Jordan scanned the pier and caught the eye of Abbie standing beside his father. "Just one second," he said to Chupacabra. He walked over to them.

"Jordan!" his dad exclaimed. "Isn't this amazing? That's the Loch Ness Monster!"

"I know, Dad."

"Abbie told your mother and I all about the Creature Keepers. We're up to speed, so don't worry."

"That's great, Dad."

Mr. Grimsley pointed at Chupacabra. "That one, there. He's no good. Watch out for him, son."

"Dad, I know. I know all about them."

"Of course you do." Mr. Grimsley glanced at Wilford. "Him I don't know. What is he, some sort of albino bigfoot or something?"

"Excuse me," Wilford said. "I'm the Yeti. Abominable Snowman?"

"Dad," Abbie said. "Maybe just be quiet now, and

let us handle this."

Mr. Grimsley nodded. Jordan glanced around the pier. "Abbie, where the heck is—"

"Hey, look! There's Bigfoot!" Mr. Grimsley suddenly blurted out.

Near the wooden platform rig, a large foot stepped over the pier railing. Syd lifted his other, smaller foot awkwardly. His eyeshades were askew on top of his head. He looked confused, and a little annoyed.

"See, you can't call him that, Dad," Abbie said. "He really doesn't like that name."

"What is all the ruckus?" Syd said, rubbing his eyes. "It sounds like a nine-point-six-Richter rock-rumbler over here. Some of us are trying to sleep!"

The crowd burst into the biggest cheer yet, which visibly annoyed Wilford. Nessie pouted as they all hollered, "SAS-QUATCH!" and snapped even more pictures as Syd began getting into it, mugging for the camera and striking his signature pose.

"Okay, okay, that's enough!" Wilford grabbed the Sasquatch and dragged him over to stand with him and Nessie. "What makes you two so darned famous, anyhow?"

"Buck would say publicity," Syd said. "I mean, no offense, dude, but you live alone on a mountaintop in the Himalayas. That's just a poor branding strategy."

Chupacabra faced the three special cryptids. "Well, if everyone's here now, let's move things along, shall we? Starting with moving you three out of my way." He slammed his Soil-Sole down on the concrete section of the pier. A massive slab broke free from the wooden section, crumbling into the water—taking Nessie, Syd, and Wilford along with it.

"That was even easier than I thought," the evil cryptid said with a grin.

32

The wooden section of the pier cracked and splintered where the concrete chunk had torn away from it. The screaming crowd on that side retreated, pushing and shoving one another back from the broken edge.

Jordan, Abbie, Alistair, and Mr. Grimsley went to run toward the gap to search for the fallen cryptids but found themselves trapped on the concrete side of the pier between Chupacabra and the chasm. They were unable to help even as innocent people dangled from the wooden side, clamoring to get back onto the pier.

"We're cut off by that monster!" Mr. Grimsley exclaimed.

"Luckily we've got a lot more friends than he does!" Abbie pointed as Kriss swooped overhead. The

Mothman grabbed the people hanging from the broken section of the pier and delivered them safely with the others before zooming off again.

On the other side, Sam and Julia, along with the kids and the Alebrijes carpenters from Flamboyanes, led the crowd in an effort to tear up nearby food shacks and gift stalls. Like an army of worker ants, they used the wood and nails to begin constructing a makeshift bridge across the gap, back toward the concrete section.

"There's no sign of 'em!" Alistair had dashed to the edge of the railing and was searching the churning water. Jordan, Abbie, and Mr. Grimsley joined him. The three super-cryptids were nowhere to be seen.

"Wait, look there!" Jordan pointed downward. A white furry tail flickered near one of the legs of the old drilling platform, splashing before disappearing into the depths.

"It's Moe!" Abbie exclaimed. "She'll find them!"

The brief flash of hope was suddenly replaced with a shock of cold from behind, as Chupacabra shot an arctic blast from his Blizzard-Bristles. It slammed into the wooden drill tower on the old platform, sending the rickety structure tipping over, demolishing the cabin and bunkhouse. The entire thing toppled into the water, right where Moe had disappeared.

Jordan, Abbie, Alistair, and Mr. Grimsley stared wide-eyed in horror at the water churning with splintered wood and debris. There was still no sign of any of the cryptids.

Chupacabra cackled. "One less obstacle standing between me and my prize. With the three elemental gifts in my control, I can now extract the fourth—and finally control the power of the Perfect Storm!"

"No!" Jordan ran in a blind rage straight at Chupacabra. The cryptid leaped with his Soil-Sole, soaring over Jordan and the others, straight out over the gulf. Jordan stopped and spun around. "Stop him!" he screamed.

"If he gets to that eggsteroid, it's over!" Abbie yelled.

Alistair leaned over the railing, put his chubby fingers to his lips, and let out a sharp whistle.

As Chupacabra descended toward the water, a white creature breached to meet him. Moe swung his great, furry body in midair. Gilligan rode atop his neck, holding on as the Trunko swatted Chupacabra with his wide tail, slapping him back up over the railing. Chupacabra hit the concrete pier hard, landing in a lump near where the *Mayan Princess* was docked.

Gilligan leaped from Moe's back as he crested, onto the dock behind Jordan, Abbie, Alistair, and Mr. Grimsley. The great white Trunko splashed back into the water below.

"Great work, you guys!" Jordan said. "Any sign of the special cryptids?"

"Guys?" Gilligan said. "I did all the work! And yeah, I also managed to get those three 'specials' unstuck down there. They were trapped under a slab of concrete. But don't thank me or anything. I only saved the lives of the three most powerful cryptids on the planet. No biggie."

"I think you had a bit of help," Alistair said.

"Who, Moe? Please. That soggy old gym sock just slows me down."

"HONK!" Moe breached again, blasting Gilligan with a trunkful of water.

Gilligan shook it off. "He does have exceptional hearing. I'll give him that."

"Thanks, Moe!" Abbie yelled over the side to Moe, who disappeared into the water. She smiled at the sight of Nessie floating on her back like a fat buoy. Standing on her great belly were Wilford and Syd waving up at them.

"Oh, bless that puffy white whale!" Alistair hollered out. "They're okay!"

A joyful noise came from across the broken pier. The crowd stopped working on their bridge to wave back to the famous cryptids below. As the news cameras rolled and the crowd pointed and cheered, Abbie's and Jordan's attention refocused toward the end of the pier, where Chupacabra was still lying in a lump.

"He's still down," Jordan said. "This could be our only chance. Use whatever means you have to, but we have to *keep him out of that water.*"

"I've got just the team to do it." Abbie grabbed Alistair. "C'mon!"

Mr. Grimsley watched Abbie and Alistair bolt toward the ship. "I'm learning quite a lot today, Jordan," he said. "About my father and my kids."

"We're glad you're here to help us save the world," Jordan said.

"Me too. I only wish your grandfather were with us. Not so I could see him. But so that he could see you."

"Thanks, Dad. I have someone I wish was here, too."

"Well, whaddya say we save the world—for Grampa Grimsley and Eldon Pecone."

The two of them shared a smile, then Jordan's father turned and ran off to join the others. Jordan climbed up on the railing and looked down at the debris floating in the water. Wilford, Syd, and even Nessie waved him on.

Jordan shut his eyes and leaped off the pier.

33

Chupacabra stood up to find himself surrounded by a very strange collection of adversaries. He chuckled. "The Creature Keepers. How sad."

Abbie stepped forward as the cryptids gathered behind her. "I think you have us confused with someone else. We're not Creature Keepers. We're Face Chompers. And we have one job: to keep your scaly butt drydocked, permanently."

"Yee-haw!" Buck suddenly broke through the

crowd as he waved his signature lasso over his head, hurling it toward Chupacabra. "I got him, you guys! You guys, I got him— *WHOA!*"

Chupacabra grabbed and yanked the rope, sending Buck flying.

"You pathetic parasites, you think you can stop me?" The scales on Chupacabra's Hydro-Hide fluttered, snapping the rope like soggy spaghetti. He glared at Donald, Francine, Sandy, and the others. "You creatures had your chance to join me. But you foolishly refused and chose to stand with humans. Now you shall see what an unfortunate decision that was!"

He took a deep breath, the frozen crystals in his Blizzard-Bristles glistening in anticipation of creating an icy blast.

"*Now!*" Abbie shouted.

Donald lifted Clarissa and flung the Colossus Crab straight at Chupacabra. Her pincers slashed the thick Blizzard-Bristles, leaving a silly-looking patch beneath his snout. The frozen storm he was about to unleash sputtered out as more of a chilly breeze.

"*AAAUUUGGH!*" Chupacabra reached out to grab Clarissa just as Sandy leaped toward him, her golden fur radiating brightly. The others looked away or covered their eyes as Chupacabra fell backward, blinded from the glare. He fumbled around for something to fight back with and found a thick tree branch. He gripped it—until it suddenly gripped him back.

"What—what is this?"

Francine's stick arms twined around Chupacabra's arm like a Chinese finger trap, gripping him tightly before lifting him into the air. The Bunyip thrashed Chupacabra against the concrete pier until the infuriated cryptid fluttered his Hydro-Hide again, this time shedding a few hundred scales in order to slip his now-naked arms out of the swamp creature's grip. The scales littered the ground, falling to the pier like sparkling sequins.

Chupacabra stumbled back until he reached the edge

of the pier. Realizing where he was, he grinned at the others and let himself fall backward.

"Oh, no!" Abbie and the others ran to the edge, surprised to see Chupacabra floating in midair, and rising. Kriss and Gavin had their claws and talons sunk in Chupacabra's shoulders, and carried him high over the center of the pier again—then tossed him like a pile of garbage.

Chupacabra hit the concrete hard, then rose unsteadily to his feet.

Lou and Paul leaped into action, pummeling Chupacabra and pinning him to the pier. The other cryptids moved in to help as Chupacabra growled menacingly. He pushed Lou backward with his powerful Soil-Sole, sending the New Jersey Devil and the Dingonek knocking into the other Face Chompers. Abbie dived out of the way, but Chupacabra leaped up again and grabbed her. He tossed her to the ground, then lifted his Soil-Sole over her.

The others froze at the sight of this. Chupacabra grinned. "So this is your new master! You finally wise up and find the strength to leave George Grimsley's enslavement only to be brainwashed by another human—and a *girl* at that!"

"You bet she's a girl, you horrible beast!" Abbie's mom yelled out.

"And not just any girl," Abbie's dad added. "A Grimsley girl!" They dived at Chupacabra, slamming into him and knocking him away from Abbie.

Chupacabra stumbled backward but used his tail to regain his balance. Alistair helped Abbie to her feet while Harvey pulled the Grimsleys back toward the Face Chompers.

Chupacabra spotted Harvey Quisling. "Another traitor!" Chupacabra sneered at the old man standing defiantly among his new comrades. "And how convenient to have you all gathered before me. All but one, that is—your cowardly ex-leader George Grimsley has abandoned you, yet again. Don't worry: he and I have a deal. I'll see to him once I retrieve what I came here for. In the meantime, you will all pay for your betrayal. With one stomp of my Soil-Sole, I will turn this entire pier into rubble. Consider this a sneak preview of Operation Pangaea. Pray you die now and be spared what is to come!"

Chupacabra went to raise his mighty Soil-Sole. As he tried, a confused expression spread over his face. He tugged with his rear leg and looked down. His Soil-Sole looked like it was stuck in a big wad of chewing gum—Day-Glo–yellow chewing gum, with multiple eyes staring intently back at him.

"'Fraid I can't letcha do that to my mates, chief," Hogie said.

"What is this? Let me go!" Chupacabra twisted his leg and yanked harder. His foot snapped back, sinking deeper into the goo as the Tasmanian Globster oozed tighter around his ankle. He tried to blast Hogie with his Blizzard-Bristle, but just a tiny puff of powder poofed out of his shorn whiskers.

"Nice work, Hogie!" Abbie called.

"Thanks, but I wouldn't mind a little help!" Hogie cried out.

They ran to Hogie and grabbed hold of his gloppy body as Abbie counted off. "One, two, three—*HOIST*!"

The entire team—Face Chompers, Mr. and Mrs. Grimsley, Buck Wilde, Harvey Quisling, and Alistair MacAlister—all pulled the Globster as hard as they could, yanking him out from under his captor. Chupacabra hit the concrete with a thud.

"This time, let's make sure he stays down!" Abbie cried out.

"You heard her, guys!" Clarissa shriek-lisped. "Cryptid-pile on this scurvy dog!" They leaped on top of Chupacabra, pinning him to the pier.

Whoops and hollers from the villagers and news crews filled the air. They were halfway across the chasm on their makeshift bridge cheering the Face Chompers on.

"See that?" Buck said to Abbie. "You can't put a price tag on this kind of promotion. We got 'em eating out of our hands now."

34

Jordan clung to Nessie's neck as she swam in circles at the surface of the debris-filled water. Syd and Wilford held on tight as well, trying their best not to slip off the scaly cryptid as she began to go faster and faster.

"Not a big fan of water in this particular form!" Wilford hollered up to Jordan over the swirling, sloshing current. "I really hope you know what you're doing!"

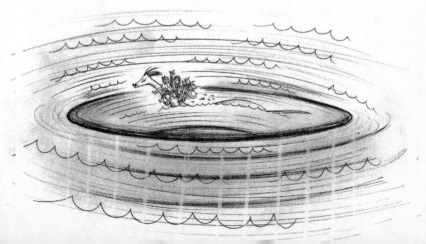

"So do I!" Jordan leaned in closer to Nessie. "That's it, girl! We need a whirlpool all the way to the bottom! You can do it!"

Nessie snorted. The scales of her Hydro-Hide shifted, and she thrust her tail and fins, bearing down on the swirling water.

"Yee-haw!" Syd held tight with one arm as he swung his other in the air. He smacked Nessie on the side. "Giddyup!"

She didn't like that and bucked, nearly tossing them all into the vortex she was creating. The faster she swam, the deeper it dipped, pulling the wood and debris away from them and gradually creating a swirling wall of water. She surged like a torpedo along the spinning current, spiraling lower and lower, until she reached the bottom of the gulf. "Great work, Nessie!" Jordan yelled when he spotted the exposed rocky bottom of the Chicxulub crater.

"All ashore that's going ashore!" Syd called out. He leaped off Nessie's back and tumbled out of the water wall into the center of the whirlpool, landing at the soggy bottom. Jordan leaped off next, and Syd caught him. Finally, Wilford let go of Nessie. They all looked up. The incredible funnel of water was spinning around and above them, all the way back to the surface. It was like standing in the eye of a liquid twister.

"Just don't stop, whatever you do!" Wilford yelled to Nessie as she zoomed past, swimming just inside the whooshing, spinning current.

"Over here!" Jordan yelled. Wilford and Syd sloshed across the mucky bottom of the gulf to where Jordan was kneeling. Embedded there was the dense, shiny black orb, staring up at them like the pupil of a giant, underground eyeball.

Syd placed his Soil-Sole on the surface of the strange stone and closed his eyes. Jordan had seen his great foot meld with rock and soil before. He was an expert

at all things of the soil and earth. "It's not from around here," the Sasquatch said. "It's like nothing I've ever seen or felt. And it's *hot*."

"This is the asteroid," Wilford said. "It has to be."

"Could there be something alive inside it?" Jordan asked.

Wilford shared a glance with him. "The fourth special cryptid."

Syd shook his head. "I'm not sensing anything living." He pointed at the blaststones lodged in the surrounding rocky floor. "But those red crystals are shocked quartz, if I'm not mistaken. When this asteroid thingy slammed into this spot, it created such a hot thermo-blast that it altered the geological makeup of the stones around it." He took his foot off the black asteroid. "Somehow this thing is still burning on the inside."

"Impossible," Wilford said, feeling the strange stone. "Nothing can burn for sixty-six million years at the bottom of the sea and stay that hot."

"Whatever it is, it's got to come out of there and fast," Jordan said. "And only you three special cryptids can do it."

"Then what are we waiting for? Let's get cracking!" Syd raised his Soil-Sole and slammed it down on the strange stone with all his might. The ground shook and rumbled, but the loudest sound came from Syd himself.

"*OWWWWWEEEEE!*" He grabbed his foot and stumbled backward, almost falling into the wall of rushing water behind him, which would have swept him away if Wilford hadn't yanked him back toward the center.

The Yeti glared at him. "Do you ever use that bark-brain before you act?"

Syd was in too much pain to respond to the insult. He hopped around on his little foot, holding his large one, whimpering and sobbing. "*Ow-ow-ow-ow-ow!*"

Syd's efforts had put the tiniest hairline crack in the eggsteroid. But the shock waves of the impact crumbled the stone floor where it was lodged. The odd object was now lying in a bed of broken-open rock laden with blaststones. While Syd gently blew on his pinkie toe, Jordan and Wilford went to work digging out the eggsteroid.

"I can't hold on much longer!" Gavin called out from near the bottom of the cryptid-pile. "I think my wings are beginning to freeze!"

"Just a little longer!" Abbie said. On the broken pier, the crowd of people was trying to make its way over to help them. Abbie wished she knew where her brother was or what he was doing. An anguished cry snapped her attention back.

"I can't feel my muscles!" Lou said. Through the thicket of wings, claws, legs, tails, and horns, his red arm was turning blue as the eerie white frost steadily spread from beneath them.

Abbie put her ear to a space between Francine and Sandy. She could hear a soft, low exhale: Chupacabra's breath seeping out of him in a slow hiss. What few Blizzard-Bristles he had left after Clarissa's trim he was using to his advantage—Abbie could feel the sub-zero air on her neck and ear.

A low sinister laugh started as a chuckle, then grew louder and stronger. Abbie heard a creaking. The pile trembled, then—*CRACK!* The ice broke beneath them, sending the cryptids tumbling in different directions. Each of them had broken ice attached to whatever part of the body was closest to Chupacabra's frozen whis-kers. They lay in pain, rubbing their wing, their leg, their tail, their claws, trying to warm them back to life.

Chupacabra stood up and shook the ice and frost off his body. "You Grimsleys are a major thorn in my side," he said. "Time for you to feel one in yours." He raised his claw to strike Abbie. *THUMP!* Something bounced off the back of his head. It was a wooden toy Alebrijes creature. *THUMP!* A snow globe tagged him in the chest. *THUMP!* A bottle of orange soda. The crowd had finally crossed the gap and was throwing anything they could get their hands on from the gift and food stands.

BONK! A scuba tank tagged the infuriated cryptid in the head, and Chupacabra reeled backward, stumbling across the pier and against the railing.

"Stop him!" Abbie cried. But she was too late. As Chupacabra fell over the side, she rushed to the rail just in time to see him fall into a strange, watery vortex that dropped straight to the center of the Chicxulub crater. His limp body got caught in the swirling whirlpool wall, and he spun off into the water.

35

Jordan and Wilford dug deeper into the blaststone rubble to extract the eggsteroid. Wilford gently blew through his Blizzard-Bristles, cooling the orb down enough so he and Syd could lift it out of the center of the Chicxulub crater.

Aside from the tiny crack Syd had put in it, the object was perfectly smooth, and roughly the size of a beach ball. Syd knocked on it. "Hello? Anybody home? *Helloooo?*"

"What now?" Wilford asked Jordan.

"Now you can hand it over to me!" Chupacabra's voice cut above the roaring sound of the water swirling around them. He hovered high above, near the top of the whirlpool. Using the Hydro-Hide on his tail and

lower body, he floated ominously, suspended between the whirlpool's rushing walls.

"*SKRONK!*" Nessie's head popped out of the water. She tried to take a nip at Chupacabra as she sped past.

"Tell that attack-cow to stay clear!" he shouted down. "Remind her that she's not the only one with Hydro-Hide! One flick of my tail and this water cyclone comes crashing down on the three of you!"

Nessie continued swimming in circles closer to the bottom, keeping the whirlpool from crashing, but staying close to Jordan, Syd, and Wilford.

"It's okay, Nessie!" Jordan shouted to her as she

circled past just inside the spinning funnel. "Keep swimming! We'll handle this."

Chupacabra's cackle echoed over the sound of rushing water that surrounded them. "Thank you for doing all the hard work for me!" he shouted down. "Now if you could kindly toss my package up to me, I'll leave you in peace."

"You mean you'll leave us to rest in peace!" Jordan shouted back. "The minute you get what you want, you're going to drop a mountain of water on our heads!"

"Georgie boy. You hurt my feelings. I promised you I would kill you as soon as I got the power of the Perfect Storm, and I intend to keep my promise. Besides, drowning is far too gentle a way for my lifelong nemesis to die. Now just give me the orb, and I'll see to it that you get out of here alive. We go way back, Georgie boy. You can trust me."

"Why does he keep calling you that?" Syd said quietly.

"He thinks I'm my grandfather," Jordan muttered. "And I've got to keep letting him."

"Jordan, what do we do?" Wilford asked.

"You heard him," Jordan said. "He wants the orb. Let's give it to him. Syd, how's the ol' foot?"

"Oh, no," Wilford said.

"Oh, yeah!" Syd grinned and stepped back, leaving

Wilford struggling to hold the orb. "Little to the left, Frosty. And hold her steady. I'd hate to shatter your hand."

"Enough of this!" Chupacabra hollered over the rushing water. "Give to me what is mine—*NOW!*"

"I'd like everyone to know that I'm against this plan." Wilford held the orb out, turned his head, and shut his eyes.

"All right, Syd," Jordan said. "Let's give him what he's asking for!"

Syd swung his great foot, kicking the eggsteroid out of Wilford's hands. It blasted straight up the water funnel, slamming Chupacabra in the jaw. As the dense orb continued to sail straight up and out the top of the whirlpool, Chupacabra fell—dropping like a stone down the center of the flume.

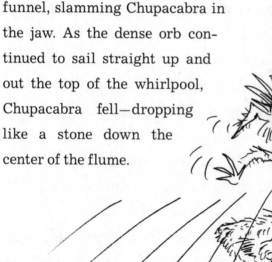

WHUMP! Chupacabra landed hard in the pile of cleared rocks dug out of the center of the crater. As he lay motionless, the nearby blaststones began to vibrate and glow. One by one, they flew toward him, slamming into his Hydro-Hide, each one burning him as they burrowed deeper into his body.

"SKRONK!" Nessie shot out of the funnel wall. The whirlpool shifted and slowed, no longer churning from the power of the Hydro-Hide but by its own weakening momentum. In a split second, Syd and Wilford were on Nessie's back.

Syd held out his paw as Nessie prepared to dive back into the water wall. "Quickly, Jordan! Before the whirlpool collapses!"

Jordan took a step to hop aboard Nessie, but glanced back at Chupacabra lying in the center of the crater, covered with stones that were burning him alive.

Jordan ran toward Chupacabra.

"JORDAN!" Wilford's yell was instantly muffled as Nessie reentered the water, shooting up toward the surface with him and Syd holding on tightly.

As it slowed, the spinning funnel of water towering overhead began closing at the top. Jordan had no time to think. He grabbed Chupacabra, avoiding contact with the smoldering blaststones, and pulled him from the rubble. As the top of the funnel collapsed on itself, its walls cascaded down like a great waterfall. Jordan gripped Chupacabra tightly and took a deep breath, not knowing if it would be his last.

SPLOOOOSH! The force of the gulf as it refilled the vacuum blasted the two of them away from the epicenter, sending them turning and tumbling through the murky water. Jordan kept his breath held, and his grip on the lifeless cryptid in his arms. When the spinning stopped, he didn't know which way was up. His arms were burning from contact with the blaststones. His lungs were burning, too, screaming for air. A dizziness overcame him, and he shut his eyes.

Something soft and wet suddenly rose from beneath him. Water rushed past his face at an incredible speed. His eyes fluttered open.

Moe was lifting him and Chupacabra toward the surface at an alarming speed.

They burst out of the water and into the air. Jordan took a massive breath as they sailed up and over the railing of the pier. Moe flopped on the pier, tossing Jordan and Chupacabra off her back. Jordan tumbled to a stop and looked around. His friends had been on a similar trip—Nessie was sitting on el Terminal Remota, too, where she'd landed after rescuing Wilford and Syd. The two soggy cryptids came running over, followed by Abbie and the Grimsleys.

"Jordan!" Mrs. Grimsley exclaimed. "Are you all right?"

"Yeah, Mom," Jordan said. Nearby, lying on the pier, Chupacabra was still unconscious. The blaststones were sizzling against his Hydro-Hide, burrowing their way into his body. "Wilford," he said, "you've got to do something. He'll die."

Wilford nodded at Jordan. The Yeti took a deep breath, then blew a pinpoint gust directly into each of the cryptid's injuries. The lodged blaststones began dimming just like the one in Jordan's room had.

"It's working!" Jordan said. He reached out and touched one of the stones. It was warm, but he could pull it out. "Abbie, help me!"

Abbie knelt beside the cryptid. She and Jordan quickly extracted the remaining blaststones from Chupacabra's Hydro-Hide. It was badly damaged, with large swaths of scales missing or burned off.

"He's going to be okay," Jordan said.

"You saved him," Abbie said.

Jordan smiled at his sister. "We saved him."

The others stared at Jordan and Abbie for a moment. Jordan could tell what they were wondering: *But why?* Jordan shrugged. "He's a creature. And we're Creature Keepers."

Mr. and Mrs. Grimsley smiled at the two of them. "Well, then you're probably going to want to see something," Mr. Grimsley said.

"Yeah," Abbie said to Jordan. "This is pretty weird. Even for us."

Syd and Wilford kept a close eye on Chupacabra, while Buck, Alistair, and Harvey kept the onlooking locals and tourists at a safe distance. Abbie and her parents led Jordan over to the Face Chompers, gathered in a tight group. They moved aside when Jordan and Abbie approached.

There on the concrete pier was the eggsteroid, split wide open. Its two halves were lying side by side, each of the thick, black shells filled with a boiling, fiery-red liquid.

36

Jordan and Abbie got as close as they could, but the radiation coming off the molten substance was even more intense than the heat of the blaststones.

"It looks like it's alive," Abbie said.

"What is it?" Sandy said from behind.

"Is this the fourth special?" Donald chimed in.

"Don't get too close, kids," Mr. Grimsley said.

"Wise advice," Wilford added. "That stuff looks like it could melt all of Mount Everest."

"Super gnarly," Syd said.

They all looked up at Syd and Wilford. "Hey, what are you two doing here?" Abbie said. "Who's watching over Chupacabra?"

"Don't worry," Syd said. "He's out cold. Besides, I

asked that jelly dude to keep a few dozen eyes on him."

"*Whoooooaaaaaah!*" A gelatinous blob of gooey Globster sailed overhead. Hogie hit the side of the *Mayan Princess* with a loud splat, then slowly slid down its side, disappearing beneath the edge of the pier.

Chupacabra loomed before them, beaten and bruised but sporting a grin as wide and as sinister as ever. "I've been as patient as I can be, but my patience has worn thin! It is time for you—for *all* of you—to die!"

"You can't kill us!" Mrs. Grimsley pointed to her children. "They saved your life!"

Chupacabra stopped. He seemed to consider this, studying Jordan and Abbie for a moment. "Well," he finally said. "That was monumentally stupid of you, wasn't it?"

Chupacabra cackled at them as he went to lift his Soil-Sole. *"Aaaarrrggh!"* He clutched his leg in pain. It seemed badly broken, and too weak to lift his heavy foot.

WHOOSH! A whipping breeze suddenly swirled around them, followed by a familiar Australian voice overhead.

"Hey, guys! I'm okay!" The flattened Globster cried out from the open side door of the Heli-Jet. It zoomed in low, knocking Chupacabra backward. The injured cryptid howled in pain as he fell back on his leg.

Bernard circled around and waved to them. Francine waved back excitedly. "It's Hogie!" she yelled. "That little snot is on board!"

Hogie's gelatinous body stretched from the open door like a long gloopy lifeline. Hanging by his tail off the end of Hogie's appendage was Gilligan. He swung from the thick and stringy Globster, flinging himself over the pier. He did a triple somersault and landed right next to Moe.

"C'mon, you soggy old mop," Gilligan said to the Trunko. "Time to get you back in the drink!" Donald and Lou ran and helped Gilligan roll their large friend toward the edge of the pier. Gilligan and Moe plunged into the water below.

Bernard hovered over the cryptids. "Face Chompers! Grab hold and hop on!"

Sandy effortlessly leaped into the side door. Lou picked up Donald and threw him into the Heli-Jet, then jumped up and grabbed its runner. Others caught a claw, foot, tail, or wing in Hogie's stringy mass. The stretched-out, Day-Glo Globster hung off the Heli-Jet with various creatures stuck to him like a furry, freaky flytrap.

Chupacabra pulled himself along the pier, painfully dragging his bad leg behind him. He reached out to grab the dangling Glob-ster, but Bernard lifted them out of his reach.

Paul, the last and slowest of the bunch, galloped his short legs

from behind Chupacabra, trampling over the struggling cryptid as he tried to leap for the rising Heli-Jet. The dense jungle walrus failed miserably, but Gavin and Kriss swooped in to help him. They gripped his scaly back and flapped their wings, carrying him off along with the others.

The crowd of people gathered near the broken pier let out a loud cheer at the rescue operation they'd witnessed as Bernard veered the Face Chompers–filled aircraft over the water, away from the pier, and blasted away, leaving Buck, Harvey, Jordan, Abbie, and their parents standing beside the cracked-open orb.

Chupacabra pulled himself onto all fours. With some trouble, he crawled like a wounded coyote toward the bubbling halves of the orb.

"Don't come any closer!" Jordan hollered at him. "We may have saved you once, but we won't let you endanger another creature or human."

"Aye," Alistair said. "We stand at the ready." He was beside Nessie, who along with Syd and Wilford were staring the wounded cryptid down, ready to attack him with their elemental powers.

Chupacabra stopped and tried to straighten himself as best he could, which wasn't much. He was on all fours, hunched over, his ears and spiky hair water-slicked back atop his head. The sight of him reminded

Abbie of something. She broke into her backpack and pulled out the pencil rubbing of the cave carving she'd done at the Mayan ruins.

"Jordan! Look at this!"

"That's a really cool sketch, Abbie, but maybe this isn't the best time."

"This is an ancient drawing! It tells the story of the Chicxulub crater. Look at it! It's him! Chupacabra is the one who was born here!"

Chupacabra broke into a coughing cackle. He grinned at Abbie. "Not bad," he said.

"This means . . . you're the fourth special cryptid," Jordan said.

The damaged creature gazed at the glowing liquid behind them. "And you have looted my birthright, George, stealing something dear to me for the second time." Chupacabra winced in pain as he pulled himself up and stood, his limp leg anchored by the heavy Soil-Sole. "I was cursed twice when I came into this world, Georgie. First, separated from my elemental gift that would have allowed me not just to survive but to take my place among the most powerful cryptids. And then the second curse—when I met you."

The injured creature tried to hobble closer to Jordan. Wilford and Syd bristled.

"I was trying to find my way back here when you discovered me all those years ago," Chupacabra said. "You photographed me, exposed me to the world. You turned me into a hunted animal and forced me into hiding. You made it impossible for me to claim what was mine. Growing without my gift made me sensitive to the blaststones that surrounded it. Even once I found a way to return, I was unable to get close to it. But I soon figured out that the elemental powers from the other three specials would allow me to overcome these obstacles. I could move the water with the Hydro-Hide, freeze the blaststones with the Blizzard-Bristles, and crack open the orb with the Soil-Sole. It was the perfect plan—until you and your Creature Keepers stopped me cold."

Wilford stared icicles at Chupacabra. "And we'd be happy to do it again."

"No, no, I surrender. I can see I've been outwitted." Chupacabra raised his arms over his head. "I should thank you. You saved me the dirty work by going down and extracting my package for me." He gazed again at the bubbling bowls behind Jordan and Abbie. "I see you even went to the trouble of opening it up for me."

"Tell us what it is," Abbie demanded.

The creature eyed Abbie. "It's the last element I need for the power of the Perfect Storm, of course. And the first step in Operation Pangaea."

The magma inside the cracked shells began bubbling aggressively.

"Enough talk," Jordan said. "If you don't want to be frozen solid, back away."

"Correction, Georgie—if *you* don't want to be burned to a crisp, you'd better *duck*!" Chupacabra suddenly raised his arms higher and spread his claws. In an instant, the red-hot liquid exploded out of the two shells, flying straight at Jordan's head. Jordan dived to

the ground as the molten blobs slammed into Chupacabra's open claws, engulfing his arms in flames. He
threw his head back and let out a loud howl.

Responding quickly, Wilford shot a shock of ice
across the pier at Chupacabra. The cryptid caught the
arctic blast in his flaming clutches, turning it into
steam. He watched, delighted, as the flames took the
form of his claws.

"Behold," he said. "My birthright and the final piece
to the Perfect Storm." He held up his arms and mar-
veled at the glowing red flames. "MY PYRO-PAWS!"

37

"Jordan!" Alistair dived, pulling his friend away from Chupacabra's feet just as the cryptid snapped an arm downward. *FLOOM!* His flaming Pyro-Paw shot out, stretching to melt a wide hole through the concrete pier, right where Jordan's head had been.

The magmalike appendage retracted back to Chupacabra's arm as he pointed his other fiery fist in the direction of Nessie, Syd, and Wilford. The three special cryptids stared

back, helpless to do anything, but itching for a fight.

"I must confess," Chupacabra said to them. "Now that I have my very own elemental power, I feel a bit guilty about having taken yours. Had you only listened to me years ago, we could have ruled the world together and we wouldn't be here."

"*SKRONK!*" Nessie reared her head up angrily and snorted at him.

His Pyro-Paw shot out, stretching across, stopping inches from Nessie's chest. "Watch your attitude, my dear. Your Hydro-Hide won't protect you from this. And if either of you two"—his aim turned to Syd and Wilford—"are getting an itch to stomp your feet or start huffing and puffing, remember: only one of us has all four elemental powers at his command."

"So what now?" Mr. Grimsley yelled.

"Yes!" Mrs. Grimsley said. "You have your Perfect Storm! What do you want?"

"What I've wanted from the beginning. To bring the world closer together."

"Of course," Jordan said. "Operation Pangaea. You're going to smash the continents together somehow, and create another mass extinction event."

"That's crazy," Mrs. Grimsley said.

"Not to mention impossible," Mr. Grimsley added.

"And stupid," Abbie said. "Moving entire continents

is too enormous to pull off. Even with the power of the Perfect Storm."

"I don't normally like to brag about my ingenious plans," Chupacabra said. "But this is a really good one. And since you're all so skeptical, please allow me to explain. With the Hydro-Hide, I'll control the great currents of the earth to do my bidding and push the loosened continents wherever I please. The mantle they sit upon will be cracked and dislodged with the Soil-Sole. With the Blizzard-Bristles, I can create massive ice floes to wedge any stubborn continents. I'm thinking Australia might be sticky."

"Sorry," Abbie said. "Still sounds like a stupid plan to me."

Chupacabra held up one of his flaming arms. "Without these, you might be right. One can't just break off continents and move them around like puzzle pieces. I required the final element: the power to dip deep into the mantle of the earth and turn solid rock into rivers of lava. You know, to get things flowing. Obtaining the power of the Perfect Storm was just the first step. Now that I have all four elemental gifts, the real fun starts."

He retracted his Pyro-Paw from Nessie and tried to strike a proud pose. Stepping back, he winced as he put his weight on his broken Soil-Sole leg. A few dozen crispy scales popped off his battered Hydro-Hide, falling like dead leaves onto the ground. A look of worry flashed across his face.

"Uh, hold up, there, buddy." Buck stepped forward. "I'm no cryptozoologist, but I did play one on TV. And excepting for those oven mitts of yours there, I gotta say, you're not really looking ready for prime time, if you know what I mean."

"He's right," Syd said. "You can barely lift that Soil-Sole of mine."

"And those Blizzard-Bristles," Wilford said, pointing at the shorn stubble on Chupacabra's upper lip. "It took me years of meditation and inner growth to get such a full, bushy moustache. What did you do, run it through a wood chipper?"

"*SKRONK!*" Nessie boomed.

Alistair chuckled. "Haggis-Breath makes a fair point. Yer Hydro-Hide is riddled with patches of burned and missing scales. Ya look like a bluefish that's been blackened by a blind man with a blowtorch. Her words, not mine."

"SILENCE!" Chupacabra's Pyro-Paws blazed as he stumbled back on his bad leg. He tried his best to flutter his worn-out Hydro-Hide. Even more burned scales popped off, scattering on the pier. Chupacabra blew with all his might through his shorn Blizzard-Bristles, releasing a tiny puff of fluffy snow.

"Okay," Wilford began moving closer to Chupacabra, his full Blizzard-Bristles twinkling at the ready.
"Let's all try taking a deep, calming breath. . . ." The
wise old Yeti began to inhale carefully.

Chupacabra caught on and thrust his blazing Pyro-
Paws toward them. "One snowflake and that breath
will be your last! I will fry the three of you where you
stand!"

Wilford backed down, carefully letting the breath out through his nose.

"You can't kill them," Jordan said. "As you know, killing another cryptid ties you to their same fate."

"He's right," Abbie said. "Those are the sacred cryptid rules."

"Your plan has come up short, pal," Syd said. "The gifts you stole from us are damaged goods now. Why don't we let these nice people all go free? Then we can work things out, just us special cryptids."

"Like we should have all those years ago," Wilford added.

A panicked expression overtook Chupacabra. He glanced around anxiously. Something caught his eye. "No," he said. "It's too late for that. And I've learned that letting humans go free was my original mistake. I won't make it again!"

FLOOM! He shot his arms into the air. His Pyro-Paws extended again, arching and stretching toward the crowd gathered at the edge of the broken pier, forming a fireball. It blazed menacingly as it hung just above the crowd's heads like an asteroid set on pause, ready to crash into the earth and kill all life in its path.

The crowd let out a panicked scream as they ducked and tried to shield themselves from the fiery death-ball hanging over them. Abbie spotted the terrified

Flamboyanes children. Julia and Sam covered them as their papier-mâché Alebrijes went up in flames from the radiating heat bearing down on them.

"Jordan, we have to do something! He's going to sacrifice them all if he doesn't get his way!"

Jordan turned to his sister. His eyes were wide. "Sacrifice. Abbie, that's it."

"That's what?"

"That's what it will take."

Jordan stepped up to Chupacabra. He could feel the heat radiating off Chupacabra's blasting Pyro-Paws. He swallowed hard. "You finally got the gift that was rightfully yours, but it cost you the three you stole. You don't have the power of the Perfect Storm. You can't execute Operation Pangaea. Face it, old friend, you've come up short. But I can offer you what you've lost. I can restore you, and give you back the power of the Perfect Storm."

"You're a liar, Grimsley," Chupacabra said. "What powers can you give me?"

Jordan nodded toward Syd, Wilford, and Nessie. "Theirs."

There was a collective gasp from nearly all gathered around. Chupacabra sneered at Jordan. "You have ten seconds to explain."

"It's not complicated," Jordan said. "As you well know, I, George Grimsley, am the creator and leader of the Creature Keepers. Under my command, these three cryptids must give up their elemental gifts to you. And they will. Right here, right now."

"They will?" Chupacabra said.

"We will?" Wilford said.

"Skronk?"

Jordan continued. "Once you have their gifts, you won't just be the only creature on earth with *all* the elemental powers. You will be the only creature with *any* of them. You'll have the power of the Perfect Storm. But more than that, they will have nothing. No one could challenge you. No one could stop you. You will be the one and only supreme special cryptid."

"I do like the sound of that," Chupacabra said.

"And you'd have no reason to kill anyone," Jordan added carefully.

At this, Chupacabra's grin shifted to a glare. "What's the catch, Grimsley?"

"No catch. All I ask is that you keep our little bet. That once you gained the power of the Perfect Storm, the first thing you'd do would be to kill me."

"*What?*" Abbie exclaimed. Mr. and Mrs. Grimsley gasped.

Chupacabra took in the collective reaction from Jordan's friends and family. The creature was grinning again. "I like the sound of that, too," he said.

"Then we have a deal?"

"We do."

"Good. The Loch Ness Monster, Sasquatch, and Yeti will give you their elemental gifts. In return, before you do anything else with the power of the Perfect Storm, you will kill me, George Grimsley, once and for all."

"Say your good-byes, Georgie boy," he said. "But no tricks." *FLOOM!* The fireball retracted from above the crowd, returning to his flaming arms. He redirected them toward Jordan and the others. "I'm watching you."

Jordan turned to huddle with his friends and family as Chupacabra kept a sharp eye.

With Chupacabra looming close by and eager to get on with ruling the world, Jordan had very little time to explain his plan to Abbie, his parents, Buck, Harvey, and Alistair. He quickly ran down what he needed each of them to do before revealing the key to defeating Chupacabra, once and for all.

"Grampa Grimsley's special ring," he whispered. "Eldon told me the secret to enhancing its powers. And I've seen it work. On our friend Morris the Japanese

Kappa. He'd turned permanently to stone. But the ring brought him back to life."

Abbie's eyes grew wide. "If that ring was powerful enough to bring Morris back, maybe it's powerful enough to do the opposite and turn Chupacabra to stone. I'm in."

"Ooh . . . That I'd give anything to see," Harvey said. "Count me in, too."

"Seems crazy to me," Buck said. "Luckily, I love crazy. Let's do this!"

Alistair rested a hand on Jordan's shoulder. "You know I'm with ya, lad. To the bitter end."

Jordan turned to his parents. Mrs. Grimsley looked worried. But through her worry, she was smiling. "We couldn't be more proud of all you've done for these creatures," she said. "You even gave that wretched beast a second chance. Of course, he then threw it back in your face. So I say we kick his scaly butt, Grimsley-style."

"Wow. Thanks, Mom."

"You both did what I wish I'd had the courage to do," Mr. Grimsley said softly. "You believed in your grandfather. I can't change the past, but I can do something now. I can believe in what he created, by believing in the two of you. Your grandfather sacrificed his entire life for these creatures. I only wish he could see how much the two of you are sacrificing for everything he believed in."

"Sacrifice is exactly what we need to empower Grampa Grimsley's ring," Jordan said. "Let's just hope it's enough to defeat his original enemy."

"Oh, you mean the one we're about to hand over the power of the Perfect Storm?" Abbie took in everyone's stares. "What? I'm still in, I'm just pointing out the brutally obvious in a super scary way. That's kinda my thing."

"Y'know, sometimes sacrifice is all you can do," Mrs. Grimsley said. "But if it's for someone you love, it's all you need."

"The biggest sacrifice needs to come from the ones we swore we'd protect," Jordan said. "Let's hope they feel the same way."

"Can we get on with it, please?" Chupacabra said. "I'd like their powers—*now*."

Jordan approached Nessie, Syd, and Wilford. "I know this goes against everything you've ever known or done," Jordan said. "But I'm asking the three of you to trust me."

"To trust *us*," Abbie said, stepping up beside her brother.

"Wouldn't be the first time I've lost a Soil-Sole to you two," Syd said with a shrug. "But I have to say, you did fight like a pair of Manitoban mountain muskrats

trying to get 'em back. I figure this must be pretty important. It's all yours."

The Sasquatch furrowed his unibrow in concentration. His Soil-Sole began to shift and loosen from his lower leg, peeling away from his thigh, down to his ankle. He opened his eyes and stepped out of it.

Chupacabra could hardly contain himself. The cryptid giggled as Wilford glared back at him. "I don't like this," the Yeti said, stroking his thick, snowy half moustache as he contemplated. He took a deep breath. "But you two taught me how to trust others and work as a team. So I suppose in the spirit of teamwork and trust, I will—"

"Cool!" Syd ripped Wilford's Blizzard-Bristles off his face with one quick yank and dropped the half moustache beside his Soil-Sole.

"OWW!" Wilford grabbed his upper lip and stared daggers at the Sasquatch.

"What?" Syd said. "We're on the same team, dude!"

Chupacabra snickered as he watched Alistair cross over to join them with a worried expression. He put a hand on Nessie's neck. "Well, old girl, it's your turn."

Nessie snorted and turned away, dramatically crossing her flippers and fluttering the scales of her Hydro-Hide.

"You drop the diva attitude this instant—and that Hydro-Hide of yers along with it!"

She snorted again. *"SKRONK!"*

"Whaddya mean, 'Easy for me to say'? All right then,

I'll make it easier for ya!" In one quick motion, Alistair dropped his kilt and stood buck naked.

"Old man butt," Abbie said. "This had better count as a sacrifice, too."

A thin smile crept over Nessie's face. Then she did something Jordan had never seen the Loch Ness Monster do before. She giggled. Her giggles morphed into big honking laughter. Alistair laughed along with her and patted her head.

"It'll be okay, girl," he said. "I promise."

She lifted her head, then shook her great green body like a big wet poodle. Her scales flew off, scattering in a big pile at their feet, glistening in the sun. When she was done, the mighty cryptid looked naked, her flesh soft and vulnerable.

"All right, now EVERYONE BACK!" Chupacabra approached the treasures laid out before him. The few dozen good scales that he had began to sparkle and flutter. As they did, Nessie's discarded pile began vibrating on the pier. Her scales suddenly flew through the air, attaching themselves to Chupacabra, filling the empty spots, building in layers, restoring his thick, shimmering hide.

Chupacabra leaned back on his bad leg in amazement and let out a laugh. "It's healed! The Hydro-Hide healed my leg!"

He stepped forward, placing his smaller foot into Syd's Soil-Sole. It wrapped itself around his ankle, meshing with the scales that covered his lower leg. Chupacabra let out another awful laugh as he lifted one foot, then the other. He picked up Wilford's whiskers and placed them beneath his snout beside the badly shorn half. The Blizzard-Bristles crackled and crystallized, the frozen tendrils reaching out and attaching themselves to his face, spreading evenly beneath both his nostrils. Then he stepped back.

Chupacabra puffed himself out proudly. "Look at me," he said. "At long last, the power of the Perfect Storm is mine!"

39

Chupacabra was so busy admiring himself, he didn't notice Harvey and Alistair wheeling Buck's stage toward him, across the pier. They positioned it in front of Chupacabra, then approached Jordan with the pink Face Chompers banner.

"What is this?" the super-powered cryptid said. "What are you doing?"

"You didn't forget our deal, did you?" Jordan said. "This is for my extinction. I assume you're still gonna kill me like you promised!"

"Right. Of course. A deal is a deal. But why do we need all of this?"

"Sorry, but are you not the world's only special cryptid, about to kill George Grimsley, your archnemesis?"

"No, no. I am. That's all true."

"So what, you were just gonna kill him with no fanfare? No snazziness?"

"Uh, snazziness?"

"You've been after me for *decades*, dude!" Jordan said. "You owe it to yourself to make it a memorable murder."

Chupacabra glanced around, a bit confused. Wilford and Syd were comforting Nessie, who was not taking her new nakedness very well. He grinned at this, and regained his confidence in the task at hand. "There is no creature who can compare to my power or my beauty! I'm going to be ruling the world, or what's left of it, very soon! I suppose I *should* do things with more, uh . . ."

"Snazziness," Abbie said.

"Yes! Snazziness! I demand snazziness!"

"That's the spirit!" Jordan was relieved that Chupacabra hadn't noticed, or if he did, hadn't cared, that his parents had slipped away. "Well, we might as well get on with it. I know you have continents to smash together and stuff."

Buck draped the pink Face Chompers banner over Jordan's shoulders and led him up to the small stage, where Alistair stood waiting.

"Are you ready to meet yer maker, laddie?" the old Scot said.

Jordan drew a deep breath. "Yes. Yes I am."

Chupacabra stepped closer, watching the spectacle carefully. Abbie suddenly burst into very un-Abbie-like drama. She threw herself at his Soil-Soles. "Please, your Destructor-ness! I beg you for your mercy! Spare him! *Please!*"

"You're wasting your breath," Chupacabra said. "George Grimsley's fate was determined the day he took my picture. Out of my way!" He turned back to face the stage just as Buck and Alistair finished draping the banner over the willing victim's head.

"What is this?" Chupacabra said. "Forget snazziness! I don't care about your traditions. I've waited too long for this moment. I want to see the face of my enemy as I extinguish him."

Buck and Alistair froze. Chupacabra stepped past Abbie. "REMOVE THE VEIL!"

"You're the boss," Alistair said.

He and Buck yanked the pink banner. Standing there beneath it was Harvey Quisling. "But not a very good boss. And I should know, *hee-hee*."

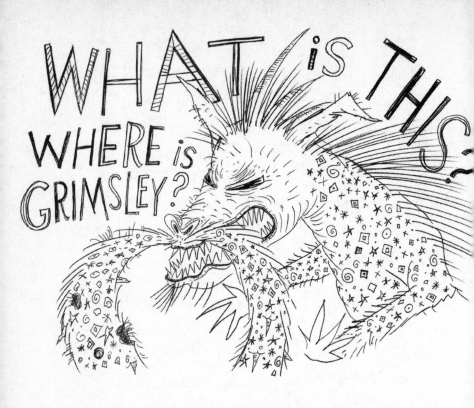

WHAT IS THIS?
WHERE IS GRIMSLEY?

Chupacabra's eyes grew wide. His eyes darted around the pier. "WHAT IS THIS? WHERE IS GRIMSLEY?"

"Sorry," Alistair said. "But a true Creature Keeper never reveals the secret behind a good *hoax*." He tossed the banner over Chupacabra's head, then leaped off the stage along with Buck and Harvey.

"*AAAARRRRGGGGGH!*" Chupacabra ripped the banner off and swung his Pyro-Paws like long flaming swords, slicing the tarp-curtains and the backdrop posts in half. Jordan was nowhere to be seen. "*WHERE IS HE?*" He leaped onto the stage, crushing it. Beneath his Soil-Soles, there was an opening in the stage. The trap door was open. Chupacabra kicked the wooden structure aside. There beneath the kindling was the hole he himself had bored through the concrete pier with his Pyro-Paw. And through the hole, in the water below, Jordan was swimming toward the waiting powerboat manned by his parents.

"GRIMSLEY!"

Chupacabra took a deep breath and flared his Pyro-Paws, just as something slammed into him, sending him tumbling into the pile of splintered wood.

Nessie's tail came swinging again, walloping him in the side of the head.

"Abbie!" Jordan's voice called from the speedboat below. She ran toward the hole. Jordan and the Grimsleys were waving up to her to jump.

Chupacabra scrambled to his feet, only to be suddenly lifted up by Syd and thrown across the pier.

"Jump, Abbie!" Wilford shouted to her. "We'll slow him down! Go!"

Abbie readied herself when a high-pitched hissing shriek she recognized stopped her cold.

"Chunk?"

Farther down the pier, lined up behind Chupacabra, were a dozen large iguanas. Standing in front of them was Chunk. He hissed again. The others hissed back in unison.

Abbie yelled down to her family, "Go! It's all right! Go without me! I have to get Chunk!" The speedboat roared off, and she ran to her former pet.

Chupacabra pulled himself to his feet. His Pyro-Paws blazed, and he shot a fiery arm out at Wilford, Syd, and Nessie. The Yeti and the Sasquatch dived to avoid being hit, but the blast winged the Loch Ness Monster's tender side. She moaned in pain.

"No!" Abbie stopped running toward Chunk and turned toward Nessie. Chupacabra blew a quick blast of ice, knocking her down. Behind him, an angry hissing sound filled the air. Chupacabra spun around.

"AAAAUUUUGGGGH!" A cluster of lizards leaped into the air and latched on to him from head to toe. They dug their sharp talons into his scales and nipped at his face, belly, arms, and anywhere they could dig in. "GET OFF ME, VILE SERPENTS!" He shook and fluttered his Hydro-Hide scales. One by one, the iguanas flew off him until there was a lone lizard left—Chunk—riding atop his head, his claws firmly sunk into the cryptid's snout.

"AIEEEE!" Chupacabra screamed in pain as he raised his Pyro-Paws toward his head.

"Chunk! Down, boy!" The iguana obeyed his ex-owner and leaped off as Chupacabra's blazing paws singed the top of his own head.

"OWWWEEEE!" He shook the fire out and turned back, wild-eyed, to face his attackers. Buck, Harvey, Syd, and Wilford were tending to Nessie's wound as Abbie stood defiantly, her devoted Chunk flopped in her arms.

"I should slay you all where you stand, but I won't waste my time! You will be thrust into extinction soon enough! But first, know this—I will crush your protector, George Grimsley, once and for all. And trust me, I'll make sure he suffers!" Chupacabra took three great strides and leaped off the pier, diving into the Gulf of Mexico.

Chunk purred in Abbie's arms and licked her face. "You came back and saved me!"

It wasn't long before the Heli-Jet came floating over the *Mayan Princess*. Bernard set it down among the debris and destruction scattered about el Terminal Remota. The Skunk Ape hopped out. "Where is everyone? And what on earth happened here?"

Abbie explained to Bernard all that had happened as Buck, Harvey, and Alistair used the Heli-Jet's onboard first-aid kit to dress Nessie's wound.

"I didn't see any sign of Chupacabra, or the speedboat," Bernard said. "But I was flying pretty fast to get back here after dropping off the Face Chompers."

"You're going to need to fly twice as fast back out."

Bernard saluted her. "I'm here to serve. We fly on your command."

"Give me just one second." Abbie carried Chunk back to his iguana warriors and crouched down. "Chunk, you and your new friends did a great thing here. I'll never forget you or your bravery. Take care of yourself." She tried not to burst into tears as she hugged him one last time, set him down, then quickly turned to go. "*Ouch!*" Chunk was clinging to her leg. She peeled him off and picked him up. "No, Chunk, you're a free creature now. An honorary Face Chomper!" The iguana's long tongue shot out and licked her nose. She giggled. "Are you sure you don't want to stay with them?" He blinked slowly, flopped back in her arms, and fell asleep.

"I guess that's iguana for 'being free can also mean having the freedom to stay with someone you love,'" she said to the others. They answered by lying down where they were and sunning their bellies.

Abbie crossed the pier to where Buck was talking animatedly to the gathering crowd. The locals and tourists had witnessed everything from a safe distance but were now cautiously approaching the Sasquatch, Yeti, and Loch Ness Monster. One of them was so taken with this incredible opportunity, he didn't even notice that his speedboat had gone missing again.

Abbie pulled Harvey and Alistair aside. "You two should stay here and take care of these three. Just don't let Buck turn this into a television show."

Alistair nodded. "And you should go and make sure your family is safe—and take care of that bogus beastie, once and for all."

"Give him an extra kick in the tail, from his ol' pal Quisling," Harvey said.

"There's something else," Alistair said. "I made one of these for your brother, and it helped him face down that creature once before." He handed her the whittled slingshot. "Dunno if it'll bring you luck or power, but I want you to have it."

"Thanks, Mac." She hugged him, then ran to board the Heli-Jet. As she, Chunk, and Bernard lifted off the pier and rose above the Lido deck of the *Mayan Princess*, the last thing she saw below was the crowd of friendly humans surrounding the three most famous cryptids in the world.

40

Jordan stood facing backward as the speedboat zoomed across the Gulf of Mexico. As Mr. Grimsley kept them on course for southern Florida, Jordan kept his eyes on a strange wave in the distance. It was fatter and rounder than the chop his father was blasting

through. The longer Jordan stared at it, the more his unsettling feeling grew that the wave was either following them . . . or chasing them.

Either way, if it was Chupacabra, then things were going exactly to plan. So long as the cryptid didn't reach them before they reached the Okeeyuckachokee Swamp.

"Faster, Dad!" Jordan shouted over the roaring motor. "Mom, hold on tight and stay down!" He checked her life jacket, then turned his attention back to the water. The rogue wave was gone. Jordan frantically scanned the horizon behind them. Nothing. "Dad, faster!" he cried out again.

The speedboat jolted as its engine growled so loudly, Jordan almost couldn't make out what his mother suddenly screamed. "Roger, look!"

Jordan spun around as the freak wave suddenly rose ahead of them. Balancing atop it was Chupacabra, his Hydro-Hide churning the water into a massive ramp, his Pyro-Paws blazing and spread wide to catch them.

Mr. Grimsley veered the boat violently, but the wave moved with them, staying square in their path. "Mom! Dad! *Abandon ship!*" He grabbed his parents and pulled them to the back of the boat as it climbed the massive wave. They prepared to jump when suddenly the Heli-Jet came zooming in overhead. It slammed into Chupacabra, knocking him off the wave's crest. The speedboat continued to climb at such an angle, even as the massive wave subsided, that it was about to capsize.

"C'mon!" Abbie was in the open door of the Heli-Jet, which hovered before them. She gestured for them leap aboard. They launched themselves from the capsizing boat, tumbling into the open door of the Heli-Jet.

Jordan slid across the floor, stopping when his face smushed against something soft and scaly—Chunk's fat belly. The lazy iguana looked up at him, then went back to sleep. It was the first time Jordan had ever been happy to see his sister's rude reptile.

Abbie slammed the door shut and yelled to Bernard, who leveled the Heli-Jet, hit the thruster jets, and blasted them toward the Okeeyuckachokee Swamp.

Mrs. Grimsley hopped into the copilot's seat. "Master Ranger Bernie!" she said. "You saved us!"

"Please, ma'am, call me Bernard."

Mr. Grimsley put a hand on his shoulder. "Skunk Ape or no Skunk Ape, you make a great Badger Ranger in my book."

"We're not out of this yet," Jordan said. He and Abbie were glued to the side windows, searching the water for any sign of Chupacabra.

"Heavens! What is that?" Everyone rushed to Mrs. Grimsley's copilot window. A bright orange light flashed at the surface of the water. Something streaked into the sky.

"Bernard, prepare to do some fancy flying," Jordan said.

The streak of flame and thick smoke shot across the sky, high overhead, then zoomed directly toward them. Chupacabra's Pyro-Paws were at his sides, blasting him forward like twin rocket engines.

WHUMP! There was a violent jerk as something hit the Heli-Jet, sending everyone tumbling. Bernard struggled to right the aircraft. "Something's wrong!"

Out the cockpit window, the Okeeyuckachokee was getting closer. "We're almost there!" Jordan yelled. "You've got to keep us in the air, Bernard!" The Heli-Jet jerked again as a red light began blinking and buzzing in the cockpit.

"It's our thrusters!" Bernard hollered back. "They've been disabled! I'm switching to the rotors, but we're losing altitude and power!"

"I need to get out there," Jordan said. "If he takes out the rotors, we're toast! Bernard, you just make sure you get us to that shoreline up ahead! If you can, take us over the Puddle of Ripeness!"

WHOOSH! The Heli-Jet suddenly dropped and slowed, slamming Jordan against the roof and dropping him to the floor. He got up, grabbed a parachute, ran to the cargo door, slid it open, and climbed outside.

The wind was tearing him as he struggled to hold on to the ladder and climb along the side runners. As he approached the rear of the aircraft, he saw Chupacabra. The cryptid was clutching the tail end of the craft, blowing icy cold air directly into the jet thrusters, freezing them solid. Overhead, the rotors whined and whirred, struggling to keep the Heli-Jet airborne. The chopper dropped as they reached the shoreline. The boathouse flew by below, then the runners crashed through the thick treetops of the swamp. Jordan scrambled up the side of the Heli-Jet to avoid getting smacked by the treetops, ducking beneath the rotors slicing just above his head.

Chupacabra gave Jordan a devilish grin, then blasted a fireball at him. Jordan slid back down onto the runners as the blast hit the rotor. The entire aircraft let out a piercing whine as a burst of smoke blew out of the rotor engine. The smoke enveloped Chupacabra, who let go of the tail and went tumbling into the trees.

The Heli-Jet skimmed across the thick cypress treetops. Jordan spotted and recognized a perfectly round, oddly dense circle of them, below and dead ahead. "The Puddle of Ripeness," he said to himself. "Way to go, Bernard!"

He leaped from the chopper and yanked the rip cord on his parachute. It immediately jerked him backward as the Heli-Jet plowed through the trees, skidding into the thick brush somewhere in the distance.

Jordan tumbled into one of the concentric circles of the cypress fortress, coming to a violent halt as his parachute got tangled up inside the thick grove.

Scratched, scraped, but mostly unharmed, Jordan swung there for a moment, suspended in the trees and mesmerized by the sudden silence. He slipped out of the parachute and dropped into the path leading to the Puddle of Ripeness—and hopefully his friend Eldon Pecone.

Jordan wandered toward the light of a small campfire dancing near the edge of the Puddle of Ripeness. Flickering all around on the ground were flashes of pink. Small silk parachutes littered the area like an exotic, rumpled carpet, giving the grove a cozy, dreamlike feeling. There was also a strange abundance of half-eaten carrots.

Eldon's voice came from the shadows. "Like what I did with the place?" He stepped toward Jordan. He was still wearing nothing but his boxer shorts, and in the dim light his face looked sickly and tired. "Care for a carrot?"

Jordan scanned the dark treetops for any signs of Chupacabra. "Eldon. There's no time to explain, but you need to get out of here, now."

"We've been over this. I'm not going anywhere. Not ever again." Eldon held out a handful of paper. "Look. Letters, from the Creature Keepers. They've been floating down to me all day. Thanking me for all I've done, for keeping your grandfather's legacy alive."

"That's great," Jordan said. "Take them with you. But you have to go, now!"

"They're meant to make me feel better. So I'll come out of hiding. But they've only made me want to hide in here forever. I failed, Jordan. I failed the Creature Keepers. It's all over, and it's all my fault."

A rustling erupted in the treetops overhead. Eldon seemed not to notice. Jordan began to panic. "Listen to me, Eldon. You didn't fail. The creatures you kept safe and sheltered from the world and from each other— yes, many of them want to be free. But you have to know that when it counted, they worked together. As a team. As *a family*. They're stronger together, Eldon. Because of you, because of all the Creature Keepers, those cryptids found the confidence to step out, stand up for themselves, and to fight—*against Chupacabra!*"

"The cryptids—defeated Chupacabra?"

Jordan deflated a bit. "Uh, well, not exactly. In fact, not at all, no."

A loud cracking of a branch in the distance startled them both. "Okay, you stubborn squirrel," Jordan said. "You win, and we're out of time. So it looks like you and I are just gonna have to team up, too. One more time, whether you like it or not."

CRACK!

WAIT.
WHAT'S
GOING
ON
?

Finally, Eldon looked up. "Wait. What's going on?"

"Chupacabra's what's going on. I led him here, away from the others. Away from innocent people. But mostly I led him here . . . for my grandfather's ring."

The rustling and cracking of branches were getting

louder—and closer. "What good is the ring going to do?" Eldon said.

"Nothing by itself," Jordan explained quickly. "But you taught me sacrifice gives the ring its power. And I've seen it with my own eyes. Morris the Kappa sacrificed himself for Abbie, and the elixir in that ring brought him back to life!"

"Oh, Jordan. I'm afraid this plan can't work."

"It will! We've all sacrificed something to get to this point! Abbie gave up Chunk. The three special cryptids sacrificed their elemental gifts, and I— Well, I have an idea I haven't told anyone about that will put an end to this, once and for all."

"Wait. Go back. The three special cryptids sacrificed what, now?"

"Their elemental gifts. They gave them to Chupacabra."

"Why did they do that?"

"Because I asked them to."

"Boy, I retire for just one day, and look what happens."

"Listen to me, Eldon. I have a plan. Chupacabra is the fourth special. And now he has all four elemental gifts. The power of the Perfect Storm. He aims to use it to create a cataclysmic event that will make him the single supreme cryptid ruling over the earth. But before he can do any of that, Chupacabra has vowed to deal one final blow to the Creature Keepers—by killing George Grimsley. Don't you see? *He still thinks I'm my grandfather.* So the final sacrifice . . . will be mine."

Eldon's face went white. "Jordan, no. You can't do this. I—I can't let you."

"It's okay! Once you give me the ring, I'll have it on when I let him try to kill me. With an ultimate sacrifice like that, the ring will have to gain enough power to stop him! That's my plan!" Jordan thought a moment. "This is the first time I've said it out loud. Now that I hear it, I sure hope it works."

CRACK! A branch came crashing down into the center of the grove. A violent rustling descended from directly above. Jordan held out his hand. "Eldon. There's no more time. Give me the ring. Let me finish what my grandfather started."

Eldon stared back at him. "I told you, I can't do that, Jordan."

CRASH! An entire tree suddenly gave way as a large dark figure fell into the clearing. Chupacabra hit the ground, his Soil-Soles shaking the grove with a thundering *BOOM!* He stared across the Puddle of Ripeness at Jordan and Eldon.

"Nowhere left to run, Georgie. Now I believe you and I have a date with destiny."

* * *

347

BOOM! Bernard, Abbie, and her parents stumbled as the ground shook beneath them. They continued running from the crash-landed Heli-Jet, making their way through the dark swamp. Bernard led them to the thick cluster of cypress trees protecting the Puddle of Ripeness. They stopped short at what they saw there.

The retired Keepers stood in a semicircle, reunited with their Face Chomper creatures. Standing in front of them were Doris and Hap. Behind were the residents of Eternal Acres. A worried hush had fallen over everyone as they stared up at the wall of tree trunks reaching for the night sky. They were listening for some indication of what was happening within.

A soft, husky voice got Abbie's attention. "I considered flying in there," Kriss said. "But this is the secret, sacred place of the Skunk Ape. I would never be so bold without his permission."

Abbie stared at the Mothman. It was the first time she'd heard him speak above a whisper.

Doris stepped forward. "I told him it was okay, that the secret was pretty much out now. But he wouldn't listen. Not until you got here."

Abbie smiled at Kriss. The Mothman hid behind his hair and looked away shyly.

"Well, I'm here now, too," Bernard said. "And I know the way in."

"Good." Abbie addressed Kriss, Doris, and Hap. "You all stay here. If the plan goes wrong, your priority is to get the older folks to safety."

Kriss nodded. Hap gave a thumbs-up. Doris smiled. "Good luck, dearie."

Bernard led Abbie and her parents around the circular grove to a shallow entryway. It looked like a cutout doorframe, formed in one of the thick trunks. He reached up and placed his paw on an oddly shaped knot just above the archway and pushed. The knot sank into the bark, and the outer circle of the cypress trees rotated one way while the inner layer of trees rotated another. Abbie and the Grimsleys watched in amazement as multiple inner doorways lined up, creating a short tunnel. The tunnel led to a winding path spiraling farther inward.

"C'mon," Bernard said.

In the center of the grove, Jordan faced Chupacabra, with only the Puddle of Ripeness between them. Eldon stood just behind Jordan.

"A deal is a deal," Chupacabra said. "Time to die, George Grimsley."

"Wait." Eldon tapped Jordan's shoulder. "You made a deal with this hothead?"

"Who is this?" Chupacabra said. "And why isn't he wearing pants?"

"Forget him," Jordan said to the super-cryptid. "This is between you and me." He then muttered to Eldon out of the side of his mouth. "I told you, I made a deal that he could get the other elemental powers, but in return he had to chase me down and kill me. Smart, right?"

"Please tell me you're kidding."

"Trust me, this will work. All I need is the ring." He held his hand open behind his back. "Just slip it to me, and my whole plan comes together perfectly."

"For the last time, Jordan, I *can't*," Eldon whispered.

"What do you mean you can't? Why can't you?"

"Because I don't have it! You threw it in the Puddle of Ripeness, remember?"

Jordan froze. He grinned at Chupacabra. "Can you give us a second, please?"

Jordan spun around. *"What?"*

"You heard me! It's not here! You threw it away!"

"I threw it right to you!" Jordan said. "It was a perfectly catchable toss! You just didn't catch it!"

"Look, we can argue about the quality of the throw all day long," Eldon said.

"You were going to fish it out! What have you been doing, just sitting around in your underwear, eating carrots, and reading fan mail?"

"I didn't know you were going to come back for it! Never mind with the worst plan in the history of plans!"

"It was a great plan. I just forgot I couldn't count on you to help me."

"Well, I'm sorry," Eldon said. "Maybe I can still help. What's your plan B?"

Jordan stared blankly at his friend.

"Please tell me you have a plan B," Eldon said. "Who doesn't have a plan B? It's, like, Badger Ranger Rule number *one*! Be prepared!"

"I guess my plan B," Jordan said softly, "is true sacrifice."

Abbie, Bernard, and Mr. and Mrs. Grimsley entered the clearing and immediately stopped short at what they saw. Standing in the center on one side of the Puddle of Ripeness was Chupacabra. On the other side of the dank goo stood Jordan, with Eldon still close behind him.

"We have to help them!" Bernard said.

"No," Abbie said. "Jordan said he had a plan. And I trust my little brother knows what he's doing." She could barely believe what she'd just said.

"So do I," Mrs. Grimsley said. "But if that monster touches a hair on his head . . ."

"What is that smelly gunk between them?" Mr. Grimsley said.

"The Puddle of Ripeness," Bernard said. "It reverses the effects of the Fountain of Youth. For years I and I alone kept its secret sacred. I guess that's over."

"The Fountain of Youth." Mr. Grimsley shrugged. "Okay. At this point, why not?"

Down in the center of the clearing, Chupacabra's eyes glowed a deep red, reminding Jordan of the blast-stones he'd packed up in his small room in the city. It all felt like a million miles and a million years away.

"Time's up, George Grimsley. And by that I mean yours."

Jordan swallowed hard. He took one last look at Eldon and turned to face Chupacabra. "That's right," he said. "Because this is between us. It always has been. It was me, and only me, who caused your pain and suffering. One man, not all of mankind. So go ahead— unleash your vengeance on me and be done with it. You will have won. There is no need for you to wipe out any species after that, be it human or creature. Rule over them all, but let them live. Show them mercy, so they can see your greatness."

Chupacabra burst out laughing. "Ah, but don't you see? Wiping out humans and creatures has been part of the master plan since the beginning! Your three hero cryptids—you think they came into this world with-out destruction? You think they acquired their powers with mercy? Each was created from an extinction event, killing millions! Only by violent disruption to this planet were they born with their elemental gifts. And so now, it's my turn."

"But you had your horrible event!" Abbie shouted. "That asteroid that created the Chicxulub crater wiped out the dinosaurs, and replaced them with the ultimate monster—*you*!"

Chupacabra glared back at her. "The only monsters born from that asteroid were those of the human race. Hunting me and my kind. Killing us. Then enslaving us and keeping us hidden. But no more. Operation Pangaea will wipe them out in one great extinction event. And I shall be reborn. The ultimate super-cryptid, ruler over all that I—"

"Oh, shut your piehole already, will ya?"

Eldon stepped forward. "Jeez Louise, do you ever listen to yourself? It's 'rule over this' and 'bring about the end to that'!" Eldon turned to the Grimsleys. "Hey, do you guys know that when I first met this blowhard, he couldn't speak? That's right, not a word! Now he never stops!"

"Okay, Eldon," Jordan said gently. "I think you may have gone cuckoo-pants. Time for a carrot break. Go and sit down. I got this."

Eldon ignored Jordan. "That's another thing!" Eldon took one more step closer to the puddle that separated the two of them from Chupacabra. "For all your blabbing, you still don't understand basic English! How many times has Jordan told you *HE ISN'T GEORGE GRIMSLEY*? He's his grandson, you loony old labradoodle!"

"Not true!" Jordan shouted to Chupacabra. "George Grimsley here, in the flesh!" He whispered frantically to Eldon. "You have to stop. You're ruining my plan B!"

"Jordan, there's something I need to tell you." Eldon put a hand on Jordan's shoulder and looked into his eyes. "Your plan B is a real stinker. What were you going to do, let him kill you, then hope he'll spare mankind? You heard him—he won't show mercy on anyone. It's a terrible plan. But I must say, you were right about one thing. There *is* a reason that ring kept coming back to me. It's because I'm the one who has to sacrifice, not you."

Jordan shook his head. "No. Eldon, you don't understand. It's George Grimsley he wants."

"I know. And it's well past time that old George Grimsley finally stops hiding and shows himself."

"Eldon, what are you talking about?"

"You're very smart and very brave," the former Master Badger Ranger said. "From the first day we met, I knew you'd make an exceptional Creature Keeper. But you're no George Grimsley. Wanna know why?" He leaned in and whispered, "Because you're better than I ever was."

Jordan's eyes grew wide. Eldon pulled back and winked at him. "Except at one thing—*CANNONBALL!*"

Eldon leaped into the air, pulled his knees to his chest, and plunged into the Puddle of Ripeness, disappearing beneath the thick glop.

"*Eldon!*" Jordan nearly fell in behind him. Abbie, Mr. and Mrs. Grimsley, and Bernard rushed to his side and held him back. Even Chupacabra was stunned by what was happening. The thick puddle churned and roiled. Then it went completely calm. A large green bubble popped at the surface, releasing a nasty-smelling vapor. And then there was nothing.

"Let me go!" Jordan said. "I've got to get him out of there!"

"Jordan, you can't," Bernard said. "It's too dangerous. It could kill you." Realizing what this meant, the Skunk Ape let go of Jordan and lowered his head. Jordan stopped struggling, then turned and buried his face in Bernard's furry chest.

"Wait, what's that?" Abbie pointed toward the puddle.

A small fist slowly emerged from the center of the muck. The green goo coated its arm as it reached into the air.

"It's Eldon! He's alive! Help me get him out of there!" Jordan grabbed the arm and pulled. Abbie grabbed Jordan and pulled. Mr. Grimsley grabbed Abbie and pulled. Mrs. Grimsley grabbed Mr. Grimsley and pulled. Bernard grabbed Mrs. Grimsley and *yanked*. They all tumbled backward in a pile, with the goo-covered survivor on top. They quickly cleared the slop from his mouth and nose, then from his face. Then they all stepped back.

"Wait," Chupacabra muttered. "No . . . It can't be. . . ."

The figure was not Eldon Pecone. But he was wearing his underwear. It was a much older man—wrinkled, bald, and hunched over, but with Eldon's aged features.

The person who'd emerged from the Puddle of Ripeness was George Grimsley.

43

" Boy, howdy! That goo can sure get into a fella's nooks and crannies!"

Bernard stepped forward. He couldn't believe his eyes. "It's really you." He gave the little old man a great big hug.

"It's always been me," Grampa Grimsley said. "But hug away, big fella. I can't get any smellier than I already am!"

"WHAT IS THIS TRICKERY?" Chupacabra was confused. And growing angrier.

"Dad?" There were tears in Mr. Grimsley's eyes as he slowly approached.

"I'm afraid so, son," the old man said. "I'm sorry I deceived you."

"YOU'VE BEEN GRIMSLEY ALL ALONG?" Chupabacabra shouted again.

Mr. Grimsley tore his eyes from his long-lost father and trained them on the creature. "And if you intend to kill him, you're going to have to go through me. Because I'm George Grimsley's son!"

"And I'm his daughter-in-law," Mrs. Grimsley said, stepping forward.

"And I'm his granddaughter." Abbie stepped in front of her parents.

Jordan stepped beside his sister. "And for the last time—I'm his grandson!"

They stood together, unified with Grampa Grimsley. Bernard was still off to the side. There was an awkward silence. "And I'm, uh—"

"My oldest and dearest friend," Grampa Grimsley said, reaching for the Skunk Ape's paw.

Bernard stood a little taller. "That's right. And adopted brother. Kind of."

Chupacabra reared up. "Fine! I'll just wipe out the lot of you! In fact, I can think of no better way to kick off my global domination than by forcing the entire Grimsley clan into extinction! Are we missing anyone? Half cousins? Step-uncles? Third nephews twice removed? Come out, come out, wherever you are! Come out and meet your doom!"

Mr. Grimsley smiled at his father, then at Abbie and Jordan. "So much for Grimsley Family Fun Time, I guess." Everyone chuckled, except Chupacabra.

"Stop that! You're all about to meet your demise! The least you could do is show a little fear of the unknown! I mean, would it kill you to beg for your lives?"

"Sorry," Abbie said. "Grimsleys don't beg."

"And I've already met my demise," Grampa Grimsley

said. "Or at least faked it. So do your worst, you mangy old mongrel!"

"For that, I will not be gentle. Prepare to be hit with all the weapons you foolishly surrendered to me. Farewell, George Grimsley. Farewell to you and your entire bloodline!"

Chupacabra's Hydro-Hide fluttered violently. The ground rumbled and shook as his Soil-Soles sank into the mossy floor. His icy Blizzard-Bristles stiffened, crackling as they crystallized. His Pyro-Paws burst into flaming fists.

Bernard and the Grimsleys huddled bravely together. "Sorry, everyone," Jordan said. Looking to his grandfather, he added, "You were right. My plan really was a stinker."

"I said your *plan B* was a stinker," the old man said. "I liked where you were going with plan A." He held out his wrinkled hand. "I think you might have dropped something again." He pushed something into Jordan's hand. "Try to hold on to it this time, will ya?"

Even speckled with the green muck, Jordan recognized the crystal ring. Flowing inside, it's bluish-silver elixir danced and swirled. Jordan's eyes lit up. "Not this time."

Chupacabra spread his arms. Flames shot out of his Pyro-Paws, extending across the grove, blasting holes

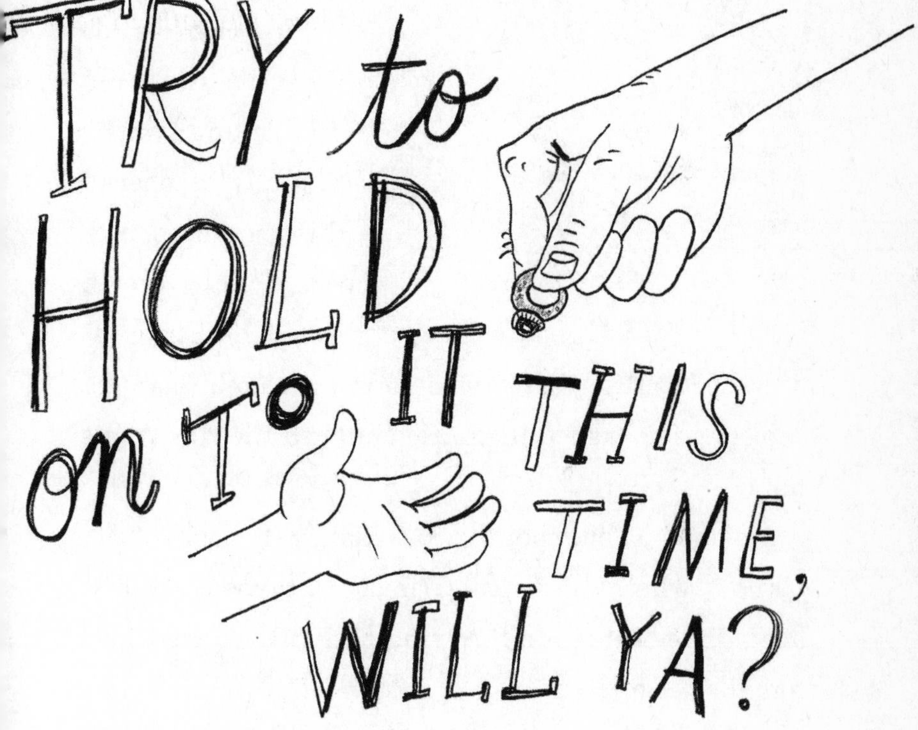
TRY to HOLD on TO IT THIS TIME, WILL YA?

through the tree trunks, setting them on fire on either side. The ground shook and rumbled as vines and roots came to life underfoot. His Hydro-Hide scales fluttered menacingly. Finally he opened his mouth to prepare a deep breath to blast through his Blizzard-Bristles. That's when Jordan caught sight of the cryptid's jagged teeth. He clutched the ring in his hand.

He had just one shot. He cocked his arm back— "Uh, y'know what?" Grampa Grimsley grabbed Jordan's arm. "I've seen your throwing skills. Let's let Abbie handle this one, eh?"

Abbie quickly pulled Alistair's slingshot out of her back pocket, took the ring, loaded it, pulled back the strap, and let it fly.

Ping!

The elixir-filled ring flew into Chupacabra's open mouth, smashing against his fang. Its contents sprayed into his throat. His exhale morphed into a wild hacking cough, which blasted chunks of ice up into the burning trees. He waved his fiery arms wildly throughout the grove, extending across the clearing, slicing the tree trunks. He stumbled back, tripping his mighty Soil-Soles over the vines and roots that he'd unearthed.

Jordan, Abbie, Grampa Grimsley, and the others scattered, taking cover from the mayhem as the sliced cypress trees began to fall in different directions like giant pickup sticks. Bernard covered Mr. and Mrs. Grimsley while Jordan and Abbie protected their grandfather, ducking beneath a fallen trunk.

"What—what have you done?" Chupacabra choked and gurgled as he continued to stumble backward, his body jerking and convulsing. His Pyro-Paws retracted, and he landed on an altarlike table of severed cypress trunks.

The Grimsleys all came out of hiding and approached him, meeting Doris, Hap, Kriss, and all the Keepers and underwear-clad Face Chompers who ventured inward,

climbing over the charred stumps. Everyone gathered around Chupacabra, who was writhing in pain.

"It's too strong," Jordan exclaimed. "The concentrated elixir from the ring is killing him!"

THUMP! THUMP! The ground shook as Syd's Soil-Soles hit the ground after suddenly slipping off Chupacabra's feet. "It's not killing him," Abbie said. "It's shrinking him!"

"Of course!" Grampa Grimsley said excitedly. "He's regressing in age! It's the same effect Harvey's elixir had on Nessie! We need more! Hap, in my tent! Go get the rest of the elixir!"

"Your tent?" Hap said. "I'll get it, but I think you mean Eldon's tent, wrinkly old dude." He ran off in the direction of the boathouse.

Doris peered at the old man, and caught her breath. "George Grimsley?"

Grampa Grimsley smiled at her, and she knew it was him.

Doris whistled to the abandoned Keepers standing with their creatures. They pulled from inside their underwear the small tinctures of elixir Hap had given them. One by one, each Keeper poured whatever they had left into the gaping, gasping mouth of Chupacabra. The cryptid choked and sputtered on it, then quickly seemed to calm as it began to take effect. Hap came running back with the box of his stash, and the rest of them took to administering it all to the shrinking patient.

"It's working!" Jordan shouted. "He's getting littler!" The Pyro-Paws slid from Chupacabra's skinny arms like molten goo, burning deep into the tree trunks. His snout grew shorter, and was engulfed by Wilford's flowing Blizzard-Bristles. Bernard reached out and gently pulled the frosty whiskers away, exposing a tiny Chupacabra face. Before their eyes, the face continued to shrink, disappearing inside Nessie's Hydro-Hide. Then, suddenly, all went quiet.

A soft whimpering cried out from within the coat of scales. Jordan and Abbie reached in and pulled out something so small they could hold it together in their arms. A tiny Chupacabra pup.

The cryptid's eyes darted around fearfully, until they landed on a face it recognized.

Grampa Grimsley reached out and Jordan and Abbie gently placed the pup in his arms. "Why, hello there, little fella," the old man said. "It's been a long time."

The Chupacabra pup purred, then stretched its neck toward the old man, then licked his wrinkled face.

Jordan Grimsley stood at the window of his new
bedroom. With the large garden wall gone, his backyard was now basically the entire Okeeyuckachokee
Swamp. This was a good thing, he thought to himself.
They were going to need the extra space.

He unzipped his duffel bag and pulled out the dead
blaststone he'd packed. He turned it over in his hand a
few times before placing it on a small bookshelf beside
his window. He began pulling out his books and lining
them up beside the blaststone.

"Unique bookend." Grampa Grimsley stood just
inside his doorway. "I used to have a pair just like it.
Ruined a perfectly good fanny pack." He picked up
one of Jordan's books. *"A Guide to Mankind's Most*

Amazing Mythological Monsters. Mind if I borrow this one?"

Jordan stared into his grandfather's face. In the few days since the strange transition in the Puddle of Ripeness, it had become easier for Jordan to find Eldon's smile behind the wrinkles, and to recognize Eldon's twinkle in the old man's eyes.

"Still a bit weird for you, I'd guess," Grampa said, reading his mind. He looked over at his reflection in a mirror on Jordan's dresser. "Kind of weird for me, too."

"You know, you could've told me. I would've understood."

"That's probably true. And I'm sorry. It was always my plan to groom you and your sister to take over the family business. Then I'd reveal who I was. I figured I'd let myself age slowly so it wasn't so much of a shock—to any of us."

"The ring," Jordan said. "Wearing that kept you young."

Grampa Grimsley nodded. "I tried to part with it. But I found the transition too painful. It nearly killed me in the Amazon. You saw me and gave it back."

"I just thought it had healing properties for whatever sickness you had."

"I welcomed the relief. I was a coward. About a lot of things."

"No. You parted with it on our way back to the Kappa's home."

"You and Abbie were more than ready to take over the Creature Keepers after that adventure. And with Chupacabra captured, I thought I could focus on surviving a gradual transition, no matter how painful, without distractions. But of course, the ring returned to me once again." He turned to the window, staring out at the swamp stretching beyond his old house. "I was happy to return it to you. The day Hap showed up with his leftover elixir."

"Of course," Jordan said. "You're the one who took the bottles."

"Again, a cowardly act. But I was very careful to leave enough for the abandoned Keepers. I filled my canteen with what I needed to get through the metamorphosis—hopefully without it killing me."

"And finally, after all that, I threw your ring away."

"At that point, it didn't matter to me anymore. I thought all was lost, that everyone I loved and trusted had betrayed me. I was going to sit in that cypress grove and let the conversion take its course. If it took my life, that was fine with me. The ultimate act of cowardice. I should never have doubted any of you. I'm sorry."

"It's okay, Eld—uh, *Grampa*." He grimaced. "Maybe it is still a little weird."

The two friends laughed.

"Hey, you two!" Mr. Grimsley poked his head into Jordan's bedroom. He held up a pair of baseball gloves. "Sorry to interrupt, *Dad*, but I was thinking maybe we might have a catch out back before lunch! Whaddya say?"

"Sure, son," Grampa Grimsley said. "I'll be right down."

"Awesome! Hey, Jordan, why don't you join us? I'll find another glove!" Mr. Grimsley ran down the hall.

"My dad has never asked me to play catch," Jordan said. "Like, ever."

"Don't complain," Grampa Grimsley said. "This will be our seventeenth catch since breakfast."

"I guess he feels you and he have a lot of *catching up* to do," Jordan said.

"I'm technically your elder now, so I say this to you as a wise old mentor. That joke was a real stinker."

Downstairs, the house was bustling with activity. The old Eternal Acres sign was carried out the door to be hung, with a fresh paint job that now read: *Harmony Acres*. In the front hall, the tenants and the retired Keepers were working side by side with the Face Chompers, busily moving furniture about, bringing strange new items through the front door.

Doris was in the foyer, barking out orders. "Easy

with that, big guy! That's a very technical piece of machinery, and we don't own it, we're just renting it!"

Just outside the front door, Lou and Donald were lugging a giant vending machine up the steps. They set it down just inside the doorway. In it was a mixture of normal snacks alongside some very strange ones. Chocolate-dipped pretzels hung beside small bags of live worms; beef jerky, along with clusters of dirty twigs.

"Hiya, Jordan," Lou said. "Yo, Gramps!"

Doris snapped at the cryptids. "Did I say break time?

We have just a week before our human students arrive for the first day of classes! Let's move it, while we're young!" She winked at Grampa Grimsley. "No offense, George."

"None taken, Doris," he said. "Keep up the good work!"

In the living room, Hogie was moving a heavy coffee table across the floor by balancing it on his back and oozing his way along. Kriss and Gavin were fluttering above the fireplace with a large banner, while Bernard and Donald were eyeballing it.

WELCOME to the
INAUGURAL CLASS of the
Harmony
Acres
Creature
Keeping
Society's
First
Academy of
Cryto-
Evolutionary
Studies

Bernard beamed proudly at his banner. "Whaddya think? Came up with the name all by myself!"

Jordan shared a look with his grandfather.

"Let it go," Grampa Grimsley said. "He'll figure it out eventually. Or not."

"Uh, George? Can I talk to you a sec?" As Bernard and Grampa Grimsley spoke, Jordan noticed something on the television screen, which was mounted in the corner.

The sound was turned off, but he could read the news graphic: *"BENEVOLENT CREATURES SAVE HUNDREDS OF LIVES IN MEXICO!"* The footage showed Nessie, Wilford, and Syd being interviewed on the day they stayed behind on the pier. Buck kept stepping into the shot to hog the limelight.

Jordan stepped up behind his grandfather, who was listening to Bernard. The Skunk Ape looked nervous as he spoke. "I know you and Eldon are—or were—the same, and so I, uh, I know you know that me and Eldon, that is to say me and *you* had a bit of a falling out before he, that is, *you* changed back into *you*. . . . So I guess I'm just wondering, or I'm really hoping, that he and I, or you and I, are, um, are—"

"Bernard," Grampa Grimsley said. "You were, are, and always will be the best friend anyone could ever have. That includes young George Grimsley, old George

Grimsley, and especially Eldon Pecone." The Skunk Ape burst into tears, and hugged the old man so hard Jordan thought he'd need a crowbar to pry them apart.

Heading out of the room, Jordan caught another quick bit of news on the television: " . . . MAYAN PRINCESS *CRUISE SHIP PURCHASED BY MYSTERIOUS INVESTOR, C. E. NOODLEPEN . . .*"

Jordan caught up with his grandfather, and also caught Doris beaming at Grampa. "Okay, so what's the deal with you and her?" Jordan asked him.

"Who, Doris? Nothing. She's just glad that I survived, that's all."

"Survived the aging process?"

"That, but also the accident, all those years ago. She was the last person to see me alive that fateful night."

"The night you were eaten by an alligator."

"The night a very helpful alligator helped me fake my own death by eating my pajamas. It was right after that Skunk Ape Summer nonsense. Everyone thought I was crazy, including your parents. So that night I broke out of the hospital they'd put me in and I came here, to my old house. I knocked on the door and begged the caretaker to keep something for me."

"The caretaker—Doris," Jordan said. "And I know what she kept for you. The suitcase, with your journal hidden inside."

"That's right. I showed her what was hidden there and made a deal with her. If she kept it and kept it *secret*, she would be richly rewarded someday by a boy who would come and claim it. A Grimsley boy."

"Me," Jordan said. "But how did you know then that I would come?"

"I didn't. The Grimsley boy wasn't you, Jordan. The Grimsley boy was *supposed* to be me. I'd discovered the elixir, and I was going to use it to hide somewhere no one would ever find me—in my own youth."

"So my happening along—"

"Was an accident. But a very fortunate one, as it turned out."

45

Abbie sat beside a child's playpen set up near the greenhouse at the edge of the Okeeyuckachokee Swamp. Inside the playpen, Chunk looked as bored as ever, sitting in a lump, while a frisky Chupacabra pup yipped and ran in circles and leaped on top of him, trying to get him to play.

"C'mon, Chunk," Abbie said. "Be a good big brother and show the little guy how to behave himself."

Chunk looked out of the corner of his eye at Chupacabra, crouched low with his tail in the air, like he was about to pounce. The iguana opened his mouth and let out a threatening hiss. Chupacabra froze in fear, then sat up perfectly still, like an obedient show puppy.

"Good boy!" Jordan approached with Grampa Grimsley.

Abbie tossed Chupacabra a slab of beef jerky, and Chunk a Crazy-Blazin' Jalapeño-Heckfire Nacho Cheezy Puff. The cryptid pup yawned, then gently snuggled up to his stepbrother. Chunk allowed it.

"Awwww . . ." A small group of people, young and old, whom Jordan had never seen before, were gathered behind them, smiling down at the playpen. Mrs. Grimsley stepped up and addressed them.

"Gather around, not too close, please," she began. "This is one of the many cryptids who will be in residence here. He's Chupacabra, a rescue, you might say."

She winked at her children and father-in-law. "He's currently being housebroken, and trained to not wipe out the human race in order to take over the world."

The crowd took a collective step back. "All right, this way, please." Mrs. Grimsley led them toward the greenhouse but turned them around to look back at the former retirement home before leading them through the greenhouse door.

She gestured toward Grampa Grimsley's old house. "As you all know, Harmony Acres will be the first academy of its kind. Once completed, it will educate potential human students like yourselves on many magnificent mysterious creatures. Students here at, um"—she paused—"*Hacks Faces*—will be taught about cryptids *by* cryptids, as each class will have its own 'Creature Teacher.' Graduates will leave our academy with a better understanding and knowledge of not just cryptids but of the world that together we all share. This way, please."

She gestured toward the entrance to the greenhouse. "Now if you'll just follow the ramp down to our underground administrative offices, our heads of admissions, Francine the Australian Bunyip and Clarissa the Christmas Island Colossus Crab, will be more than happy to answer any questions you have and help start you in the application process. And please help yourselves to a carrot on your way down—they're nature's toothbrushes! Watch your step, thank you!"

"Nice work, Mom," Jordan said as his mother rejoined them. "Super professional."

"Thank you! That was my last tour of the day. It does get tiring."

Hap ran up to them, quite out of breath, from inside the swamp. "Oh, glad you guys are all together. Mr. G wanted you all to meet him by the boathouse. It's urgent."

"Urgent?" Nervous glances were exchanged. "Is everything all right?" Jordan asked.

"You'd just better go quickly," Hap said. "I'll go and find Doris."

Abbie scooped Chunk into her arms, and Grampa Grimsley grabbed Chupacabra. They all quickly made their way deeper into the swamp.

Mr. Grimsley stood at the foot of the dock, grinning ear to ear. Floating behind him was the former *Mayan Princess*. The lettering on the side of the boat had been painted over, rather crudely in what Jordan suspected might be a Skunk Ape's sloppy handwriting. The bow now read *GRIMSLEY FAMILY RAMBLER II*. A large pink, silk banner hung from the railing running alongside the boat. Beautiful stitchwork on it read: *CREATURE CRUISES! TOURS AVAILABLE NOW!*

Standing at the railing were Syd, Wilford, Alistair, and Buck Wilde, waving down at the Grimsleys.

"All aboard!" Mr. Grimsley held out his hand for his wife and accompanied her down the dock.

A gray streak dived out of the sky as Kriss dropped Bernard on the deck of the ship. He then zoomed over and scooped Abbie up in his arms, setting her down on the deck before tumbling to a horrible landing. Jordan and Grampa Grimsley were the last to board, laughing as they ran down the dock and onto the ship.

Once on board, the Grimsleys found the swimming pool up on the Lido deck occupied by two and a half tons of Loch Ness Monster and a white, furry Trunko. Nessie and Moe were lazing about in the water, taking in the warm, late-summer sun. In the adjoining hot tub was Gilligan, grinning ear to ear.

"Now this is livin'!" the Feejee Mermonkey said, sipping from a pineapple.

Jordan and Abbie turned to their grandfather. "Did I read somewhere that C. E. Noodlepen had something to do with this purchase?" Jordan asked.

Grampa Grimsley shrugged. "Name doesn't ring a bell." He smiled. "But then, I'm pretty old and my memory isn't what it used to be."

Abbie rolled her eyes. "You may be my grandfather," she said. "But you're still a first-class dorkface."

BEEEEEYOOOOOO!

The *Grimsley Family Rambler II* let out a loud horn blast as it pulled away from the end of the dock. Abbie, Jordan, and Grampa Grimsley moved to the stern. Mr. and Mrs. Grimsley joined them, along with Syd, Wilford, Kriss, Harvey, Alistair, and Buck Wilde.

Back on the shoreline, Doris, Hap, the Face Chomper

creatures, and their Creature Keepers ran down the dock, waving bon voyage. Doris pulled a carrot out and winged it onto the Lido deck of the ship.

A bus-sized blur of white fluff suddenly came bounding out of the swamp. Peggy hopped over the entire dock, landing squarely on the ship's lower deck. Perched on her back was Harvey Quisling, holding on for dear life but laughing his heart out.

The little ship bucked and rocked as it absorbed the impact of the giant Jackalope. But the *Grimsley Family Rambler II* easily steadied herself, then slowly sailed away from the Okeeyuckachokee Swamp, straight into the sun setting over Ponce de Leon Bay.

P O N C E D E L E O N

C E N O O D L E P E N

E L D O N P E C O N E

Acknowledgments

For their never-ending love and support, we thank our families and friends. To the many humans who helped us hatch Creature Keepers, we send humongous Skunk Ape hugs:

Editor and First-Class Badger Ranger Jordan Brown, who kept our wild stories from wandering away from us but always protected their ferocious fun.

Brenda Bowen and Tina Wexler, our agents, friends, and biggest (grown-up) fans.

Everyone at HarperCollins Children's Books, including layout, lettering, and digital artists Alison Klapthor, Annemieke Beemster Leverenz, and Rick Farley. Also, CKCC West computer artists Jenny Yurshansky, Lovemando, Charlie Nelson, and Indigo Perez.

Lastly, to our young fans everywhere—thank you for your letters, artwork, book reports, videos . . . and most of all, for reading!

Gratefully,

Ro & Peter